Darcy's Education
of Miss Elizabeth Bennet

A *titillating* Pride and Prejudice Variation

aJbishop

Darcy's Education of Miss Elizabeth Bennet is a work of fiction.
Names, characters, places and incidents are products of the
author's imagination.

Cover Design by Joelle Fhima Berdowski
Cover Image by Fragonard, The Bolt (1777) with permission
Excerpt from *Fanny Hill*, by John Cleland,
retrieved from the Gutenberg Project
(https://gutenberg.org/ebooks/25305)

AUTHOR'S NOTE

This novel is a lightly titillating literary sequel to a novel, *Pride and Prejudice*. Physical intimacy is this novel's subject. Desire a natural product.

This novel contains nudity, conversations about sexuality, and tenderness. It is written with deep gratitude and respect for love and its many forms of expression.

for Daphne Williams

Book I: Rosings Park

Book II: Longbourn

Book III: London

Book IV: Pemberley

ROSINGS PARK

INVITATION
TO ESTATE MANAGEMENT,
LADY WORSHIPPING,
AND INSULT RECEIVING

It is a truth universally acknowledged that all romance ends with the word *yes*. The happy ending is assured in the deliberate absence of any further information, for no one knows how the Prince and Princess live happily-ever-after as it is never written. Few of us want to know that all good romance must suffer a little, that a marriage whose happiness is well decided is decidedly unhappy on a few occasions. Cinderella's glass slipper, transparent and light at first, will shatter with daily use. Sleeping Beauty, serene and compliant in her dormant grace, will and must wake to confront the trials of eating, working, and fornicating. If a romance is generated from a tension of absence, then marriage is created from an equal proportion of presence.

And how that is acquired is what we now seek.

We arrive to this well-known story of Elizabeth Bennet and Fitzwilliam Darcy at the cusp of such an ending wherein the lovers have survived obstacles of dislike, misunderstanding, confusion, prejudice, and passion, to resolve, finally, on betrothal and love. We arrive where so many good fairy tales end. The betrothal, however, is somewhat anti-climactic. There are no sweet touches or kisses, no expression of desire, no lightning strikes to commemorate this grand finale. The slipper fits. The wedding happens as a footnote. The prince and princess will forever be happy in our minds. And yet, we know that this cannot be true, for we ourselves have dared to live the reality of love, the little miracles of finding oneself at this momentous juncture peeking into our future completely new, from individual to betrothed, ready to become a partner in life, to shed our childhood ways, our bachelorhood, our independence, even our name.

In a fairy story, the to-be-princess is a hidden jewel brought to meet the prince's family as his beloved and chosen one. She does not yet wear the crown, but his family must ask where he found her for there is a small pool of other aristocrats and they know them all. This one, this handsome waif, has no aristocratic name, no history, no relations who will heighten her value. She cannot broker any greatness. She will empower his family not at all.

Will their Prince tell them – say it is not so! – that she lives in a little house beside the dwarves? Or that she washes floors for her stepsisters and rides pumpkins to the ball? The glass slipper fits, he says, with a shrug and a grin, sheepish with boyish charm and love-lust. And will the family believe that she is marvellous for these commendations? Not long after her arrival, they will discover her charms, for although unknown, she is bred for this moment: to be a princess, to be queen perhaps. And thus, they sigh, roll their eyes. Another one to thin the blood. Soon there will be no blood at all worth mentioning, and what then?

Our princess entered the great home of Lady Catherine de Bourgh on Darcy's arm, arriving in a regal carriage, the footmen jumping to their posts opening doors, the butler standing ready while most of the household lined up in military silence. It was an entirely different matter from her first visit to Rosings Park when she walked across the lane from Hunsford Parsonage with Mr. and Mrs. Collins to ring the bell. The same butler accepted her coat, the same smell of lavender infused the hand towels in the water closet, the same imposing portraits studied her every move, but these now held different meaning. The portraits were no mere representations of proud people assembled for posterity, but were, some of them, her intended's relations. The butler lingered more as he took her coat and assured himself of her comfort more directly than before. She watched every movement of every servant thinking that one day, one day soon, she must manage a similarly large household.

Her mother refused to let Elizabeth travel in a carriage alone with her betrothed for that would show far more freedom than was correct. Carriages were dangerous places for unwed lovers, she affirmed. Mr. Bennet, as an aside to whoever cared to listen, reminded them that their daughter Lydia had spent several weeks living in sin in London with young Wickham. "It is late to pretend that we have a firm handle on the proprieties of our young ladies' travel arrangements," he elaborated. "And may I remind you that Elizabeth is not Lydia."

"Well, that is quite clear, Mr. Bennet, for she is the second not the last of our daughters. You test me, but I *can* count. However, there is no reason to assume that because we have once made a mistake that we should be free of it on further occasion. Mistakes are not like the influenza which travels generously but from which one can gain protection. The dangers for our Eliza are no less great than those for Lydia."

And thus, Elizabeth arrived not merely on Darcy's arm, but with her overly serious and sincere sister Mary in tow, like a duckling following along behind the swans.

There are some astonishingly evil women characters in fairy tales who deliberately and determinedly attempt the ruin of innocent lives for no apparent reason but rage, jealousy, greed, spite and other such irrational causes that a psychologist might have a field day unpacking and examining under a proverbial microscope. The evil stepmothers of Hansel and Gretel, Cinderella and Snow White, as well as the inexorable and terrifying cruelty of Cruella de Ville are a few which come easily to mind.

Lady Catherine de Bourgh, née Fitzwilliam, married a knight, and from being an earl's daughter and thus sister to the current Earl of - something, she remained of high status, deigning not to marry beneath her, but choosing a man with Sir before his name and property worthy of her tastes. She was not evil, but rather overly determined. She would prefer fools and sycophants at her table; yet she could not help but admire Elizabeth's wit, which she had noticed on several occasions. She would rather this wit find new lodgings and admirers. She detested that Darcy had fallen into a trap with a village nobody, but she would do her best to ascertain the girl's ability to become skilled in society and if not, to make sure that Darcy was well apprised of her failings. Lady Catherine was confident in her ability to do so and of the tests she planned, for, as we shall see, there were many ways for a girl to fall in Regency England. Elizabeth was merely an obstacle to overcome, a silly girl who must go back whence she came and find a more suitable husband.

In the days before her departure, Elizabeth's family and friends had offered advice on proper conduct with Lady Catherine. Kitty suggested she refuse the invitation to Rosings as it would be impossible to live with such a tyrant. Mary offered Elizabeth several books in which to hide herself. Bingley suggested that Elizabeth find a way to present her most wise proclamations with a smile that did not seem a mockery, to which everyone laughed, especially because Bingley had been quite serious in his advice and thought it might work. Miss Bingley scoffed at the idea that an old Lady cloistered more or less from society might have anything current to teach a peasant girl. And then she laughed, knowing of course that Elizabeth was not a peasant. Jane instructed in a ladylike silence in which contradictions and thinking were mastered by pleasant acquiescence. Curtsy often, her mother agreed, not divulging the occasions on which such a thing should be done. Her father handed her *Lord Chesterfield's Letters to His Son*, a book in which he had found a great deal of sound advice. In it he had tucked a short list of three quotes: "assent without being servile or abject", "always do more than you say", "let her quietly enjoy her errors in good taste". Darcy agreed that it was rather hilarious thinking of Elizabeth being demure but agreed that Chesterfield's letters had also served him quite well.

"I will study Anne for suggestions," Elizabeth replied. "No doubt, as perfected daughter of that great lady, she can be a model of how to simper, become anemic and inarticulate."

"I will lose my Miss Bennet in the process," he laughed.

"But you will have me under her thumb nevertheless?"

And nodding, he admitted that he would rather comply with his aunt's wish to prepare Elizabeth for a life on a grand estate. "She is good at it and you might learn something," he shrugged.

"And you are under her thumb as well," she teased him.

He grinned. "I prefer not to think of it as such. It is a compromise position. I refuse to marry Anne and instead marry a country waif, and she gets to educate you. Tit for tat sort of thing," he teased back.

ANNE'S SORROWS

Dear reader, here is Elizabeth's prince, Mr. Fitzwilliam Darcy. Darcy is a name that suggests something old and something French, as from the Norman conquest, but is not. It is used liberally by all his acquaintants, as in 'Mr. Darcy' in public when sir is not applied by a servant as in "Yes, sir", or by his chums, like Charles Bingley and others, as in "Darcy, would you kindly hold the reins". Even his bride-to-be Elizabeth, in her mind and to his face, will often call him Darcy as if it were his first name and she his school chum at Eton.

His given name, Fitzwilliam, is in honour of his mother's maiden name. He is not an earl, although his grandfather on his maternal side was an earl; yet is it not conceivable that at some date, and with many relatives dying, that he would inherit the title? Fitzwilliam comes from that earldom, therefore, and worthy of his pride, yet it is a name reserved for his stationery and rarely for his friends. He is Fitz, Fitzy, Will, Willy (by school peers teasing him) and Billy to as few people as he can contain the spread of nomenclature applied to his first name. To his ears, there are few who can use any of these nicknames with any authority, with few exceptions, namely his sister Georgiana, his dear friend Bonnie Stately, and his uncle, an illegitimate son from the Darcy line who was raised as, and has kept, the name Sherwood.

What we know of Darcy is through Elizabeth's confused and often prejudicial eyes. He has certainly seemed arrogant on more than one occasion, proud and privileged. He has also been fair, honourable, and has gone out of his way to mend his faults. But other than these views of him from a distance, his dark silence and our ignorance of him, our ability to imagine so much of what he might be are his great appeal. That we know not very much about him but that he is a fairy tale Prince riding into Elizabeth's simple village life and expanding her potential horizons with a nod of his head would seem his true greatness.

Alas, we must construct this man from almost nothing and deny him some of the mystery. Alas, he shall be known. Alas, matrimonial intentions will and must lead to companionship, knowledge, and care. Therein lies the delight and the danger to both fairy story, romance, and marriage.

He comes to us somewhat like a blank page. For even his beloved does not know him quite so well as she would like. This is the man who has fallen in love with Elizabeth, the girl he might have had contempt for in his more privileged mind. She was not raised with a hundred servants and can but try to imagine a life at Pemberley Estate and in London society. And even as he has seen the error of his assumptions, the one in which she would automatically agree to being married to him, he will continue to make more assumptions. He believes that she will agree to his aristocratic castle of precepts which have stood many generations. It is simply a matter of education. In this he agrees with his Aunt Catherine.

On his first day at Rosings Park he wakes with a task assigned to him almost immediately via a little note in his aunt's quick scrawl. *You must tell Anne yourself.* In response, he sat at his late Uncle's great stately desk and wrote to Elizabeth.

My Dearest Lizzy,
I will call you Lizzy in that tender way that it is spoken by Jane. Not Eliza, the scolding in the word as with your mother.
Dear Lizzy,
I am sorry that today we will not meet, nor perhaps for several days as I have agreed to leave you with 'Auntie' to 'manage you'. I do wonder who will be managed, however, as I have every faith that you will learn a great deal from her and perhaps (and this is my hope) that you will learn to respect one another, if not to like.
As I mentioned previously, my Aunt Catherine has lately been in London to visit a doctor of some unusual notoriety who might cure my cousin Anne of an ill-defined ailment. I suspect — though I will not wager on any of my insights regarding their unusual relationship - that dear Auntie has in her mind that I will be more inclined to think of her daughter as marriageable once she has cured the poor girl of whatever it is that keeps her in such a state of decline.
I have, of course, and many times, dispossessed her of the idea that I should wish to marry Anne. I do not for a minute believe my mother intended but as a sweet sort of ruse this sisterly pact regarding their two babies and, had she lived to know Anne as a young woman, neither would she dare insist that I be saddled (oh, please excuse this rudeness!) with the girl as my wife. My Great Auntie has given me instructions to be the one to 'break our

engagement', fictional though it is. We (Anne, Mrs. Jenkinson and yours truly) set off today for an adventure. I think a day away from her mother's ministrations will provide Anne some relief as will my news to her of our marital intentions as I have no doubt that Anne is as little interested in marrying me as I am in marrying her.

I will find you later in the drawing room. And we shall look into each other's eyes. And I will touch you with my look. And not one person in the room shall scold us. Best regards for a fruitful day... I believe you walk with Mrs. Collins later if I am not mistaken. Send my regards. D.

Anne de Bourgh is a challenge to describe for what little we know of her until now is that she is a somewhat mousy and stifled creature, with no voice of her own and an ailment sometimes described as a heart issue, but which most of us believe hides something less polite. She is not particularly attractive, to our minds, though that is never really said, and yet with her propensity to be indoors over protected by her mother and Mrs. Jenkinson, her paid companion, we are not surprised that she is pale and wan, with a slightly hollowed-eyed countenance of perpetual surprise and hesitation.

It is for this reason that Darcy invited her for a visit to Rochester Castle to do what he felt was his duty in an environment pleasing and fun. He walked beside his dour and silent cousin with whom conversation was more like extracting words with prompts one must find on one's own and be content with the monosyllabic replies, answers dull and unadorned by any voluntary enthusiasm or apparent effort. Yet, he was aware that his cousin's life had been painful, and so he had a great deal of sympathy for her even as he dreaded every moment he must spend at her side.

Anne did seem to interact with the world as if listening to a different language. Of course, the metaphor is limited, for the language of society is fraught with difficult nuances and unconscious signaling. Poor Anne seemed terrified and pale and twitched in the carriage as they drove to the nearby village, pulling at her fingers terribly so that he felt he must reach down and hold them. It occurred to him that this formal meeting, the fact of his taking the time to entertain her, must seem to her that she was about to receive the proposal that had been promised to her by her mother these many years. She stared resolutely at the floor until they were let off at the garden gate where he bought both their entrances.

He led her through the various by-ways, strolling at his ease, and she, small and unhealthy as she always seemed, walked by his side, on his arm, with an almost smile on her lips as she admired turrets and narrow stairwells and talked of the imaginary creatures who inhabited her mind and who came alive whenever she visited castles.

When she begged to sit, they left Mrs. Jenkinson to shop for trinkets and found a terrace on the esplanade where they could take tea and biscuits and scones, served with little pots of jam and a thick dollop of Devonshire cream. And it was when her mouth and eyes and soul had been amply filled with these little treasures that he told her he had something of importance to relate. As she looked up past her narrowed eyes and her lowered forehead, her breath seemed to stop. He smiled indulgently and took her hand.

"I would like to tell you that I am engaged to be married, dear Anne."

Immediately Anne looked at him and smiled. Then her eyes fell back to the ground. "I suppose Mama was terribly upset."

"It is possible to survive her wrath," and again her eyes popped back up.

"It is that girl who arrived with you yesterday?" she asked.

"I believe you were previously acquainted with Miss Elizabeth Bennet."

"I think she quite dismissed me Fitzwilliam. She seemed overly self-possessed. And unkind. I'm sorry to say so, but I tried to like her, yet every time I spoke to her, she made a mockery."

"I am sorry to hear that, but I believe that on further acquaintance you will find that she is neither unkind nor invulnerable."

"Well, I suppose then I must wish you joy." She bit her lip and worried her fingers into knots in her lap and once reached to draw a piece of hair to her mouth, but then changed her mind and let it drop.

He nodded and she said no more. He stood and held out his arm, but she stayed in her seat, still and shaking. Her mouth trembling as if she would cry soon, like a young baby, letting its mother know it will soon scream if one does not do something quick to stop the hunger, the pain, the fear, the ... He sat again and marveled that taking her to a public place did not serve to arrest the possibility of a scene, now pending.

She started to speak several times, opened her mouth and peeked up at him momentarily and then stared again at her lap, opening her fingers as if the words were lodged in her palms. He stood again, as uncomfortable to watch Anne as she seemed to be watched. His standing forced her words, and so he listened awkward in his stance, ready to leave.

"Oh, Fitz. Free me. From them."

"Who?" He sat again.

"I have nowhere to hide. Please, make her stop. We go from appointment to appointment and... Mother has me seeing doctors and, also, other people, in order to help me. It is unpleasant, all the tests and the bloodletting and the terrible questions they must ask. And the others, well they are very strange and ..."

"Excuse me for interrupting, but who are the others?"

"She would not like me to say."

"But how can I understand your question if I do not know?"

"But she will hate me."

"Then she will not need to know." Her face was a riot of discomfort. "But who?" he was completely frustrated. His voice rose sharply despite himself. "Who?" She began to cry. "Anne, she will never hate you. She wants only to see you well. How can I help you?"

Anne sobbed quite openly and received his handkerchief gladly. He looked around and smiled at the family at a nearby table who were now pointing and noticing her dramatic display of emotions. But she gathered herself and managed to speak again without tumbling into further outbursts.

"Stop her from them all. The doctors, and the people who do séances, and call on the dead for answers. I must be free of this constant barrage of her meddling. Can you not do something?"

He told her that he could hardly see how he might be of assistance in the matter. "I suppose you have spoken to your mother about your hesitations?"

"Yes. In a manner. But no sooner do my words form in my mouth, she has dismissed them."

"Yes, she does like to have her way. Have you considered writing her a letter...?" He watched as she nodded quietly. He knew he had offered her nothing. "Have you refused? Just refused to go? Anne. It is your right."

Anne stood, and offering her hand, said, "Thank you

Fitzwilliam, I believe we have taken quite sufficiently of your time."

He nodded. "I will do my best, but you must know I have little authority with her. She does as she will."

Darcy stared out the window into a crisp night. The day had been especially magnificently unfruitful. A fresh rain had drenched the yard and that was the only consolation, for afterwards there was a purity about the air, a perfume light and sweet, which he welcomed. He was terribly restless knowing Elizabeth was within reach. He opened and reread Elizabeth's letter, the one she wrote, presumably, from within the same walls as he now stood, in which she refused to believe that his aunt had any delight in their matrimonial intentions. But as he read the words, he thought instead of his cousin Anne and worried about the strange meeting he had had with her.

As he lay in bed, he deliberated that the work of relieving a young lady of high rank from the miserable confinement of a solitary existence with a bitter overbearing mother was hardly a realm in which he felt himself to be competent. The entire affair made him feel somewhat uncomfortable and he would rather not have been charged with the request. He fervently wished, as sleep refused to arrive, that his dear Lizzy was beside him now, that he could share these thoughts with her while holding her close, feeling her warmth, seeking her advice which he always admired. The thought of her in his bed aroused him as it had often done in previous months. He closed his eyes and allowed himself to travel on the rich delight of entertaining Miss Elizabeth Bennet in the privacy of his imagination. We will not here trespass to what he did in his mind with Elizabeth but be assured that in this world of his fantasies, she had long ago stopped being a virgin.

THE GREAT GRENDEL

Elizabeth Bennet to Jane Bennet, Longbourn, October 1812
Dearest Jane,

I can't imagine what possessed me to think that coming to Rosings Park was a good idea! My impressions of the dear Lady were already quite well formed as to know that it would be oppressive and unbearable. I call her Grendel to Darcy, who laughs and asks when I read Beowulf and which translation. The trip was pleasant, though Mary was morose and read constantly despite the terrible motions of the carriage and Darcy, instead of sitting by my side, spent most of the time on his steed begging my forgiveness as he cannot bear the motions of the carriage. He re-iterated that he believed his Auntie Cate (can you see the little facetious grin he uses when he names her thus?) will have a great deal to teach me about estate management, lady worshipping, demure parodies and insult receiving. These are all to be a test which we must pass with flying colours as he will have her blessing before we are married.

The turrets of this house are dark as caves (as old as the hills) so his cousin, Anne, keeps saying as if she has no other vocabulary and will repeat things like a parrot who has been trained to this or that speech, performed exactly, but with little comprehension). Yes, see? I am already scattered and cannot complete a proper thought. The turrets, which I had not noticed before, nor how many rooms there must be cached in places which seem isolated from the main living quarters, are servants' quarters and more I believe (more: rooms for ghosts and dragons?). Where there are fairies in the gardens of Pemberley, there are evil gnomes here... no that is quite unfair, and I am exaggerating for effect. The gardens are actually quite lovely and the house is beautifully furnished and pleasant. What is not lovely is that Mary insists on keeping her job as chaperone quite righteously and follows me everywhere as if she hasn't a thought in her head for her own pleasure except to parade with me without even offering conversation to provide entertainment. I see Darcy peek occasionally to find me already occupied with her. He waves or tips his head in a nod and goes away again. Bother her righteous and overzealous sense of responsibility. I will have to have a word with her.

Apparently, Darcy spent some time here as a young boy, when his mother was ill (I believe that is a euphemism for "birthing Georgiana"), and then most summers thereafter. He knows it well and understands the ways of the world here. He takes my hand occasionally, in a paternalistic way, much the way father might, and which I quite hate from him, but even this small sign of chaste affection elicits a "Too Close Too Close" from her worshipfulness, the Great Grendel, at the other end of the room, so you see, what little freedom we had before to walk with you and Mr. Bingley these past few weeks is now quite obliterated.

Grendel keeps awful company. Her friend Dowager Fontainebleu is tolerable, though as much a snob as Lady C. and turns her nose at anything that is incorrect (I have been tapped on the hand for conversing with a servant while in the dining room, and on another occasion at the main entrance, for laughing - which you know I do not and will not restrain - and for making a comment about the men's affairs). I am well aware of how to behave, but there is a little something in me which wants to test this woman and determine the lengths to which she will peer down her nose at me.

Lady F. is fine in drawing room conversation and relieves Lady C. of the workload with rather interesting topics as well as making a fourth at whist so I must not have to join. Mary keeps to a corner absorbed in her book or, occasionally, is allowed to play the pianoforte. Anne and her keeper, Mrs. Jenkinson, are barely in existence as much of what they say is yes and yes and yes; although I must say when Lady C. is not in attendance, Mrs. Jenkinson is vociferous on a single topic: she speaks of the imminent end of the world which, according to reliable prophecy, will happen in three years. Yes Jane, we shall all die in 1815.

But horrible, horrible is an Earl of Somewhere and his wife who seem to have nowhere to live (so Darcy whispered to me for they have spent all and sold all and are bereft yet living as if it were not so... you know such cases). He is a once favourite of the late Lewis de Bourgh. Darcy is not sure why the Earl and his wife are present. This couple have worse manners than Mama except that they are elephantine snobs and parade like royalty with their opinions and demands. They smother themselves from head to toe with cologne and perfume so that there is no air remaining in the room after it has been suffused with the stuff. I keep sneezing and Lady C. makes disparaging comments about me! As if I could control a sneeze! Relief is on its way soon in the form of Col. Fitzwilliam (who takes a short leave to rescue Darcy in this hour of need- I am not sure what Darcy meant by that, but I think he asked for fortifications against his aunt). I believe the poor man has yet to find his rich bride (you do know that he was most plain to *me about his requirements).*

On the more positive side, for you see this is my first letter to you and a single eve does not give ample time to adjust to new circumstances, I am quite well ensconced in a lovely eastward facing room where, now early in the morning, I watch the sun rise through the thick bedposts. I have a canopy of beautiful lace, a large divan, majestic desk, two adorable armchairs at the fire, and a settee at the end of the bed. Even the chamber pot is quite elegant. The room is big enough to be called both a bedroom and a sitting room and I would like to invite Charlotte to visit me here for tea one afternoon. Also, I would invite another person who I will not name because too too scandalous by far! The One who holds my hand when he can. (Oh, dare I tell? After dinner we met, as by accident – but do not believe it – as we both approached the stairs to retire, and he held me in an embrace, with his breath on my neck and … yes… he kissed me. And he whispered 'bonne nuit, mon amour' in my ear. Jane, it was wonderful).

And you, but of course. I would love to have you here as well.

Oh, and I hope to soon be off with Charlotte for a walk to receive news about her little olive branch.

Your most loving and desperately missing you,

Lizzy

Before she had broken her fast and as she signed her name to the letter, she received a note from Darcy in which she understood she would see little of him during the following several days. No sooner had she read this note than she was presented with a missive to a private audience with Lady Catherine. She ignored her hunger and went, with Mary following to sit in the hall like a hound at her master's door, quite content to read her book.

Lady Catherine's private study, the room Darcy facetiously called The Throne Room, was of generous proportion, full of books both antique and current, and contained pieces of such lovely elegance that it could more accurately be described as museum than room, the furniture more properly called art than desk, table, or chair. Elizabeth was particularly taken by a large secretary cabinet with two symmetrical cupboard doors, a tower of little drawers hovering above a folding desktop. Perched at its peak like a great owl was a porcelain clock at which Elizabeth stared, inspecting all its marvellous details.

"It is Italian," Lady Catherine noted. "It is old, almost a hundred years, and it works without correction for a week or more. Which tells you something about the reliability of age and good breeding."

Elizabeth nodded and cocked her head a little when she replied, "If I am to understand correctly, it is precisely why I have come. To be schooled in whatever you may find lacking in my education."

"Perhaps we will provide a young man for her, your young chaperone," Lady Catherine offered. "We might raise your entire family somewhat and challenge the rumours that we have fallen in with a tribe of country peasants."

Elizabeth, practicing being demure and wrong, held her tongue. She was quite convinced the Great Grendel would provoke her to behave badly and then prove to Darcy that she was unfit as his wife. Many minutes passed. Lady Catherine flipped another page of her book and looked up again as Elizabeth had turned to examine a portrait of a fine lady.

"The lady is my sister Anne Fitzwilliam Darcy. She is but two years away from dying when it was rendered."

Elizabeth noted that Darcy was similar in appearance but with eyes much more deeply set and a stronger chin. "Darcy's mother," she acknowledged.

"Darcy went through terrible hardships. He is a man of confidence and ease, but his life has not been without many trials and grief. I am glad to see that he is happy but surprised at its source. You are attractive, but there are many more beautiful. You have neither a gentle nurturing sweetness that a man might want as a comfort, nor the beauty which might make him feel quite proud to have you on his arm; and you have intelligence which is quite without reasonable restraint for you neither hide your opinions nor moderate them, a trait from which most men shrink for how can they believe themselves ruler of the world if their wife is an intelligent challenge to their own poor brains?"

Elizabeth could not ascertain if Lady Catherine was being serious or facetious; in either case she decided to remain silent. She remained silent for quite a lot of time. But then she spoke. "It is also a mystery to me, your Ladyship."

"You must learn to stand. You must learn to appear comfortable and relaxed while standing in a ballroom. There is an art to it. I see how you are well formed, like a princess born in a barn, a small westward facing stall and a pretty little paddock as your entire kingdom and mules as your companions..." Elizabeth began to object to the terms used against her. "No. I will not be interrupted. I concede that at the very least you do not mistake the footmen, dressed as they are in fine livery and seeming quite handsome, with a gentleman of some worth. Is that your finest assembly dress? You will wear it all day to practice movement with heavy dresses and with much fabric to control as you walk and move. More fabric than is reasonable, but that is the fashion, yes? You must move as in a dance, a ballet in which you are on stage with the entire London society inspecting your performance. I have a seamstress coming to fit you. You must have better gowns than these for London."

Elizabeth said thank-you, but Lady Catherine waved away her words, swatting at the fly that Elizabeth was certain she had become.

"Darcy has chosen you. If he will not mind me and refrain from this terrible crime, I will at the very least make sure that he is not embarrassed by you in society. I will test you at every step, Miss Bennet, and all flaws will be reported. So mind. Now, let us find out what talents we can improve upon. I understand you cannot ride a horse. That is unacceptable. You will make dates with Col. Fitzwilliam who will teach you. A lady must be able to mount a horse in a London Park and ride in comfortable circles with her society. Now, what else do you not know? I have asked Mrs. Romero, my housekeeper, to set a setting for a typical meal. And Mrs. Dawson will teach you all the good habits I have taught her so that you know what to expect from a lady's maid. Now, you will now tell me appropriate behaviours for a young woman at table..."

"Madame, I have used a fork or two..."

"...and then we will examine the rules for conduct at an assembly."

"But I have been to many..."

"And they were in a barn or such common places? Have you been a fine lady in London society? No, I thought not. You will now listen."

CHARLOTTE'S MATRIMONIAL BLISS

Marching at a good pace, their laced boots stirring dust from the lane, Charlotte and Elizabeth laughed and talked, sharing little hugs and holding hands occasionally as their friendship revived exactly where it had left off. Charlotte commented on Elizabeth's shining eyes, her fresh face full of love wonder and delight.

"I believe you quite disliked Mr. Darcy. In fact, you spoke of him with something of a hiss the last time you were here. And I know you, Lizzy, it's not for his fortune that you will suddenly accept him."

"Mr. Darcy and I have completely and decidedly resolved our differences."

Her friend tossed her head with a look that said, I do not believe you. Charlotte knew very well Elizabeth's ideals about love and marriage.

"Darcy told me recently that my poor opinion of him made him reconsider his attitude. And yet, it was his housekeeper's high opinion of him that made me reconsider mine of his."

"Ah, now I see the passion!" Charlotte teased. "You hated him less because the housekeeper was fond of him."

"Yes, that is it!" Elizabeth laughed. But then she tried to explain. "I don't know what love is now. I love Jane and father. I love you. But my sentiments for Darcy are not in the least the same. I don't know him, cannot anticipate him as I can the others. I ask myself do I love him because he has desired me with steadfast conviction for a year and not quit his attentions? And that by removing my prejudice against him, I have allowed his devotion for me to flow into that gap?"

"Lizzy, that kind of thinking is strange. Do you not feel for yourself?"

"I do sound confused. I can say that I'll never again meet a man who understands me as well as I believe he does, who seems to mind my impertinence as a favourable delight. He calls it intelligence and wit. I do like that I can be myself with him. That is it, Charlotte. That once I removed my prejudice against him, and he resolved his sense of privilege towards me, I saw that I liked myself very much when I was in his company."

Eventually they left the road to climb a nearby hill, following hedgerows and stone walls, gradually rising higher out of the valley and away from the village. As she paused on a stile, Elizabeth turned to stare down into the valley, past the speckled fields of sheep, across the hills and the houses with their pot chimneys and warm slate roofs, to the horizon of mist lifting gradually in the increasing warmth. "It seems that I have been terribly mistaken about Mr. Darcy. When I think back, I remember caring what he thought of us even though I didn't like him at all. If I thought nothing of him, I would not care what he thought of mother's prattling or Mary's musical taste."

She climbed down the stile to allow Charlotte access.

"That you cared whether he liked your family was the first sign that you loved him?" Charlotte asked laughing.

"I know, but how does one explain the oddly paradoxical intensity of love? The more I'm with him the more I experience distortions of ardour. Is that love? And as we get to know one another, the things which I once thought I hated in him are exactly the things which present to me as most desirous. The twist of his mouth, which I once saw as disdain and arrogance, I now know is a sardonic wit not unlike Father's. And his seeming to be aloof is actually a shyness in large company and disinterest in gatherings in general."

"And that pride...? Can you dismiss it?"

"No. It's there. But he listens and agrees. So there is hope."

"And this is love."

"Of course not. It's that I see him in a different light which favours new attitudes," Elizabeth foundered. "It's like a weight..."

"Which has been lifted?"

"No. It gets heavier. Stronger. More insistent and appealing."

"And this is love. Now I understand you perfectly!" Charlotte laughed. "Love is a terrible weight we misunderstand as dislike only to be replaced by a terrible weight we no longer misunderstand as dislike and because the one whom we once disliked has a big fine house, we will reconstrue our original impressions to forge them into something workable."

Elizabeth sighed with exaggeration, batting her eyelids and looking lovesick, wringing her hands and sighing again. "You sum it up perfectly."

They walked a little in silence, happy and content in each other's presence, their strong bond well established and fine. Then Elizabeth, having so many questions about Charlotte's matrimonial life, asked Charlotte how it had been with her the last months that they were absent from one another.

If introductions are necessary, Charlotte had been married less than a year to Mr. Collins, who is Mr. Bennet's cousin. He had arrived at the Bennet household with the intent to choose one or the other of Mr. Bennet's daughters as his wife. He was confident of their acceptance for there was an entail on the property which left it to him should Mr. Bennet die. He felt that he was doing the family a kindness in offering himself to protect them from losing their home. Agreeing wholeheartedly, Mrs. Bennet directed him to her second daughter Elizabeth who was horrified by his blustery buffoonery and refused him emphatically. He, not to be dissuaded from his matrimonial quest, walked across the village to propose to Elizabeth's dear friend, Charlotte Lucas. On a recent visit to her friend, Elizabeth found the two sequestered in their own separate lives, quite not the adoring couple that she had envisioned for her own matrimonial bliss.

"Do you now have little secrets which you keep with one another?" Elizabeth asked.

"Little secrets," Charlotte repeated under her breath. "No. No little secrets."

Elizabeth, hearing something catch in Charlotte's answer, studied her and found there a great sorrow. She did not like Mr. Collins and she liked even less that her dear friend Charlotte had married him.

"Mr. Collins is a good man, he is not unkind at all, but..."

Elizabeth watched her friend struggle to speak through overwhelming emotions and placed her arms around Charlotte's shoulder, and petted her head, and Charlotte fell to the ground sobbing uncontrollably. Elizabeth worried that some death had occurred, that Charlotte had lost a child prematurely, or some such tragedy.

Charlotte accepted a handkerchief from Elizabeth as hers had become well used, and she blew her nose and wiped her eyes, and composed herself, but as she began to speak, the words caught in her throat and she shook her head crying as Elizabeth soothed and rocked her. It was some time before Charlotte suggested they should walk again and so they continued to climb and ambled along the ridge with few words, noting a bird or a beautiful tree, but otherwise quite silent until Charlotte began to express what was weighing so heavily on her heart.

"Elizabeth, all I can say is that matrimony is not a simple matter...I am very confused, for wanting some things which I thought would naturally be mutual, and that the purpose of this union was clear, and should one get married and yet not express that implicit purpose, not even with words, much less in action, and then should that implicit purpose be disclosed by one party become a thing that horrifies the other party...so it becomes a dark and uninhabitable subject which creates a distance, like a hallway one keeps between each of the rooms, so that when one steps into the room the other leaves..."

Not quite realizing to which matrimonial purpose Charlotte referred, Elizabeth nevertheless understood that a great chasm had opened between Mr. and Mrs. Collins who, she knew, were not entirely close in the first place. Her only models for matrimonial relations were offered by her own parents. She considered how her mother mollified her father by ordering his favourite food before introducing the topic of a new purchase, or other slightly trivial matter. Yet for any more demanding and conflictual topic, she was so upset that there was only drama, the common refrain Send for Mr. Jones (the apothecary), while pressing hot compresses to her head with her girls providing soothing words in a dim light. Meanwhile, Mr. Bennet rushed to solve the problem, should he be so lucky. That Charlotte should take to her bedroom with a melodrama of compresses and shrieking was poor advice, but Elizabeth could think of nothing to say.

Charlotte shook her head. "I know what you're thinking. I thought so also. That the layers of our public face would peel away as we grew to know one another. That all would happen naturally as we are now bound together and must create a life. That is what I imagined. We are happy except for the most important thing, Lizzy. The one in which..." and she searched the horizon as if it might produce the words. "I wish you were not a maiden that I could speak more openly about what is in my heart."

Charlotte began to cry again, more softly this time. Then she whispered that she too was still a maiden. Elizabeth felt like she had been struck. Charlotte explained that the more she suggested that she should like to be a mother, the more Mr. Collins withdrew. He, unable to accommodate her wish or communicate in any way about it, sent a letter to their friends announcing an olive branch as if her being with child were already a fact.

"It was his way of agreeing to my intention. And I could not bear to write to you how he had misled you by announcing something not true...I just hoped that we could make it true soon thereafter."

"He is not a man of the world, Charlotte. You knew it when you married him."

"And I liked him for it. I didn't want a man accustomed to women and ready to follow any skirt that would have him."

"Well, no woman does, but he is far from that. I don't think he has ever, in his life, imagined what lies beneath our skirts."

"I have tried to..." Charlotte paused, searching for words. "I try to make myself... available... Oh, he runs from me. Lizzy. And what do I know of the matter? Nothing! Oh, it's too unbearable! It's too catastrophic to contemplate."

"Why be impatient?"

"I want children. Isn't that why one marries?" Charlotte paused, and with a slightly mirthful look at Elizabeth, she announced "If this continues, what choice have I but to claim an annulment?"

"That is radical! I know you don't mean it; it would ruin your reputation. Perhaps you could go around the village and purchase children from mothers who have too many? Some families with twelve or more might be quite willing to sell them for a few dozen eggs and a handful of potatoes."

"Oh you - this is serious!" Charlotte scolded.

A hawk circled in the air before them and gave its sharp kwei kwei cry and Elizabeth took Charlotte's hand and pulled her to a standing position and gave her a hug.

"Patience dear. He'll come around. He must!"

Charlotte started shaking. At first Elizabeth thought she was again crying, but when uncontrollable laughter finally escaped, they both laughed for such a long time that they had to run into a bush and pee.

BILLIARD ROOM TALK

Evan, the Earl of Somewhere, was standing with his cue as if armed, with a cigarette perched delicately between two fingers and his head cocked slightly at an angle, a pose Darcy knew he had constructed carefully in the glass as a young man seeking a persona of intrigue and casualness both. Col. Fitzwilliam, known to them as Tod, was at the table, as unassuming as ever, pragmatic and sensible to the point of having little personality.

Darcy, trying not to think of Elizabeth for it aroused him too much, paid attention to the game in progress. But as Col. Fitzwilliam's ball rolled to a stop at the point of falling, the Earl whispered Lady Catherine's refrain with calculated mockery. "Too close! Too close!"

They burst out laughing while Darcy, tired of the joke, shook his head and reprimanded them for their sad lack of original material. The Earl took his snuff box from his vest pocket, pinched the tobacco and snorted it. He closed the lid and returned it to his pocket. "Darcy, I have a minor complaint. I have been here almost a fortnight and you have not yet offered to bring me into the library. Your uncle was far more generous."

"Evan: we snuck in as boys," Darcy objected.

"He left the doors open, you simpleton," the Earl chided.

Col. Fitzwilliam leaned into his shot. The Earl swirled a brandy in his glass. "It is one of the finest such libraries I have seen – and I have seen many examples, none quite so replete as this one. When I was still pretending I had the means, I inquired into purchasing it."

"From my uncle? He would not sell," Col. Fitzwilliam proclaimed.

"No. I put out feelers after his death. But the servants told me that Lady Catherine had no knowledge of it, and none of us were about to change that…"

"She might destroy it," Darcy interjected. They laughed. "But of course, technically, it belongs to Anne as she inherited the estate."

The Earl nodded. "Yes. I thought so as well. Though you couldn't get anything from that one without going through that other one. Inquiries were made and I decided not to pursue. My dearest

23

convinced me I should buy some meat for our supper instead."

Darcy was unsure why his uncle had collected a library of erotic material, literary and visual, scientific and deviant, from everywhere in the world. He was from an old and respected family, and Darcy himself loved the man; however, he had established a racy tone on his side of the manor that was as distinctive as it was hidden. The library was as complex as the man, from tastefully chosen materials of ancient manuscripts to salacious pamphlets and coarse humour.

"Is it true you have a collection of your own, Evan?" Col. Fitzwilliam asked.

The Earl shook his head. "Alas, no more. All sold."

"Were you hoping to find something in particular tonight? That Eastern manual you keep going on about?" Darcy asked.

"Yes, that and others."

"Still a connoisseur," added Col. Fitzwilliam.

"I haven't been in the room for years," Darcy told him, signaling his disinterest.

"All this time with the library at your disposal and you neglect it," the Earl reprimanded. "Do you know how to access it?"

"Certainly. Though, I must admit, since we were boys, I have lost the taste for it..."

"...Not when you have a fine filly at the end of your passage," the Earl suggested, referring to a well hidden passage linking the former Lewis de Bourgh's bedchamber and study, through the secret library, to the mistress bedroom, the one currently occupied by Elizabeth.

"Believe it or not, I have not used the mistress tunnels," Darcy replied. He was determined to maintain proper relations with Elizabeth. To control his desires. To be as chaste as she.

"Fitzy! I am disappointed in you," the Earl exclaimed. "And with your reputation? Not even to use a maid?"

"I have noticed that maids do not like being used."

"But why do you wait now to be married?" Col. Fitzwilliam interjected. "It is not as though you are in need of money or a home."

Darcy smiled to himself. "Tod, I want her to know me better," he alleged, hoping these few words explained sufficiently his intentions. "I want to know her. And I suppose I want to appease Lady Catherine. Despite what we all think of her, she is my close relation and I want to honour her wishes, if only a little."

"Marriage will cure both!" Col. Fitzwilliam laughed.

"And then what? If I hate the smell of her mouth or the way she... no that is not the point. I just want to know that we will be compatible in many ways."

"Darcy: you astonish me. You will ruin her before marriage? Would you respect her if she gave in to you?"

Darcy ignored the Earl's pretense at chastity and propriety. He had "ruined" his fair share of women. Instead, Darcy confessed that he had not had a mistress in over a year.

"You? The great and renowned Don Juan?" The Earl teased.

"How tired that reputation is. How passé. I am no Byron. My mistress suffers from my absence. She has taken up with Bonnie Stately's brother instead."

His mistress. It sounded, to him now, somewhat puerile and dull to say it. When he was a younger man and he took up with married ladies, married for convenience to tired old bores (their words), he thought himself quite the dapper and enlightened man serving these women. But he did so with such kindness and attention that he gained a reputation, one in which he was desired, sought and solicited. To most of these invitations, he was also absent. Despite the circuit of tattle regarding his skills, he chose but a few women during his mistress years and took great pains to care for them as much as circumstance would allow.

"And Elizabeth is in the mistress chambers. Did you plan that?" Col. Fitzwilliam asked.

"My dearest Auntie Cate arranged it. I couldn't tell her why it was inappropriate without explaining why…"

"Auntie Cate can't possibly have a clue that we call it the mistress room," Col. Fitzwilliam suggested.

"Auntie Cate is more likely to be ignorant that you refer to her as 'Auntie' and 'Cate'," the Earl mused. "It is possible she has done the thing intentionally…"

Darcy looked up.

"Really Evan, you think it is likely that she wants Elizabeth to be compromised?" Col. Fitzwilliam asked.

The Earl merely cocked his head a little. "I will say no more. It is speculation and conjecture. Now…" he said, pouring another glass of brandy, "there is a maid in our household I am quite fond of. My dearest has sometimes allowed her to join us. You should get to know her, Darcy. Take the edge off. Or else you are all piping and fiddling. Oh, dear boy, you can't tell me that you are reduced to such?"

"Do you remember Darcy, when we came upon the library by accident?" the colonel asked, peering down the table at a line of red balls. Darcy saw that they were all ready to drop if Col. Fitzwilliam could but correctly place the cue ball after each shot.

"How old were we? Ten? What a find!" Col. Fitzwilliam mused, sinking another ball.

"It is no wonder we are so well versed in female needs," the Earl added. "My darling says they all come for me and my prowess!" he laughed. "Most men must not have any abilities at all if mine is to be deemed prowess."

"Yes, and you leave little earl's everywhere," Col. Fitzwilliam mumbled.

"It is simply not true. To have unclaimed children shrugging about is not much my style, as much as you may think me a delinquent. I am merely irresponsible with money. And I blame that entirely on my beloved whose tastes I didn't curb. It is Darcy who has dropped gorgeous brats this way and that."

Darcy winced. "We were discussing your failings, Evan. Tomorrow we can book mine."

"Have you told your bride about your little transgression and subsequent progeny?" the Earl asked.

Darcy shook his head.

"Might not tell her - maybe not ever," the Earl advised.

"She will bite off your head if she finds out," Col. Fitzwilliam agreed.

"Yes, you have caught a live one, there Darcy. Good shot!" the Earl exclaimed as he moved to the far side of the table. "Quite right. Don't tell her that you have a daughter living happily with some ill shod plod in a beastly village in nowheresville. That floosy Augusta was trouble. And we all knew it. I know you and she were dear friends as children, but you were like parading aristocrats, she bossy and you silently proud, and I don't know what you did together when you were alone beside the unmentionables... holding hands and kissing and making a daughter, but she was after you, my boy, and we all saw it."

"I do not blame her at all for what happened."

"And I would blame her entirely," Col. Fitzwilliam stood from a missed shot.

"She was a trollop," the Earl insisted. "I know. She trollopped me. And others, but we didn't believe that story about the first time being safe. I am surprised you did." He sank the last ball. "Darcy, will you play?"

"You say the most remarkably untrue things, Evan," Col. Fitzwilliam declared. "Even amongst friends who can call your bluff. We all know that she despised you."

"The precise truth is irrelevant," the Earl argued. "Whether it was me or another, she was not as chaste as she ought to have been. I am merely making Darcy see that he is the victim. I'm on your side!"

"I feel responsible because there was a child produced and a young woman who lost hope at a happy life."

"Well, there is such a thing as being too honourable," Evan added.

"All of this is far too much seriousness for an old single man. I am off to the comfort of my own bed," Col. Fitzwilliam yawned.

The Earl snickered. "Do not stay long with her..."

"Ah, Evan. Your mind is torturously single minded. Have you considered that we are not all alike?" Col. Fitzwilliam goaded as he replaced his cue in the rack.

After Col. Fitzwilliam departed, the Earl waved his hand, "I wonder to which room he travels?"

"He chases that French heiress, Sophie, to no avail. She can barely remember his name. Somehow he has managed to have her join us when Georgiana arrives."

"Ah, good man. Still seeking his gold." The Earl nodded to the upper floor, Darcy's study and its secret salacious library. "Shall we?"

"Soon," Darcy nodded, "but not tonight."

"Ah yes, your blood boils too much for a titillating romp. Good. To bed with you. To piping and fiddling. Well, bonne nuit, alors."

HOW DEBUTANTES WILL FALL

Dinners in the de Bourgh household were sober affairs. The Earl of Somewhere made slightly coloured jests, Anne and Mary were entirely silent, Mrs. Jenkinson agreed to everything, while Darcy set in with a word or two and failed to ignite any conversation. Col. Fitzwilliam was the most dynamic participant and told funny stories but failed to make an impression on the silence once his story was complete. Elizabeth felt the silence deeply for at home their meals were always filled with the chatter of many voices in a steady bickering cheeriness. For this reason, she chose on several occasions to dine alone in her room with Mary, finding in that lonely company a more enjoyable experience. She also felt, in this capitulation, that Lady Catherine was already winning the battle to reveal how unfit she was to be Darcy's bride.

A week after her arrival, Mr. and Mrs. Collins, the Miss Webbs and Lady Metcalfe were invited to dine with them and the atmosphere improved a little. Lady Catherine presided at one end of the table and Darcy at the other. Neighbours leaned in to speak to one another and the room became almost noisy. The candles were more numerous so that the room was bright and one course followed the other, each more rich and delicious than the last.

Elizabeth had not seen Darcy but once or twice, to nod or to have her hand momentarily held and kissed, her eyes admired. All week, he was busy with errands for his aunt who, he whispered, Keeps me from you. And if perchance they should meet somewhere and touch within Lady Catherine's scope, she continued to yell Too Close! Too Close! forcing them to once again part. And now she was too close too close beside Grendel with Darcy at the far end of the table. Whenever Elizabeth sought his eyes for a moment of commiseration, the Great Lady diverted her with a question.

Elizabeth was grateful for the training she received as she now knew exactly what was expected of her at Lady Catherine's table. The rigorous syllabus of her estate management training lasted all day every day as various members of the household, staff and guests, provided the lessons. Col. Fitzwilliam taught riding, the Dowager elocution, the butler and housekeeper details of staff management and the ever interesting problem of silverware. Lady Catherine instructed in accounting and budgets, the conditions of formal address and peerage laws, to name but a few. At night, Elizabeth could barely keep her eyes open to read, and this was only partially due to the fact that Lady Catherine provided the books. Ledgers, lists of Aristocrats and their titles, the history of British monarchy, and other such highly engaging material did not keep her awake at the best of times. Although she would be surprised how often their information proved useful.

The noisy cheer at the dinner table was interrupted when Lady Catherine announced she would tell a story. It described the fall of a young debutante and her entire family when she tripped as she climbed down from her carriage in front of the palace entrance, a catastrophic failure at her coming out. She was shunned from society with subtle silences and turned backs.

"High stakes etiquette, a friend of mine calls those balls," Col. Fitzwilliam commented.

"Her chances were ruined," Lady Metcalfe said.

"Yes, she will now have a hard time making a good match if she has nothing else to distinguish her," the Dowager Fontainebleu agreed.

"Her father was so embarrassed, he resigned from his club," Lady Metcalfe added.

"That is excessive, is it not?" Elizabeth asked. "That we have misfortunes is not indicative of our true attributes. To trip is but an accident."

"That we have misfortune when we are under inspection has everything to do with our attributes, and our luck, and both are found wanting in such a circumstance, accident or not," Lady Catherine contradicted.

"Quite right. Quite so, for who wants a wife with poor luck," Mr. Collins parroted. "An accident is a sign of God's restricted approbation."

Elizabeth listened as everyone contributed to the list of requirements for young ladies of noble birth to find suitable husbands in high-ranking London society circles. She would like to have pointed out that despite not fulfilling most of the requirements - except that she had not fallen from her carriage when being introduced as a debutante - she had nevertheless been chosen by a high-ranking man.

"And what of the men?" Mary suggested, in a little voice, not at all confident, but sufficiently loud to penetrate. "What do they do to deserve equal approbation?"

Anne squealed. It was a reflex that she apparently could not contain, a mixture of horror and laughter, of delicious delight and terror at the consequences. Elizabeth glanced down the table to Darcy whose face was a perfect mask. But was there a slight curl of one side of his lips? She peaked across at Col. Fitzwilliam. He had begun to hum a little under his breath and she was sure he was trying not to laugh.

Anne mumbled an apology and visibly sank into her chair. Mrs. Jenkinson blushed as if this was a sign of her own failures, and Mary, unable to hide the contradictions of her own thoughts and feeling both fierce and frail, stared at her food.

The Earl of Somewhere filled the ensuing silence by recounting a story about a debutante who had similarly been trussed up at her coming out after a faux pas, yet had survived the experience, coming back from it as from a poor showing in the first half of a polo match by becoming one of the most entertaining, delightful, and precocious creatures of the ball (his words). Thus, followed stories of various declensions describing infamous debutante coming out stories, most of which veered from the tragic to the comedic, all focusing on the women's failings.

Elizabeth, pondering Mary's question about the privilege of men, nodded as Col. Fitzwilliam, who sat beside her, offered to pour wine into her glass and she replied A little, yes thank you, when he asked if she would like duck confit. He picked it delicately from the serving platter and placed it on her plate, then served himself. She peeked as all the men served the woman to their right and then themselves, providing this little service which suddenly seemed to mask a terrible imbalance. He offered carrot puree. Yes, thank you a little, she answered, watching as he served her. Perhaps it was good that he had all the work to do and she none. She watched as Darcy served the Countess, barely paying attention except to mind that the food was landing on the plate.

Elizabeth had earlier in the week made the mistake of whispering to Mrs. Jenkinson to please pass the salt. In the ensuing silence, while her great indiscretion was suspended in the room like inopportune flatulence or the crash of a glass, a manservant rushed to the rescue and delivered the salt. She had almost laughed out loud imagining her own father running around the table to serve all five of his household's women while they sat in silence hoping he would anticipate their needs. Here she was to be mindful of eating too slowly and too quickly, to pace herself according to the hostess, to wait until something was offered, to speak only when asked, in other words, to acquire invisibility. Eating had never been as dangerous nor as succulent. After Mary's outburst, she wondered if Mary would also be brought into the Throne Room for lessons on social etiquette.

This thought led to the next, that within a day of their arrival, Mary's dogged attention to her job of chaperone had ceased and she, Mary, was nowhere to be found most hours of the day. When Elizabeth sought her sister in the drawing room, Mary told her plainly that Lady Catherine had ordered her to desist in her duties.

"Perhaps she wants you to get into trouble, Elizabeth," Mary proposed. Elizabeth agreed and looked about the room for Charlotte. She had studied Mr. and Mrs. Collins all evening for signs that their marital life was improved, but while Mr. Collins was prodigious with praises, his Dear Dear Mrs. Collins, and his How she is quite so very very good to me, Mrs. Collins, and his Oh she is quite the model of perfection, Mrs. Collins, Charlotte's patient heeding to his words and her static facial expressions revealed nothing.

When Elizabeth caught Charlotte in the corner of the drawing room, she asked, Will you speak to me? but immediately Mr. Collins arrived and led Charlotte away by the elbow. Lady Catherine shifted in her seat and squinted at Elizabeth and puckered her lips as if she were thinking of something eminently distasteful and beckoned to her.

"I must ask you a question about a delicate matter," she began as Elizabeth sat beside her. "Mrs. Collins is not with child and her husband is a muff... Do not peer at me with such eyes, missy, I am not blind. And I can see from your response that I am on the right track."

Elizabeth felt herself get hot and lowered her eyes.

"Thank you. You have provided as much information as I need

in your silence," Lady Catherine mused. "She threatens to leave him, I suspect. She desires motherhood. I will not have my curate compromised in such a way. Scandalous that she remains barren. And for lack of trying, you tell me?"

"I said no such thing."

"Ah, but we both know it is true. Do not pretend to be a pure creature. You must yourself have had some wiles about you to have trapped my nephew in this scandalous plan. You have already been compromised by him I have no doubt. But I will respect his need to be honourable. To behave correctly in this affair. It is his way, to be honourable. Now, will you deny that Mr. Collins is a fool?"

Elizabeth was happy to reply affirmatively to the fact that she believed Mr. Collins to be a fool.

"Thank you, that will be all."

Elizabeth, eager to be released from this great meddler, bowed gracefully and fled to the protection of Anne and Mary. She had noticed that the two had become friends in the interceding week while she had been busy with her tutorials in standing, abiding, and groveling. They were in the midst of a discussion about perception, which she heard Anne saying was such an extremely personal matter that it was impossible to determine whether what one person saw was the same as the other except by agreement. To Elizabeth, who had never heard Anne speak more than a few mediocre sentences such a How do you do or You are quite well? Anne seemed fairly enlightened in Mary's company. But when Elizabeth arrived, the conversation shifted and Anne bent her head as if suddenly ashamed.

"We are talking about husbands," Mary told Elizabeth as she sat. "We cannot decide why one should want one."

"One doesn't want one," Anne announced, "One needs one. And then one hopes that one is engaged to one whom one should like to want."

"One can live without one," Mary challenged. "One can live in one's estate all one's life and inherit it."

Anne nodded. "One might. But then there are no babies to make the inheritance. And for Mummy, that is distasteful. The line must continue and all that."

Elizabeth wondered what had happened to the epistemological conversation she had interrupted. "May one ask if thou knowest any reason why Mr. Collins should be upset with me?" she interrupted with exaggerated formality.

Anne giggled behind her hand. Mary answered with her straightforward monotone.

"Lady Catherine suggested that Charlotte has not the breeding to be your close companion."

"That is absurd. She is a better person than any I have met anywhere."

DARCY'S ASSIGNMENT

Intimacy is not a thing that is lost or gained with any ease. For some people, it is acquired slowly over many years, a precious and well-polished treasure the value of which is well known for the work that has been done to acquire it. And yet, it can be lost to situations both of choice or circumstance. In the case of Elizabeth and Darcy, their eagerness to know one another was in reverse proportion to the amount of time they had to acquire knowledge of one another, for Lady Catherine was relentless in her demands to keep them separate. Following some weeks of tedious finishing school à la Great Grendel and her associates (the housekeeper, butler, Mrs. Jenkinson, and the Dowager), Elizabeth was released for several days without further notice and immediately went for a walk.

When she returned with Mary and Anne by way of the grand lane which was the main entrance to the estate, a carriage with four proud horses was parked at its entrance and they agreed it must be Georgiana who had finally arrived. The house in the distance dominated with its wide roof line and multiple windows and two distinctive turrets. Two pillars marked the doorway in a classical style at the head of a wide and rounded stair. The lane between was lined with large and sculpturesque trees, most over a century old and losing their leaves as winter set in. The gravel lane was impeccably maintained. As Elizabeth was eager to see Georgiana again, she picked up her skirt and trotted down the lane, leaving the other two to arrive at their own pace. As she came around the carriage, she found Darcy alone playing tug of war with a chocolate and cream coloured pointer. "Ah, my Miss Bennet. Well timed. I am quite delighted to introduce you to The Dog."

"And what is his name?" Elizabeth asked.

"Well, it is in fact The Dog. You know, spoken with caps and as if he wore a crown, for I have never known a dog to have so many fastidious routines. He is so named because he began living in the house and Mrs. Reynolds, our housekeeper, would occasionally point out that fact and ask, 'What sir, do you suppose we should do about The Dog?' He has arrived with Georgiana and a French woman, Mlle. Sophie Turin, who has accompanied her, but who is a stranger to us."

Darcy's countenance was fresh and beaming, his tenderness for the dog evident. The dog dropped the rope and visited her with his entire body wagging, a face of joy and smiles. Elizabeth bent over and greeted him enthusiastically. She picked up the rope and tugged, the dog leaning hard into the game. Darcy grabbed a section to help Elizabeth and they both wrestled The Dog until they were out of breath and sat on the bottom of the stairs.

"The Dog is not an appropriate name for your dear companion, Fitzwilliam," Elizabeth laughed, regardless of Mrs. Reynolds' approbation. "You will name our children The Child the First, The Child the Second, and etcetera?" And then blushed at the change in his features as she spoke of children, looking more like he would have them sooner than later, his eyes peered into hers until, despite herself, she looked down. But then, when she raised up her eyes to him to meet his gaze, to say yes, I can speak of these things, he had looked away.

"Yes, until The Child the Thirteenth, which just sounds awful and then we'll name him Sam or her Petunia."

She nodded, "Of course. I should have known."

"Things are bound to become lively," he warned, mocking a yawn. He gently squeezed her arm. "Thank you. For tolerating this."

"No matter, dearest. One of these days you will have to learn how to tolerate my mother."

To which he made a face. He had successfully avoided Mrs. Bennet, her voice which grated his ears and her inane conversation.

"Your riding is worse than you have described."

"It was better than I had hoped!" she answered. "The Colonel recommends I return to ponies."

"I was jealous when I saw you with him the other day. There was a smile in your eyes as you spoke and a proprietary way he took your elbow..."

"Your cousin is enchanting. Haven't you noticed how green his eyes are? How his hands fly?" she teased. "Not to worry. I was merely talking to him. I do hope that every conversation I undertake with a man will not raise your ire! But I do not like the Earl, nor the Countess, his wife. She touches you in ways that are rather invasive, if you ask me, and Lady Catherine says nothing to interfere. I would be whipped if I were to touch you in such a manner. I believe every time I look at you, she yells…"

"Too close too close." Darcy chimed in, imitating his aunt as they had both had quite enough of the refrain.

"Are you jealous?" he asked. "But you have nothing to fear, my dear, it is just her way, she is coquettish with every man who moves."

A footman arrived with a message from Lady Catherine, to which he nodded but did not move.

"I believe the Countess is paid by your aunt to interfere," Elizabeth confided, resuming the conversation. He laughed and shook his head disbelievingly. "But your Col. Fitzwilliam is sweet. He does not test me at all. He told me all about how you raised your hunter, like a pet. He described how you'd play with it in the field when it was still too young to ride. What is the hunter's name? The Horse?"

He nodded.

"But it cannot be!" she exclaimed.

"No. But I named him when I was young. He is poorly named."

"Worse than The Dog?"

"I named him Harrumph."

"I prefer The Horse. Please do not become involved when it is time to name our children!" she laughed.

He spoke in a Yorkshire accent. "My certy. My father war Yorkshire, which makes me a bit Yorkshire too. So, we knows nottin' 'bout naming and Grand Folk from London shocked at war 'incivility'; we like weel enough to gi'e 'em summat to be shocked at, 'cause it's sport to us to wath 'em turn up the whites o' their een, snf spreed out their bits o' hands…"

Elizabeth laughed so hard, she pushed at his chest to make him stop. Yet, he continued, explaining the horse's name.

"It t'wer my favrit book – Gul'var… and them hosses which talked grand like. There's a deal about me you do not yet know, Miss Bennet. I learnt, shall I say, 'to nip my words short like!' But it will be our little secret, for there are few people who have met farmer Fitz Darcy."

She leaned into his shoulder with her own, for just a second. "Darcy, I do believe that we have not had any time to be together. This is the first good conversation we have enjoyed since I arrived!"

He took her hand. "No matter. Soon we will tire of each other for we will be at one another's side all the rest of our days!"

"Never."

He stood and bowed politely, excusing himself to obey his aunt's request and, as he turned to leave, his sister Georgiana flew out the front door and ran into Elizabeth's arms squealing, "Oh, I am so delighted to be your sister, Miss Bennet. We shall be the best of friends."

For the first time since she had agreed to marry Darcy, Elizabeth felt a joy of making a new home, of having new family, of being welcomed into something that would become her life. Georgiana immediately agreed to go riding with her and they went off together to enjoy an afternoon with Col. Fitzwilliam.

That very evening, Darcy and Elizabeth were in the drawing room, their two chairs side by side, talking together as if they were alone in the room, their heads bent together, their voices carrying directly to each other quite comfortably. No sign of touching could be noted by any person in the room and so no words of criticism interrupted their conversation. And since the Countess was not well and had dined in her chambers, her flirting was noticeably absent. Darcy had told Elizabeth that the Countess's attentions were ostensibly to show Anne ways of attracting a husband, a ruse in which Darcy was a player. They admitted that Lady Catherine may have other secondary objectives, to provoke Elizabeth to behave badly for example. But Elizabeth was quite adamant that Grendel would not win the game, for she had found in herself the tame and pretty Elizabeth, Fanny Burney's good Cecilia, who knew enough to hold her tongue. "It is not terribly hard. One does nothing, says nothing but your ladyship yes, your most masterful mistress yes, and goes about learning what is good to learn. I know more about the lineages of the finest British families than they themselves."

Elizabeth asked what that great Grendel had desired of him earlier, joking and teasing because she could not have imagined the answer, and if she had imagined the answer, she would not have posed the question. He raised his eyebrows at her and shook his head as if to say, oh, do not tread there, but she frowned, and worried that Lady Catherine had spoken of some essential attribute which had been found wanting. And so he must reassure her and then, of course, she reminded him of their agreement, to be friends to one another, which required a certain level of disclosure, to which he said

I am not sure that this qualifies. And then her curiosity was piqued, and he saw that if he could not speak to her of this topic, then he was something of a hypocrite if he wanted close intimacy with her.

He felt something adjust within him, a sense of something new happening, as if a slight gap between them was suddenly offering a bridge by which it might be closed, and on which he could walk quite safely, for the topic was far enough from them both personally to not touch at their own physical intimacy, but to skirt around the topic and create pathways by which, in the future, they might tread.

He peered into the room and there were but the whist players at the other end of the room, quite loud and not attentive to their conversation. Darcy bent his head a little closer to her and whispered, "My aunt pressures me to speak to Mr. Collins as if we were friends."

"Oh?"

"She told me I was the best and only man for the job." She turned her head, attentive. "She does not want her parson running off every time his wife feels an absence in her womb. I am to give Mr. Collins manly advice."

Elizabeth blushed, fell silent, horrified, and then laughed a little.

"She meddles a great deal." Darcy took her hand but did not look at her. "And it is not compassion which drives this request. She cannot abide chaos. I exaggerate of course, but she will have order and whatever is needed to maintain the appearance of order."

"And she asked you to provide…?" Elizabeth would not say another word but nodded. "When Charlotte first confided in me, I too considered asking someone to help the poor man. He has been without proper… guidance." She paused and touched his arm, then removed it before notice could be taken of the action, and then "And how are you quite fit for the job?" Elizabeth probed.

Darcy started. "Anyone who knows anything is suited for this job. It just happens that I am a man. I think that is what she meant."

"Really?" Elizabeth replied as if not believing him. He smiled a cheeky grin, the one he used for years when his aunt confronted him. Fitzwilliam! Do not think you can sneak that on me, she would say, and Elizabeth shot him a look which said much the same thing, that she would not be bribed by his adorable face. "But the question is, Lizzy," and he leaned way in close to her so he could smell her neck. "I will not broach the subject with him if he has done what he was supposed to do last year."

She giggled. He sat back, astonished. She began to laugh with a sort of nervous laughter all the while shaking her head. "I do not know!" she was finally able to say.

Elizabeth's dark eyes shone into him with an open expression of delight. Were they actually having this conversation? He rolled his eyes and she laughed loudly. He took her by the hand. "Dear Elizabeth. I don't even know who I am with you. I feel a liberty that is unfamiliar with anyone except, perhaps, my cousin. But you, it is even stronger. I want to hold you to me, and to never let go…"

She took his hands and leaned forward and kissed him – not once – but several times on his neck, slowly moving from just under his ear into his collarbone. He stretched his neck out a little for her to find her way and shivered with the incredible pain that tightened throughout him as desire for her crushed him. "My, I grow fond of your impertinence."

As she met his eyes, he could see it in her. She wanted him also.

She shook her head, blushing. "Perhaps you could suggest that he start by kissing her," she whispered.

Lady Catherine called her away and she went, obediently, to sit with Grendel and talk of something mundane.

At the end of a long day, back in her room with her hair down and her slippers on her feet, wearing nothing but her shift and a night coat, her body released from the confinement of the highly stylized and constrictive clothes she must wear all day to suit Lady Catherine, Elizabeth stared from the window and recalled her excellent day. She had met Darcy on his way to bed, an orchestrated encounter she had no doubt. He had pulled her aside, into a broom closet or some such thing, for it was quite unlit by candle or window, and he pressed himself against her with hips and lips and then, with a ferocious moan, had pushed away from her and fled the room.

She crawled under the covers and blew out the light, but she was wide awake thinking about the urges which these intimacies with Darcy had produced in her. She touched her lips, let her tongue move across them, her hand to her breast, pinching her nipples, imagining these to be his hands. She felt her body jerk awake, to come to attention in a way, igniting inside outside all over, she could not be precise. She felt simultaneously light and heavy, as if the weight of these sentiments was a force which lifted with its momentum.

As she followed these thoughts, experiencing her body as she imagined Darcy with her, there was a knocking nearby which startled her. Her hands flew back to the top of her quilt and she grabbed her book as if reading, and listened. The banging repeated. If it was coming from the hallway, she might not have trembled, but that it seemed to come from behind the large cupboard was terrifying. She pulled up her covers to her eyes and listened with hyper vigilance, straining her hearing beyond breath and heartbeat. She heard a handle rotating. She bolted up from her bed, ready to face whatever was coming.

"Sophie. Viens. C'est barré," yelled a deep voice.

Elizabeth screamed. "Go away. I am not Mademoiselle Turin!" and then, as the voice cursed and retreated, she wished she had at least discovered who it was occupying the strange room behind her wall. She climbed out of bed and opened the two side by side doors of the massive oak garderobe and peered in, but all she found were her clothes, three dresses and five shifts. She stepped beyond these but found nothing which seemed like a latch. However, when she banged against the wooden frame, there was a hollow sound which seemed to echo and she was sure there was a door hidden somewhere.

THE SALACIOUS LIBRARY

Darcy and the Earl of Somewhere went to the drawing room to bid the ladies goodnight. A few were playing whist and Elizabeth was ensconced in letter writing. Darcy took her hand, bowed to her, and gave her a loving kiss on her gloved knuckles saying Goodnight my dear in the most formal and loving way. She tossed a smile at him and caught his eyes with all the words she could not speak and all the touching she could not do and bade him good night with equal formality.

In his personal chambers, Darcy poured two brandies and handed one to the Earl. He led the Earl to a large bookshelf, reached into a shelf beyond Spinoza's *Ethics* and flipped a lever, pulled a handle and opened the door to the hidden room. He stepped in with his candle in one hand and brandy in the other while the Earl delighted in the appropriate choice of Spinoza to hide the secret access, a choice deft with inuendo and irony. Darcy lit a few more candles and handed the candelabra to the Earl in order to read the titles. It was a reading room with several armchairs and a small table. And it was unusual and hidden because all the material within contained works relating to human sexuality. It also contained a second door, the entrance to the mistress tunnels and the primary reason Darcy didn't want to indulge the Earl.

While Darcy swirled his brandy in his glass and drank little, the Earl perused a section of the bookshelf which contained eastern manuals and began the tedious task of checking each title. He spoke with his back turned as he lifted titles from the shelf to glance and return them, not finding what he was seeking.

"You know, my wife chastises me for never having invited you to join us. She is disappointed that you have decided to marry without giving her the pleasure of your company."

The Earl turned and spoke to Darcy directly.

"I saw you wince at that door. If you would like to make your way to our chambers later this evening, I don't think either of us would object."

"You're too kind," Darcy laughed. The Earl cocked his head as if to say, I am serious. But then he turned again, speaking as before to the books.

"I must admit, when we were boys, I saw nothing of the fraternizer in you. You were quiet, slightly withdrawn and even quite unattractive in the way boys can be. Chubby and ungainly and..."

"With a slight stammer. Have you not found what you are searching for?" Darcy asked, disappointed that disparagement remained the Earl's habitual way of seducing a lover.

"Yes. The stammer. I had forgotten it. And then I did not see you for two years and you became a man, well formed, as you remain, and a man, no less, with a reputation."

Darcy regretted the reputation and wondered how he might make it go away.

"The rumours exaggerate."

"Even if exaggerated, one does not acquire such a reputation without some truth lurking within."

"It is true that I am capable of satisfying a woman. Perhaps that is sufficient to make me noteworthy."

"I have been told that you are adventuresome..."

"I believe I was with women who felt free to enjoy themselves, Evan. And that allowed for a spirit of adventure, yes, but not an artificial search for newer and bigger exploits. If you must know, even though it is not your business. Perhaps you might put some of these rumours to bed for me, (no pun intended I am sure)..."

"Of course, none! That was terrible, Darcy," the Earl chuckled while pulling more titles.

"It was my drug of choice, Evan. Sex. It saved me from worse distractions after Mother's death."

"You feel too deeply."

"I felt that too deeply, yes. I might as easily have chosen opium or drink to temper the pain. I believe, under the circumstances, I have done more good than harm in taking a mistress or two..."

"...or seven or thirty," the Earl interrupted.

"...and I do not regret anything except that everyone must continue to talk of it."

"I assure you, there are a few young buccaneers who have replaced you."

"Is that what they call me? A buccaneer? Not very flattering..."

"I beg to differ. It conjures a flashy hero, does it not? A

compelling Byronic figure."

"Yes, but will any person remember that the man writes poetry?"

"George Byron wrote a poem for a dog – you have at least two things which favour an introduction: love of women and love of dogs."

"I cannot speak for Byron, but I am no longer seeking flashy dalliances. I have found something far more compelling."

"Don't tell me you have relieved the mighty Elizabeth of her maidenhead?"

Darcy shook his head.

"Then it is Love? Oh, don't be a fool," the Earl added. "Oh, look here! *Fanny Hill.*"

"You've left the Eastern Manuals section."

"Yes. Didn't find that compelling little pamphlet. But this," he held *Fanny Hill* aloft, and then opened its cover with reverence, "this is a rare original. The underground pamphlets that have been copied have faults – inconsistencies. If you don't mind, I will borrow it to compare. In my room of course – wouldn't think of removing it from the house." Darcy nodded. "There is a passage, among many I might add, which I just adore. It is from the point of view of a flashy woman, paid to please, and a young man she must service. Ha, isn't language absurdly ambiguous? Ah, but here there are no ambiguities. It is quite clear, which is of course the reason why this book is not widely distributed. And I quote: *But what was yet more surprising, the owner of this natural curiosity, through the want of occasions in the strictness of his home-breeding, and the little time he had been in town not having afforded him one, was hitherto an absolute stranger, in practice at least, to the use of all that manhood he was so nobly stock'd with; and it now fell to my lot to stand his first trial of it, if I could resolve to run the risks of its disproportion to that tender part of me, which such an oversiz'd machine was very fit to lay in ruins.* How delightfully hilarious. A virgin man with a machine! Is that how you think of your cock, man? My lady, I will perform great acts of mastery on you with my machine. And she will reach out for it and say Let me repair it for you. Gawd, Darcy. Love has nothing to do with sex, which is quite another thing. You'll see. A year or two and your love will be certain, but your appetite will roam. I am lucky that my dearest will roam with me, and it is quite a lot of fun. Perhaps, this evening, you could bring your princess also? You yawn. Oh dear, you are already a fossil. Thank you for your hospitality. It is a fascinating collection."

Darcy stood, blew out the candles and led the Earl back to the study where he poured two more brandies and they sat in two wingbacks next to the fire. "It has occurred to me that my aunt has brought you here to tempt me, or Elizabeth, or both, so she can have cause to disparage my engagement."

The Earl nodded. "You are on to us, ol' man. That is precisely why we were invited."

"I hear that mocking tone. Forgive me for asking, but she is determined to intercede."

"The Countess is here to instruct Anne – to make her desirable to men. You see: you have ruined her chances at a match by refusing to marry her. Now your Auntie Cate must see to her future another way."

"That is ridiculous. She is fine as she is."

"Well, if living as a spinster with her ageing and overly oppressive mother is fine...I don't believe your Auntie Cate wants Anne to marry... then who would she oppress? Perhaps she wants a timorous man (for who else might Anne drag home?) so as to have little Annes to continue the oppression. A little tribe of pawns?"

Darcy smiled, but with sadness. "That may be the pretext. But you are here to tempt me, or Elizabeth, to lure us away from one another."

"Ah, well ol' man, that is for you to decide." And he blew Darcy a kiss. They spoke of other things well into the night, of people they knew in common and of the Earl's story about his declining fortunes, which were not entirely his fault, though he admitted that for some time he neglected his debts and continued to spend by way of not acknowledging his situation. Yet, he did not regret their unmitigated spending, and when it became obvious that the debts had accumulated beyond his mastery to delay their payment, they had sold everything and lived in a little townhouse in Cheapside, which was not really as bad as everyone had said it would be, and were away visiting their many friends as often as possible in great manors and halls, eating their fine food and entertaining them in the way that only the Earl and his beloved knew how.

After the Earl left, Darcy could not sleep. He had avoided the library for a very good reason and now, having broken the rule, he was experiencing its effects. He paced. Or perhaps it would be better described as an attempt not to pace, for he was quite still standing at the fireplace, leaning against the mantle and staring at the high flames. The heat was amassing so that soon he would have to step away, but for the time being he hoped to burn what occupied his mind. Theoretically, relief was close at hand in several forms, but the first, Elizabeth, was prohibited and the other, the library, was less satisfying now that the first was close at hand.

"Damn this!" he shouted, stepping out of the hearth and leaving the rage of flames, he tore open the curtain and stared at the moon. It was large in the sky, clear and cold in a night that had no humidity and no clouds. He could trace the silhouettes of the trees and outbuildings and little cottages beyond the limits of the park. He could see a horseman travelling along a ridge. All was a blue tinge, and his mind wrestled with his body as he stared. He stood, tall and rigid, master of the world, of the buildings and trees. He was restless as a beast and caught by animal instincts, and he imagined bounding from the balcony and running through the woods with The Dog, howling and chasing, and he felt his body grow wild with claws and great huge arms. The mere thought of running loose in the woods seemed like a relief to the cravats, the stiff-backed chairs and the maze of forks and knives that were his daily life.

He unlocked the French windows and stepped onto the balcony, raised his head, and grabbed the balustrade tightly between both hands, gouging into it with his frustration. She rose in his mind, waiting in some lonely place, vulnerable and scared, tied to a tree maybe, or guarded by some awful thing, and he comes upon her, and in his care of her, even as he is beast, allows her to see through his beastliness to accept him as saviour, and opens to him, gives herself to him...

"Oh, for God's sake, this is ridiculous!" he cried out loud. Both ridiculing himself and amused, he slammed the curtain shut, if such a thing was possible, and felt that he was quite unable to sleep until something radical was done. He took up the candle and went back to the secret library. He sat in the armchair and opened his pant buttons. The picture on the wall sufficed as he was already almost entirely on the verge of delivery. His frustration at having Elizabeth so near, her smell, the singular way she would shift her leg and reveal her little ankle for him when no one was looking, her laughter, all this so close at hand and with no satisfaction, was made worse by the fact that they had barely had a moment to speak since they arrived.

His body was on the verge of chaos.

The picture on the far wall was of a woman on a bed, a carousel of cloth draped here and there about her shoulders and torso, softening her nakedness, one leg up and shod with a buckled shoe, and the other leg spread to focus on the central detail of her labia. Her fingers rested on her mound where soft curls of hair snaked around them. He stared at that place, imagining that it belonged to Elizabeth, that delicious feeling of rounding those soft folds, circling until she was rising and arching to him, circling until he could crash into her without resistance, circling until her face was full of an expectant tension of bliss.

Circling until he was far into her, inseparable.

INTIMACIES IN THE GARDEN

Although Elizabeth could be impulsive, she had thought a lot about what she was about to say to Darcy, but she had not found an easy way to broach the subject. They had been quiet together some minutes and she decided to dispense with any preamble. Their conversation the previous day about the plight of Mr. and Mrs. Collins' matrimonial bed had opened a pathway to converse about their own relations.

"Darcy, I hope we don't have children immediately after we are married. I should like to have you to myself before we are parents."

"It is a beautiful day," he said, kissing her on the nose. "We are laughing and enjoying it with these good friends, and you speak of children. What an impetuous, strange girl you are. Is this a conversation we need to have this minute?"

"Of course not."

"I will tell you one thing: I will not be a Mr. Collins if that is what you mean."

Elizabeth giggled. "Oh, I should hope not. Now Fitzwilliam, you managed not to tell me why your aunt said that you are the right man for the job."

"You use Great Grendel's tone precisely. You have been listening."

"I should. She seems to get you to do all manner of things! Now, do not try to distract me."

They were alone on a little lane in the wood, a tract designed especially for horse or pedestrian, and their party was behind and before them in untethered groups as they meandered beneath a canopy of glorious oak, elm, aspen and beech.

"Here. I will begin first," she said. "I have not kissed a boy. I have, however, thought of kissing Daniel Adams, a boy who brought us milk and was astonishing in his good looks. But it was a thought which did not linger, and I have not ever been like my younger sisters who pine constantly over boys. There. My entire history. Now it is your turn."

"Lizzy. I cannot believe you want me to disclose the details of my life prior to our meeting. What value is there in knowing that I have not spent the past ten or more years of my life unaccustomed to the attentions of women?"

He paused, hoping that perhaps he had said enough, but she looked at him insistent.

"But you may hear, occasionally, rumours of my reputation. As rumours are often mischievous, the rumours about me will also be misleading. For instance, to some, you are an impudent over opinionated bold girl. However, I see you as an intelligent, free spirited and adventuresome woman. The two are the same, but the gaze of the rumour mill never views with compassion, nor is it generous with the complexities of human character. It takes a facile stance – which is invariably negative - and presents it with single strokes."

"You are exceedingly proficient at avoiding questions to which you wish to offer no answer."

"I am." He grinned impertinently like an eight-year-old boy, the smile offered as fake apology when one is caught in the cookie jar and the smile will excuse every transgression.

"And you will not tell me."

"What good would it be to know that I have a past? I have not spent the past ten years, since adulthood, without occasion to be... affectionate to certain women. I do not come to you uneducated as to their needs." He arched his eyebrow at her and she blushed.

"Will you hate me now?" he asked as her silence continued.

"I hate that you know more in these matters than I do. I hate that you are an expert and I am ignorant. It is not jealousy I feel, for I am quite certain you no longer think of these women..."

"Most were married."

"Darcy, that is shocking."

"Is it? There are women whose fate it is to be married to old men, cronies of their father's, for the sake of alliances which are no doubt as distasteful to you as to them. But it is a custom that continues from quite some time ago and they are expected to produce heirs. Is it any wonder that they seek, in discreet ways, a liaison with a man of comparable age, or younger, who wants also to learn something of the ways of women without committing himself?"

"You present yourself as quite a shining knight."

"If you knew anything of the romance stories of London's court, you'd know that my experiences are tame. The salons run by some of its most influential women are breeding places for challenging political conversations, sexual prowlers, and artistic fodder. Elizabeth, I do not indulge at all by comparison. But I am not a prude. Please, let us stop this quarreling. I cannot bear to have you hate me, even just a little. It was a long time ago now. And I am quite cured of it, I am afraid. I find myself pacing before a fire every evening trying to disabuse myself of a singular woman who, for the moment, will not give me the satisfaction I found elsewhere; but from whom I have no hope of escape."

"Oh, really? And will you visit her tonight?" Elizabeth asked, thinking of the man in her garderobe.

"I don't dare. She does not yet want children..." he whispered in her ear.

Elizabeth stopped walking suddenly, and he was ahead of her before he realized that she was no longer on his arm. "What is it? You seem ill. Shall I fetch water?" he asked, much concerned by her countenance.

She shook her head and pulled him towards her. "It is nothing. Nothing," and she did not know how to describe the feeling of his breath on her ear, the words he spoke, the sudden crushing need she had to put her mouth, her hands, her body against his, to feel him fully naked, to touch his hair, his mouth, to have him with her, to receive all of him. Speechless, she wrapped her arm into his and continued walking, confused and overwhelmed with desire she knew not how to express. She must remember to be a lady, but his tantalizing words were provoking her in a way unfamiliar and new.

"I wanted, immediately and manifestly, to have children with you," she whispered in his ear, trusting that the word "manifest" would push the point that it was not the children but the creation of them that she sought.

As they walked, he felt the weight of her on his arm, he felt the rich texture of their exchanges as a relationship unlike any he had before experienced. It was as if she allowed him, just in her being, to be himself. This was an opportunity to tell Elizabeth about his daughter, Lettice Rose. The girl he had never seen until his solicitor Higginson located her not far from Rosings Park in a village just east of the South Downs. After a meal in a local Inn, he had ridden casually through the village to stop in front a brick house with a significant workshop off to one side and a garden to the other where several children ran about. The blacksmith for whom this was clearly both home and work, was in the large doorway of his shop, hammering. Darcy saw a woman, the blacksmith's wife, hanging laundry at the back of the house. The scene was simple and bucolic.

The blacksmith looked up and saw Darcy sitting on his large, dappled stallion, and he waved, casually, the way a man might tip his hat at a passing acquaintance. It was a friendly wave, but a casual observer would note that it was both familiar and yet not beckoning. Darcy raised his hand also, in a casual salute. His horse shifted its weight from one foot to the other, but otherwise stood quite still in the middle of the lane while Darcy watched the children running and playing in the yard. The man stopped his work and watched Darcy watch his children. Darcy had sent a letter ahead, which had merely stated a time and day with the request that the children be out where he could see them.

One child, a girl, he followed with special attention. He was glad to see her playing with the others, fit and happy and without a care. Suddenly she laughed. Darcy's countenance didn't change, but his body experienced a strange thrill, the kind which arrives with an equal portion of joy and anguish, for the girl's laugh reminded him exactly of his mother.

Before he could broach this difficult subject, Elizabeth probed further into his history with other women.

"After all the choices you must have had," Elizabeth mused, her hand resting lightly on his forearm. "The opportunities, the women of society and rank. And you want me?" she asked sincerely.

"I do. Is it so remarkable?"

"It is. Yes, it is. It is not often a man of your rank marries for love."

"And yet, you refused me because of you thought you did not love me."

"Indeed, I did. But I am not you! I wonder that you also choose from preference," she laughed. "What of you? How think you of this?"

She surprised him again, this tenderness, that she wanted to know him.

"If I had a choice, Elizabeth, I would explain the reasons I chose you. But you see, my dear, I have none. You fell into me, like an invading army, and I have not been able to defend myself. I have no choice."

She laughed as she leaned closer into him. "Oh, cruel man, to represent me thus."

"Sherwood – you will like my uncle, Elizabeth, and I am eager for you to meet him - he gave me good advice when society was hounding me to marry. His language is so colourful, I'll never forget it. He said, wait man, you're bidin' the biddies, chasin' the ought of a small-minded drawin' room! Go away instead. Travel. Do somewhat other! Which of course, I did. And then the war... and... well that is another story."

"Then your hesitation to set a wedding date has nothing to do with doubts about me?"

He squeezed her hand. "No, darling. Of course not. If anything, it is the reverse, that you should know me a little. That we should know one another better."

"I could not stand it if you tired of me in a few years and hated me. Being married, loving you as I do and residing in matrimony with you tired and bored because you took me prematurely, before you were certain..."

"But how do you know it is not you who will tire of me?" he asked. "I have been in love before. I know what I want. It is you who are young."

"You have been in love?"

"Or so I believed. A long time ago. She was nineteen and I was younger by almost three years. She was much like a cousin we saw so much of one another growing up. I believe she seduced me first," he smiled. "She was not as innocent as I was."

He gathered his courage to tell Elizabeth about Lettice Rose, this daughter of his who had made him swell with pride and love despite being a stranger. But the Countess approached them from behind and took his other arm. She began a conversation in which she neglected to speak to Elizabeth who grew bored and excused herself with a wink and went merrily off to pick chestnuts.

"I do not imagine what you see in her, Mr. Darcy," the Countess of Somewhere interrupted her own chatter.

"Ah, but I beg your forgiveness, my dear. I learn from her daily."

"You see with different eyes than I."

"You have been with Evan for many years. Do your eyes change in that time? You lose your financial position in great galloping strides. You take refuge within the halls of those who have not yet lost their wealth…"

"I love him. It is simple."

"Yes. And you accommodate his interests."

"I do. Better that than that he sneaks everywhere. We have accommodated each other. I was wrong about you, however, Mr. Darcy."

"I believe that is true. I am not such an adventurer as my reputation suggests."

"Yes. No. It is that you have more depth than I had imagined. I am sorry to say it, but I begin to even like you."

"Why, thank you."

"The rumour mill is not a good place to know one's society. I am afraid it is misleading. I should know! I am its subject often enough. And I have grown used to not caring. My life with Evan. We grew together in ways that I would once have found unimaginable. We have expanded each other's worlds."

"I too begin to understand that I am a better man when I am with Miss Bennet."

THE TUNNELS AND THE TURRET

Jane Bennet to Elizabeth Bennet, Rosings Park, November 1812

Dear Lizzy,

I am so sorry I have not yet replied to your two previous letters. And now it is finally quiet here and I breathe a little to absorb your absence. I do miss you, though what a time we are having.

As Mr. and Mrs. Hurst have gone to London for reasons which seem quite uninteresting to everyone, Miss Bingley (who prefers I call her Caroline now that we are almost sisters) has invited me to stay with them. Her dear friend, Miss Grantley has come and we formed a merry little troupe until Kitty complained that she would not stay home alone with Mother, who then complained that she would not be left alone at home, and father looked over his glasses and decreed that he should not be left with no one but Mrs. Bennet for company and that he would quite prefer to be alone, so it was arranged that they join us at Netherfield for several days except for father who will be most delighted to have some peace, as he calls it. Charles, (oh yes, I will call him so to you. My dear dear Charles) smiles and is delighted and has that look about him that says to me that there are far too many women in his life and that he misses your Mr. Darcy quite as much as I miss you. Yet, he encourages his sisters to come and visit from the north so that we shall all meet. They arrive soon and stay a fortnight.

We go riding quite often in the countryside and – oh Lizzy! I almost forgot to tell you. He has made a present to me of a fine gelding. I have never ridden an animal quite so astonishingly perfect in its gait and elegant in its jumping. You know how I have learned to love to ride and to have such a beast under me has quite ruined me for our dear Molly. The other day he said to me that he does not have estate enough to manage to keep busy, that his sister manages the household and he has little to do but manage their income... and then you will not believe it. He has started to paint! We ride out, choose a location and paint together. Miss Bingley says it is the occupation of ladies who have nothing better to do (which I did not take as a disparagement to me since I am quite busy at home and do much more than she of sewing and gardening) to which Bingley said, "yes perhaps that is true, but" and he named many admirable artists of whom only a few I had ever heard, all of them of course men.

As for you, a little discomfort with Lady C. will not be anything more than disagreeable, and since you have been agreeably situated for most of your life, with so little constraints on your movements and your pleasure, with a doting father and a silly mother, who both love you quite well enough to make you one of the happiest people (have I emphasized enough how happy your life has been?) that it must seem quite like a prison to have to be in the narrow shadow of a great Lady of deep manners. And I am sure you will manage quite well once you remember the reason you are there. It is time, poor dear, to put your lovely romantic ideals about love to the grindstone, as they say, and see how they sharpen (Oh, sorry my dear, that seems quite wrong now that I read it but I have to leave soon after breakfast and will not restart this letter. See what happens when we hurry the pen and do not think properly on our words before we put them to paper or, in some people's cases, to air?). And kissing! Oh Izzy, do be careful!!!!! Girls are so easily ruined by a kiss that leads to more than a kiss.

November is almost come and we begin to speak of the Christmas season, to have you by our side again, perhaps with your Mr. Darcy and Georgiana as well, for Charles tells me that he has invited and encouraged Mr. Darcy to join him. His cousin, a young man currently studying at Oxford, also begs to join us. Then the halls will ring and the bells will toll! I have already begun to plan a few little events.

Oh, it is late and I am not yet dressed. Be well Lizzy. Love love.

Elizabeth, after spending an hour in her room replying to Jane, sealed the envelope and rang to have it picked up. As she waited for the lady's maid, she stared at the garderobe which she suddenly found quite a lot more fascinating than she had previously. Although two days had passed since the voice had spoken to her through it, this was the first occasion in which she had an afternoon to herself in which to explore. After delivering her letter into a sweet Miss

Carole's hand, she lit a candle and pushed past her dresses. She ran her hands along the edges of the cupboard walls and found what she could not find in the evening dark, a hole which seemed more flaw than design which, when she pressed a finger into it, found a latch. She gave a little tug, heard a click which announced the release of a cable, and the back wall of the garderobe disengaged. She swung it open and peered into a tunnel which led immediately to a very narrow and steep stairwell. She frowned, returned to her room and studied the ceilings both inside her room and outside and realized that the ceiling in her own room was much higher than that of the ceiling in the hallway. Place to put a passageway she speculated. She took off her shoes and re-entered the tunnel where she climbed the stairs, rising into a low and arched passage with a single exit at the end where there was a choice of stairwell or left turn towards, she assumed, Darcy's quarters. The floor was cold and damp through her stockings, but the walls were dry. The air was not as stuffy as she might have imagined, and there were no signs of skeletons or dragons or spider webs as in a fairy story. She climbed carefully, emerging into a circular room as if rising out of the floor, and there in the middle of the room were Anne and Mary kissing. She frowned, looked away, looked again, and backed out of the room. She heard Anne's distinctly small voice saying I love you Mary Bennet. Elizabeth paused at the bottom of the stairwell and coughed very deliberately and recommenced her climb. Changed her mind and started back down when Mary called to her. Elizabeth peered up through a forced smile, "How perfectly medieval this is, to have hidden passageways and dragon lairs."

Anne's turret was a splendid round room, small, with windows facing every quarter, a bundle of blankets, candles perched everywhere, and crudely made stools and tables.

"Anne has been sneaking into this room since she was thirteen. Look here, she has a secret drawer where she keeps all her writing," and Mary pulled at a stone to reveal a thick stack of paper.

"What do you write?" Elizabeth asked Anne, who did not reply, but who handed her a mess of papers. Elizabeth, glancing quickly, saw that there were fairies and dragons and invisible cloaks and wands, and she asked Anne to read a little. Anne nodded enthusiastically, picked papers from a nearby stack, shuffled through and took a little stool. She turned to Mary who, knowing what was meant in the look, introduced Lady Anne de Bourgh with an official voice. When Anne had finished reading a lovely little story about a fairy queen who was misguided in her attempts to find love in a tree, they clapped and told her what a good writer she was. This woman who does not speak puts volumes to paper.

"These stories would be brilliant for children," she exclaimed.

"It is a secret," Anne whispered. And Elizabeth did not ask whether she referred to the place, the writing, or the kiss.

"Well, perhaps your stories should not be. And this room! Well, it deserves secrecy. I wish I had been a child playing here. What a lot of fun we would have had, wouldn't we Mary?"

Elizabeth rose and excused herself.

To her dismay, Mary followed her out. Elizabeth let her pass and followed Mary down the stairs. She did not want to lead Mary directly to her own chambers and give away her own secret. As they clambered down two flights of tightly twisting steps in dim light, Mary spoke to her openly.

"I have once before kissed a woman, Elizabeth. I know I am not meant to tell you, but you saw us, I know you did, so it is too late for secrecy. Besides, secrecy will make us all into hypocrites. However, my concern is not for my proclivity to be attracted to the female sex, for I have quite decided that there is such a thing as a woman who is bent that way and I find men dull in the extreme, ill smelling and ill mannered. Their bodies are…well, I simply cannot imagine allowing a man to touch me."

They paused at a landing.

"Mary. You know it is considered wrong. An illness to be corrected. How do you know that women are known to be attracted to women?"

"Do not argue with me based on ignorance. What of those 'sisters' Mrs. Genworth and Miss Tartingham?"

"They are sisters, Mary, it is quite right for them to live together. One is a widow and the other a spinster. Of course, they support one another."

"And what makes you so sure they are sisters?" Mary glared at Elizabeth. She continued a little along a narrow hall and arrived at a door of thick oak and unleashed some kind of a contrivance and peeked into the room beyond. Apparently, it was empty, and she stepped out.

"I believe you are confusing my principals of right and wrong from my doubts about the validity of cultural propriety."

Elizabeth, who had never seen the room before, understood how many little corners there were for men to get away, to be private, to do what men do when the women are not with them. Mary continued with her arguments as if she had rehearsed them all her life and Elizabeth the first recipient to her ideas.

"I am very decided that there is a right and wrong, that one's ethical decisions are based in universal themes, but humans are absolutely incapable of determining these."

"Mary. You are trampling me with your thoughts. What have you been reading? Surely you do not obtain all these insights from Lady Anne? Do you mean to say that there is nothing wrong with loving a woman? That despite it, you remain the high principled, morally superior, and haughty person you've always been despite this character trait?"

Mary, who had a face which assumed a kind of fastidious superiority when she was challenged, stopped talking. But not for long. "The problem, Elizabeth, is not one of morality or ethics. It is the problem of Anne."

She put her finger to her lips as they tiptoed into the entrance hall and began climbing the stairwell. Lady Catherine arrived above them on the second floor landing and, as they passed her with gracious nods, Elizabeth worried about the obvious lack of shoes and bent low in her dress to hide her stockinged feet. Once out of earshot, they fled into Elizabeth's room. Elizabeth carefully closed the garderobe doors to hide the tunnel entrance as if tidying her room for her visitor.

"Now tell me: what is the problem, for I am fairly certain I already know!"

She was quite surprised by the answer.

"Anne has fallen in love with me and I have not fallen in love with her. She is sweet, but she is also strange. I cannot tell exactly, but her thoughts run in a way that seem to fragment."

Elizabeth nodded. She could agree to this.

"I think we should leave before planned as I cannot think of any other way to extricate myself from her devotion without causing her grief. Can we not make up some excuse as to why we must leave?"

"No Mary. I am not leaving early because you have to *extricate* yourself from an entirely absurd situation. I won't. You'll have to resolve this some other way."

"Like what?"

"Well. You might stop kissing her."

"I am going now for I cannot tell if you are offering that as good advice or because you think I should not be kissing anyone."

"Mary! You should kiss no one to whom you are not betrothed!"

"Elizabeth, you have not been listening to me. I will never be betrothed. I will never accept a man. I will die an old maid and I wish to. But does that mean that I should never kiss, ever, in my entire life?"

As she sat before her glass arranging her hair and tidying up after her adventures in the cobwebs and dust of dragon's paths, Elizabeth shook her head trying to rid herself of the strangeness of the situation, the shock and sense of disgust for her sister's preferences. An hour earlier, she imagined that the most exciting thing she might face in her day would be Darcy visiting her in her boudoir through a secret tunnel.

"I can easily imagine how you feel," Mary claimed, staring at Elizabeth through the glass. "It is the same as everyone everywhere. You are conventional. But Elizabeth, think of it from my point of view. Is it wrong to disparage anyone for the way they love? Love is hard to find, one that is lasting, where there is friendship and passion and which accompany people throughout their entire lives. Something so rare should not be judged superficially."

Elizabeth had never thought of herself as particularly conventional. She considered Anne's adoration, that she was *in love* with Mary. Not an illness, but a love. A thing she, Elizabeth, felt for Darcy. A thing he felt for his hound and his horse, and she for her sisters. Could one set limits on how equally important all these loves might be felt? She laughed, imagining Darcy kissing The Dog or she kissing Charlotte.

"It isn't funny!" Mary admonished.

"It is funny to think of kissing Charlotte. I believe she would slap me."

Mary dropped onto the little divan. "I don't know what to do."

Poor Mary, Elizabeth thought. Not because she was misguided, or caught in a love conflict, but because when marriage was the only option for a woman, how would Mary spend her life?

MR. COLLINS
IS IN WANT OF AN EDUCATION

Becoming Mr. Collins' confidante was a grotesque task. Darcy listened to the bobbing Mr. Collins flatter the late great Sir Lewis de Bourgh's study, its fine desk, rug, art, vase, handles on said desk, choice of curtain and curtain rod, listing without actually noting that the Spanish walnut desk was carved with doves and designed as a wedding present and was set perfectly on a large Flemish rug with verdure landscape. He did not identify the Islamic brass vase set perfectly on a simple 15th century three-legged drop table. He did not establish provenance nor quality in his flattery for he knew nothing of these but that they were desk, vase, table, and curtain, of which facts Darcy could only nod and agree.

Darcy was desperate to make the man stop talking, to interrupt the list and the bobbing, but he had no idea how to broach the barbaric topic of Mr. Collins' matrimonial relations. As Mr. Collins' effluvial speech listed his respect of the lady of etcetera, the place, his station, his responsibility and what a great humble honour, Darcy was reminded of a conversation he'd had recently with Charles Bingley in which he was likewise asked to provide matrimonial advice.

They had paused to watch a dozen or more bohemian waxwings dance in the air currents above a shallow fall where the water rippled. Darcy stripped and dove into the water, shook the cold from his head as he surfaced, and called to Bingley that he should jump in as well. He lay back floating like a large upside-down turtle, his ears entirely muffled in a glorious humming silence. When he looked up, the clouds rode past with marching insistence, great white beasts like a herd across the blue of the sky. He swam swiftly to warm up and pulled himself out onto a rock and shook his hair.

As he dried in the sun, he told Bingley that Elizabeth had accepted his marriage proposal.

"Your affair is full of contradictions," Bingley replied. "You pursue this girl all year, despite her apparent dislike of you, and now suddenly she will have you. It is a mystery to most of us."

"A congratulations might be in order," Darcy teased him.

"Yes, yes. Good man and all that," Bingley laughed.

"Your confusion comes from a lack of information. Elizabeth and I have had private exchanges; thus, we are less confused than the rest of you," Darcy replied.

As Darcy put his legs into his breeches, he considered the subtlety of physical love, the satisfaction of care expressed as desire, of the woman he had loved long ago and of the women with whom he had shared a bed, giving and taking pleasure, but without love, without the feeling that burned to be with Elizabeth completely. To have her by his side all hours of every day. This was entirely new to him. And entirely shocking. He had asked when her sentiments for him had turned. She had leaned into him, touching his breast lightly, and whispered, just now, when you asked. She had smiled up at him, her eyes shining with a clarity and generosity.

As they returned up the path to their horses, Bingley stopped suddenly to face Darcy.

"May I confide in you?'

"Of course."

"Jane: she is so full of purity and blissful generosity and tenderness. I must admit, I harbour none of those appetites for her that you seem to suggest wanting, or even of having, for Elizabeth. Is that a problem, do you suppose? I never imagined that my parents had any pleasure in their procreating. It was duty, yet with Jane, I would like to think of her as more than just some creature on which to relieve myself ..."

"Of course."

"Yes, well, the other extreme, that she remains so chaste that I can barely touch her is as intolerable. I wonder how it will be with us, to be together that way." Bingley paused. "Forgive me for asking," he continued finally. "I believe you are the only person to whom I would not only ask this question, but to whom I would entrust a decent answer. I do want it to be a good experience for her, for her first time."

Darcy waited. He thought of his first woman, a girl slightly older than he was at the time, also a virgin. He remembered that he had little memory of it, that it paled in comparison to his more recent entendre with mature women. He wondered what he might say to Bingley that would not embarrass either of them. Bingley started to speak again, apologizing and retracting his question.

"No, it's fine. You know the usual escapades a young man is likely to find, but in these you don't always pay attention to your partner. With Jane, where there is care, it will happen naturally and remember one thing only. Above all, wait for her."

"Wait for what?"

"Her pleasure of course. Seek it. Make it your pleasure. Seek it slowly."

It was good advice, but the subtlety of his answer to Bingley was not likely to edify Mr. Collins.

"Dear Mr. Collins," Darcy stood to sit beside his new best friend. "I would like to ask your deepest confidences in a matter which causes me pain and with no true friend to whom I might turn."

"I am deeply indebted that you would consider me..."

"You see, Mr. Collins, it is the matter of how a husband must...on their first night of married life... I, well..." and here Darcy pretended to struggle.

Mr. Collins spoke up. "You are unsure how to show your affection to Miss Bennet?"

It was too easy, Darcy thought. "Exactly. And because your wife is her good friend, I thought you might have insight for me."

A deep silence tortured them both as Mr. Collins failed to complete any subsequent sentence. The man, with every well-intentioned start, crashed the minute any words of substance were required. His hands folded in his lap like writhing snakes and his face, used to maintain a picture of blissful decorum, had turned a shade close to fig.

Darcy could not help but think of Mr. Collins' marriage proposal to Elizabeth who had described it in detail with expert impersonation. Darcy frowned, reminded that he also had been refused by Elizabeth and wondered whether she did impersonations of him. Mr. Collins, upon receiving her refusal, had assumed she was merely being coquettish. Mr. Collins, like Darcy, had assumed that she would accept his offer of marriage. Mr. Collins thought all women liked to be asked more than once. Darcy thought that this might be true since he had proposed to Elizabeth twice. And he frowned again. The parallels in their situation were far too absurd to be taken seriously. That he was tied to Mr. Collins in an unlikely commiseration made him somewhat uncomfortable as he watched the man's face contort.

"I am sorry," he stammered. "I am well versed in all the scriptures for good spiritual conduct in this matter. I believe that you would do well to read Genesis as it discusses marital relations..."

"Very good suggestion," Darcy agreed. "I too have access to literature, far more than is good for any one man, yet it fails to provide the right tone for the evening after one's marriage and has far too many suggestions for the many evenings following. There are myriad instructions about the procreative act, but I find none which succeed in showing me the tenderness and delicacy with which I should like to proceed on our first evening together."

"Indeed. I cannot believe that Sir Lewis de Bourgh would allow books with more than a trivial example of tender...."

"Would you like to see this library?"

As they entered the room, they surprised Mary and Anne bent over a book, the library's second entrance open to a tunnel behind them. They dropped their reading on a low table and stood like guards in a parade. Their faces were a cross between serious and horrified. Anne nodded and ran into the tunnel and Mary, after stammering a few words of explanation, said Please excuse me, and elegantly retreated. Meanwhile, Mr. Collins' face had gained a pallor not common to healthy people as he peered at the lewd poster on the wall, the similarly suggestive books and pamphlets displayed on the table.

Darcy, who had earlier perused the shelves for a particular manuscript, handed it to him. "You see, this one is very scientific. And in English." He handed it, casually open, into Mr. Collins' other hand. "See. Read this. The Germans have done much work in their scientific explorations of ... um... marriage contracts. This is popular, as you see it has been reprinted many times over the past hundred years."

Mr. Collins, voice shaking somewhat, read: "*Man consists of an egg, which is impregnated in the testicles of the woman, by the more subtle part of the man's seed; but the forming faculty and virtue in the seed, is a divine gift, it being abundantly endued with a vital spirit, which gives sap and form to the embryo...*"

As Mr. Collins read from the anonymously published *Aristotle's Masterpieces*, he seemed to become more, rather than less, confused while Darcy worried if he might have made a mistake in corrupting Mr. Collins' vestal purity.

Darcy's uncle, the library's collector, disapproved of prudes. He claimed that they merely sought to imprison primal instincts so that, instead of flowing freely and easily, these natural urges seeped out wickedly from corners, leading to ridiculous behaviour. Sir Lewis believed in dancing and music and galloping. He believed in dangerous boar hunting, of conversing with men who traipsed through Africa, and of defending his honour with duels. He especially believed in having sex, of talking about having sex, and of laughing about having sex. That there should be a man with no idea how to approach his wife would have been monstrous to him.

"Do you see?" Darcy asked hopefully, handing Mr. Collins another text, *The Mysteries of Conjugal Love Reveal'd* which had revealed very little to him, but he hoped the words "kindle secret parts" and "coitus" might stir Mr. Collins' imagination.

"And here is another fairly useful little pamphlet, the *Midwives Book*, written by a woman who has described with some flavour and metaphor, about ... well, here." Darcy read, "*True conception is thus when the seed of both sexes is good and duly prepared and cast into the womb.* It is very old, and much outdated, but it has value, you see? For we are too much reliant on word of mouth for so many of life's little mysteries, especially as regards those between a man and his wife."

"Yes, yes..." Mr. Collins agreed absently. He had instead picked up the book Anne and Mary had lately been inspecting, the *Kama Sutra*. Mr. Collins was instantly lost in the diagrams this sweet little tome provided.

"Quite an excessive proposition of different ways to distribute one's affections," he murmured as he turned the pages. "Not delicate in its diplomacy. Not restrained in its portrayal of the mutual pleasures... see, her face?"

"I believe it predates Christ. Not this copy, obviously."

"Yes, indeed, indeed, obviously, so obviously...Yes, very many ways to - uh – attain a connection...Oh, dear. Oh, excessively explicit. Not a place for gentlemen."

Darcy did not know to which 'place' Mr. Collins was referring, the library or reproductive tract. Mr. Collins was so enraptured that he seemed to forget that he was not alone. After turning the pages slowly and deliberately for several minutes, he finally spoke with a voice quite constricted, "This is quite an astonishing room. You say that all of these materials are of a similar nature?"

"They are."

Darcy, not trusting that he could remain serious, begged to be allowed to return to his study and asked Mr. Collins to please stay as long as he should wish.

"I understand a man of your significance would not want to remain in a circumstance as uncomfortable as this. I will stay and ponder your question, Mr. Darcy, with the most and gravest attention to detail so that, when you ask it, I might be able to share my wisdom with as much efficiency as my mind will allow."

Darcy bowed deeply and departed from the room.

"I will be but a few minutes," Mr. Collins yelled after him.

Darcy completed his ledger, read a note from his steward, wrote a reply, and began a letter to Bingley before Mr. Collins emerged from the library.

"I had no idea." He bowed low and departed without another comment, but immediately returned.

"Perhaps you would like to sit?" Darcy invited.

"No indeed! I must go. I quite forgot that you had a question for me. I wonder if you would repeat it as it has quite left me."

"I too have forgotten, Mr. Collins. I think I am quite relieved now that I have shared my burden with someone."

"I am so honoured and glad to be of service to one so distinguished and..."

Eventually, after several bows and bobs, Mr. Collins left the room.

A POST ASSEMBLY TREAT

A letter from Jane arrived by the afternoon post. She was painting a great deal with Charles. Kitty was in love with a very handsome farmer's son and would not be dissuaded. Mrs. Bennet had retired to her room with distressed nerves and was taking all her meals there, croaking The shame! The shame! Mr. Bennet simply shrugged and announced that silly girls would be silly. Miss Bingley's advice to Jane regarding London society were all about gossip and who was in Bath and Jane thought that Lady Catherine's advice to Elizabeth seemed sensible and valuable in comparison.

Elizabeth immediately wrote back.

Elizabeth Bennet to Jane Bennet, Longbourn, November 1812

Dear Jane,

It is quiet here today. I cannot believe that Mary and I have spent a complete month surviving her worshipfulness. Our plan is to leave in several more weeks with Darcy and Georgiana, who will stop in London and then he will move on to Netherfield. I can't wait to see you. These letters are barely satisfying compared to having you with me. We have discussed spending some time in London over the early spring – perhaps convincing father and others to let a house there. I am excited about it now that I have been well stocked with opening conversational phrases thanks to her worshipfulness (no, Jane, I am actually – for a change – not being facetious).

Lady C. has told me that we are done with my training. Thank goodness for it has been four full weeks of intense studies and learning. I learned to keep the books, to use accounting methods, and a myriad of other details which I find I cannot now forget. Quite astounding what Grendel thinks useful! She provided a graduation exam in which I was studied for faults of dress and stance, and quizzed. You would be proud of me, for I bowed and scaped and agreed. She has organized a large assembly for my miniature coming out – the one in which I am not a country waif, but a fine lady. Ha. It is tonight and she has given me two ball gowns. Quite beautiful and tasteful, as you know I like. She and I have not exactly become chums, but I suppose she is resigned to have me, whether or not she likes it.

She then gave me time to peruse her library and choose some books of my own liking. I decided to re-read Cecelia.

"Romance," Lady Catherine said dismissively and, also probably, somewhat incorrectly. And then I found A Vindication on the Rights of Women by Mary Wollstonecraft, which was only partly cut. I picked it up and she smiled. "I believe that was left behind by someone." I must admit, Jane, I believe she left it out for me! She then said, "I could not bear to throw it out, for I do not throw out books no matter their subject. It is not the usual reading syllabus for young ladies in London, but Darcy's favourite women will apparently read such things. I think you will find the supercilious women of society quite abominably dull for your mind and vapid to your character, so the ideas expressed in these will help you garner favour with women of intelligence and ambition who derive pleasure in inviting great men and women of letters and politics to their soirees. It is to these homes you will want to be invited. Darcy, who no doubt you have noticed can prowl and remain at the outskirts when there are more than ten people in a room, will be of no help at all in procuring these cards to their events. Except for his good looks and desirability to the women, which he has now lost since he has not chosen any of them, he would prefer to visit his close friends and break fast with them than go to balls and ballets."

I told her I thought she was being unfair and she told me I must hold my tongue.

Have you read it Jane? You must!

As for other events, I will not detail the trouble that Mary is in, but rest assured that I believe she needed a chaperone more than I.

My relations with Darcy grow increasingly tender. We have had a few moments alone, and these I treasure for the promise of more once we are married. I cannot describe to you the stirrings which occupy me, for they are of a base nature and not at all ladylike; yet he does not seem to mind *that I respond in some way. In fact, I believe he is trying to encourage me.*

Yours with love,

Lizzy

At the assembly, Elizabeth danced often with Darcy and others, including Georgiana, Mlle. Turin, and Mr. Collins. She teased Darcy that it was sad Col. Fitzwilliam was not present as he probably danced quite well. Most impressively, there were no Too Close Too Close ministrations except once, when the Earl came near she and Darcy and whispered it mockingly. She did her best to look delightful and charmed while engaged in vapid conversations, and said nothing but yes indeed, and no indeed not. She even received a compliment from the Countess who smirked at her and commended her performance with a wink and a nod.

Then Charlotte grabbed her elbow and asked if they might talk privately. Mr. Collins is away for a moment! she urged. Tugging Charlotte to a little known terrasse overlooking the east fields, Elizabeth begged details of her friend's matrimonial happiness. To which Charlotte replied, "Mr. Collins is marvellous. Just you wait. It is marvellous! He came home for morning tea and kissed me. He kissed me on the forehead!"

Elizabeth smiled indulgently. She would not disclose how Darcy had several times sequestered her in a dark corner to kiss at great length with much passion and hands here and there, her own tongue finding his and... Well, she smiled and was glad for her friend's experience. A kiss. On the forehead. Well, that was something, was it not? She congratulated Charlotte on her progress, and then asked why they had not been able to spend more time together since her arrival.

"Mr. Collins believes you have sullied Lady Catherine's esteem of us, by association. He prevents me from indulging in any communication with you for fear that it will compromise his position at the parsonage."

Elizabeth began to object, for objectionable it was, but Charlotte dismissed her with a singularly direct look and grimace, and with these she told Elizabeth that she agreed with Elizabeth's objection, but there was nothing to be done but sneak to a terrasse for a few brief words. "And what of you? How is it to be a lady in this great hall?"

Elizabeth curtsied prettily, with a slight tilt of her head and an endearing smile on her face and said, "As you see. I am transformed."

But Charlotte could see through Elizabeth's little ruse. "I do not think it possible for you and Lady Catherine to be truly reconciled. You think too highly of your opinions and so does she of hers. It makes for very little leeway and no harmony. Unless you find a way of respecting her, Eliza, you will find her quite out of reach."

"But how can I respect someone who takes no trouble in knowing me, sees me but from a single attitude of self-serving righteousness?"

"So, you see. It is as I said."

"Perhaps. I will try."

"Did it occur to you that she also tries?"

"Perhaps she does. She has been generous in some ways. This dress, for instance, is a gift from her."

Charlotte nodded. "It suits you well. I have heard that you have travelled as well. A little. With Georgiana, Mr. Darcy and other members of your entourage?"

"Yes. With Anne and Mary as well. We went for several days into Dover, to see its white cliffs. And we went also to Canterbury, to the cathedral. And what a charming village it is! Yes. We have had a few little excursions to 'educate' me of the world. Have you been out that way? It is not terribly far. The weather was not perfect as it gets cold, but we dressed well and walked easily about. It was glorious, actually, even as it blew a gale!"

Charlotte shook her head, no, but her attention was turned towards the large French doors to the room beyond where Mary and Anne were seated in conversation.

"I see them out in the little pony cart. It is – of course – just for one person, but they squeeze side by side and traipse about the country when it is not pouring. I see them often passing as they must go my way to gain the main road. It is fortunate for Lady Anne."

"She always seemed dour and cross. So pale and thin and sickly."

"Indeed, she never seems happy, but I believe there is some change in her."

"Really? Yes, I do suppose that's true." Elizabeth worried a little that, since Charlotte noticed their intimacy, might not others who would see in it something sinister? Would friendly glances be construed as illicit love.

Charlotte squeezed Elizabeth's arm and bid her good night and walked away rather more quickly than was appropriate for a lady of good breeding and high station in London society. Elizabeth made a mental note to edit the way her thoughts had adopted Lady Catherine's loud refrains.

Late that evening, after thanking her hostess for the lovely graduation party, Elizabeth retired finally to her bedchamber, blew out her candle immediately and was so tired that sleep was already upon her when a loud bang close by woke her and a man's voice, muffled as if behind a door, yelled in pain. "Lizzy. Are you there? It is me."

"Darcy?" she exclaimed, perhaps a little loudly as she lit a candle and opened the garderobe door. "Darcy, what are you doing with my dresses and how long have you been there?" She could hear his suppressed laughter.

"Come. It is locked," came his voice.

"Of course, it's locked. I have kept it that way to keep out the marauders."

She pushed around the dresses to unlock the door to find Darcy standing in the narrow tunnel, his forehead bleeding. She retreated quickly, rummaged for a suitable cloth with which to create a compress and handed him her clean undershirt.

"The weather has been quite cold of late," he observed as he stepped gingerly past the dresses.

"I do believe winter will start earlier this year."

"It seems that we are all in agreement as to this observation."

To which Elizabeth could only reply by giggling. She was cold, so she grabbed the quilt from her bed and added coal to the fire. Darcy, having waited patiently just inside the room, formally asked if he might come join her as if greeting her at a theatre box or a parlour.

"Please sit, Darcy," she replied and they each took an armchair by the fire and sat in silence, she waiting for him to announce his intentions and he seeming uncomfortable with their unaccustomed privacy. "How long have you known about this passageway, Fitzwilliam?" she finally asked. "And why have you hesitated to use it? But wait, I should examine your injury." She moved in front of him, raising the candle to see by. "It has almost stopped bleeding." As she started backing away, he grabbed her arm, holding her motionless above him while his other hand held the bloody undershirt. He lifted his face and carefully roamed from her eyes and face, down along the line of her body and then back up to her eyes. She blushed.

"Elizabeth. I am sorry. But I can see the shape of you and the curves of your body through your nightdress. The light makes it… change my mood immediately."

She tugged her arm slightly and he let her go as if agreeing that under the circumstances they should be more, not less, circumspect.

"I trust you Darcy… I just want to, I want not to, I…"

"I don't trust myself Lizzy. I want too much to draw you near and touch you. It would not be possible to stop. I came because I wanted, for once, just to be alone with you. Not to cause you discomfort."

She gathered the quilt around her in a cocoon and sat in the armchair. He threw the undershirt into a far corner and pulled his chair next to hers.

"My uncle housed his mistresses in this room and I am occupying his former chambers at the end of the secret passageway."

Elizabeth reached up with one hand to touch his lips. His proximity overwhelmed her; their privacy shocked her. He nibbled at her finger and she drew back, laughing. He took her hand again and put it on the armrest while she apologized for being too forward, and he thanked her for her caution, and her affection, and apologized for their awkwardness. For a long while, they kept their silence while the fire snapped and their fingers played together, twining, stroking, and occasionally exploring up and down each other's wrists. Eventually, she fell asleep with his finger in her palm, circling. She awoke in his arms as he put her to bed. She awoke again in the night to find him beside her on top of the bedspread, his hand still in hers. In the morning, he was gone and the cupboard door was closed.

"Oh Darcy," she mused, "Why do you wait to set a date for our wedding? How will we avoid the terrible temptations of proximity?"

TEMPTATIONS
IN THE MISTRESS TUNNEL

In fit of frustration, Darcy left his study the evening after he had slept on Elizabeth's bed. He careened into the tunnel via the secret library. He did not know where to go. Out and into the Earl's chambers where, for a single evening, he would show the Countess a good time while her husband watched? It would not be the first time a husband had sat back and watched he, Darcy, perform. Some men enjoyed seeing his wife dominated by another man. Darcy asked himself if he would want that with Elizabeth, some young stud, eager and stupid, having his way with her, while he sat on an armchair pulling at himself.

He turned. He would take her now. This evening. He would go and he would make love to her all night so that his imagination, racing with desperate longing, might be appeased. He would lift that nightdress, which revealed so much even as she wore it, her soft creamy breast, nipples high and...

He turned away. He had promised himself that he would patiently, gladly, slowly, awaken her body to its own needs. He had promised that it would be Elizabeth herself who would be calling him to make love and not the other way around. Soon, you'll have her. You bastard. Be patient, he said to his erection.

He had sat alone in his study, away from everyone, reading a good book and enjoying his own company, and then he had hit upon a single sentence in which the word "shape" appeared, and the memory of her the previous night, the contours of her loveliness backlit though her nightdress, distracted him so that the book was subsequently without any charm. He was not a heavy drinker, but he poured himself a brandy, and then another, and then took the bottle into the tunnels.

He arrived at the stairwell where he had a choice, to ascend to Anne's special hiding place in the turret, or to descend past the exit into the billiard room to the guessing room at the bottom of the stairs. Darcy sat on a stair and imagined himself in that room, its small turret-like roundness, the innocuous rope which rang a bell somewhere in the servant's quarters. He paused with aching insistence, anticipating the hand or mouth behind the wall on his member. He and Col. Fitzwilliam had secretly named it the guessing room to disguise their conversations about the heaven's hole.

As younger lads, they studied the servants, guessing whose hand, whose mouth. It might be the butler. It might be the old gardener. It might be whoever draws the short straw. It might be whoever is still awake. It might be, he thought now, impossibly unsatisfying.

As he sat on the stair, he heard steps coming from below. His mind raced to consider the men who were currently staying at Rosings' and could think of only one resident who might be tempted by the heaven's gate, but the footsteps produced a boy.

"Sir!" the boy exclaimed, surprised at finding Darcy occupying the place of his next footfall.

"Is this now the purview of servants? This room is being abused by boys in livery?"

"No sir. I mean, well, me and my gal, we use it. But not the way it is meant. I mean, we sit on opposite sides of a wall. She sits up and waits for me and we talk, see...through the hole."

"Talk."

"Yes. Yes sir. We been friends since we was kids and figure this way of talking – separated like – makes it safe to share talk, private talk sir, without the risk of ..."

"Complications."

"Exactly the word, sir."

Darcy stood.

"Would you pass, sir?" the boy asked, waiting for Darcy to get out of the way so that he might make room for Darcy's descent. Darcy nodded. "I will take out that bell rope. I'm cutting it down. What is your name?"

"Yes sir. Robert. Or Bob. My friends calls me. No, but you wouldn't no, that's right. Sorry sir?? (Sire? Lord?). Must be the circumstances, sir, of us meeting here in this place, makes me want to be friendly. I don't think many of us down there would mind much if you was to kill that tradition. It don't get used much anyway, now. Not like they say it was in the old days, when the master was alive. There's some here who still talk about those shenanigans."

"I bet they do. Good night, Robert."

"Mr. Darcy, sir," the boy bowed awkwardly on the steep stairs and offered his pocketknife. Darcy smiled and pulled one from his own vest.

"I'm sorry sir: I never thought you lot did anything for yourselves. Oh, I'm sorry – they keep me in the kitchen 'cause I talk too much!"

"Good night, Robert," Darcy insisted, but almost laughed as he careened down the treacherous stairwell.

As she brushed her hair, Elizabeth waited for the sound of tapping inside her garderobe. Darcy had not indicated one way or the other as to his intentions, but she was excited and anxious and curious and wanting and not wanting him to visit. Her desire for him, so strong even in public places where his smell, his character, his voice, all of it infused her like a potion that transformed itself immediately into something unbearably physical. In the privacy of her chambers, these emotions might not be contained. There was no good reason for having him visit again and risk its temptations. Yet, waking beside him had infected her, as if nothing else could improve on the simple act of lying in his arms and sleeping.

After cutting the bell string in the heaven's hole, Darcy made his way to the Earl's room. He changed his mind several times, walking like a jaguar in a confined space, up and down the hallway. The Earl answered the door.

"Evan, I must ask you to leave," Darcy whispered loudly. "I cannot stand the temptation you have offered me. Tomorrow you pack." But as he spoke, he heard a muffled sound, a simpering kind of noise that he knew well. He pushed the Earl out of the way and entered the room. Seated in a straight-backed chair, her arms wrapped around herself as if providing her own comfort, the girl (for that is how he thought of her despite her nine and twenty years), stared up at him with such a look of pleading that he thought he would murder his aunt for her terrible interference. Darcy turned and punched the Earl and by the time he turned again, the Countess was off the bed, scampering to him, seductively half clothed, and using a soft crooning voice. "Will you not join us, Fitz? We are teaching the girl how to seduce, but she is not a quick learner..."

Darcy took Anne's hand and led her away.

He did visit her, but late, tapping as before to rouse her from sleep. Darcy stood in the doorway with a big silly grin on his face, his vest open and shirt entirely undone and disheveled. When he stepped into the garderobe, he took her shoulders and leaned her against the wall and frenetically covered her in kisses. His hand went all over her in a hurried, pushy way, and she was unsure how to respond. The door was open and she worried about being visible despite the tunnel's apparent emptiness. She considered reaching for the door in a way which would avoid bothering Darcy, then, as she was thinking all these things, she realized that she did not feel any reciprocation of desire.

"Darcy," she pushed him a little on the chest. He resisted, ignoring her.

"Darling, please stop."

"Damn it," he swore. "I don't know how a man is to survive on so little."

"Are you drunk?"

"I am not entirely sober."

He pulled away slightly, though his hands were still on her hips. She pulled at the soft cotton of his shirt and ran her hands across his muscled torso, over the sculpted curves of his shoulders, and he yanked the shirt off. She closed her eyes and roamed down his chest, abdomen and around to his back. He took a deep breath and squeezed hard on her hip bones, pulling at them slightly, bringing them into him, and that is when she felt it through her flimsy shift. His desire. His hands pulled her into him and pushed her away, slowly, easily, gently, and again, pulling her in and pushing her out. And he kissed her slowly, and she kissed him back, eager, opening herself to him. She felt the chaos of her body's wishes obstruct her completely.

"Yes, Lizzy. Yes," he whispered.

After a few minutes, he stopped and she smiled up at him. His eyes had narrowed and he was breathing as if with a terrible weight and pain in his chest. He growled, or that is the closest thing she could think of to call the noise he made, then he pushed her gently but decisively against the wall and left. He stormed noisily down the tunnel, the light bobbing against the walls with each stride. "Be careful of your head," she whispered loudly and he raised his hand in acknowledgement but did not turn or speak. She stood unmoving for a few minutes as it was all she could do to keep herself from running after him.

FRACTURES

Jane! Several days have passed since the last letter entry — so sorry I have not sent it yet but will do so tomorrow sans faute. Terrible things have happened. This afternoon, I was called into the Lady's private chambers and she informed me that a doctor would inspect my virginity! I told her I would not succumb to such an inspection, even by a doctor and... well you can imagine what ensued. She accused me of ... oh, Jane. I will not relate it for you can imagine. I was reduced to tears. She timed it perfectly for the men were all away hunting for the day. The doctor, it seemed, was already in attendance. I fled. I ran to the protection of Anne's secret turret! Imagine!

Later, when I sought Darcy and his protection, I saw from a stairwell landing the Countess of Somewhere talking to him in a corner. They did not know they were seen. She had her hand on his elbow and she was very close to him. His face was unmoving, but she was whispering in his ear in a very familiar way. I do not know what to think of this. When he saw me, he moved away from her, as if guilty of something, and she smiled at me in manner that was unfriendly and provocative. As I arrived and begged his audience, he would not speak to me but rushed off. And that is all. He went away without speaking to me. The Countess took me by the arm and walked with me saying: "You must be praised for arresting the attention of a man to whom quite a number of women have thrown themselves, Miss Bennet, women who have wiles and aptitudes that would quite astonish most men. I wonder whether you shall be able to keep his attentions..."

The Earl informed me that Darcy's hunter has been in an accident and he has had to shoot it. He will be most upset about this. He is as proud of Harrumph as a parent is of a child, but I would have expected Darcy to confide this information to me. Instead, he flees from me. What am I to think of this Jane? The drawing room is mostly empty as I write this. Anne and Georgiana are absent. The Dowager and countess are the only two people who make any effort at sociability. The men are all away this evening and seem to have dined in their own chambers. Mary is in her corner reading and I in mine writing this letter.

Before leaving the drawing room to retire, Elizabeth asked Mary if she was aware what was wrong in the household.

"Besides the horse being shot? Only that I have asked Anne to stop following me, but that would concern no one else."

Long after Elizabeth was asleep, Darcy came to her chambers through the cupboard door. He stood and bowed formally, asking if he might come in. The Dog, wagging and greeting her happily, was at his heels and entered with him. Darcy went straight to an armchair and collapsed there. The Dog to the hearth rug.

"I have had to speak to Evan," he said, his eyes closed. "He and the Countess are to leave tomorrow morning. I do not like the way they have been harassing Anne."

Elizabeth wrapped in her quilt, sat beside him.

"Yes, I like neither of them, as I have said, but I'm sorry for Anne. And I'm sorry to hear about your horse," she offered finally. "I too have not had a pleasant day."

To which he made no reply. She wondered why he had bothered to come when it might be better to be asleep. As he made no move to speak, nor to move his chair nearer, nor to pace the room, which might have been a relief, she soon became uneasy wondering the purpose of the visit and disliking the discomfort of this awful silence. It was as if a third person had stepped between them to interfere with their rapport. When she was about to tell him about her escape from Lady Catherine and the doctor, she noticed tears in the corners of his eyes.

"Oh, my poor dear," she went to him, bent in front of him, and held him by the knees. Darcy wiped his eyes but did not otherwise move.

"I raised him myself," he moaned. "We grew into adulthood together. He knew me, my every whim and need. It is unbearable. And I am shocked at how hard it is."

He did not speak again but sat controlling his emotions.

"But I did not come here to seek solace..."

"But you might have, for I am happy to give it."

"Thank you, but I must explain myself for I was embarrassed to speak with you today."

"You were embarrassed?" she asked, confused.

"I was terrible last night. I do hope you will not reproach me for it?"

"Last night?" she asked, not remembering any act for which he should be apologizing.

"I was drunk and violent."

"Come, let us be comfortable," she replied, "You have had enough for the day and I have nothing to forgive in you."

"I was not a gentleman..."

"No, you were a lover, a friend. I almost chased you down the tunnel," she confessed, blushing. "You excited appetites… well I was not quite sure what to do with them."

He frowned.

"You were not particularly frightening," she insisted. "I trust you, Darcy. I trust you with my every bone to care for me. Last night, well, it was special in its own way." She walked him to the bed and they lay down, as before, with him above and she below the covers. The Dog jumped up and lay at their feet. Darcy, dressed except for his shoes and jacket, wrapped himself in a blanket and, when she hugged him, he began to cry in earnest. She talked to him soothingly and listened. She coached him to calm himself and stroked his forehead. She rubbed his back and held him. His breathing finally settled and he slept.

She wondered at the mystery of such a creature who one night could be a beast and the next a boy.

EXILE

As soon as Elizabeth arrived in the foyer on her way to the conservatory for breakfast, she knew something terrible had happened. Servants, who were normally invisible, were whispering and scurrying, and the housekeeper who was usually in attendance was not. A doctor was escorted upstairs past her as she descended, but when she begged information of a maid, the girl knew only that something had befallen Lady Anne.

Elizabeth waited for Darcy, but he did not come, and as she and Mary were the only two eating, she gained no enlightenment. It was a beautiful day with a blameless sky, open to possibilities of rushing away as much as it presented an uninterrupted pastel. She and Mary immediately went out of doors and walked far, then as they circled back, arrived accidentally at the court where they had previously played pall mall. They accessed the little garden shed in which the mallets and balls were kept and enjoyed themselves by practicing complicated shots.

Most of their walk had been in silence, as Mary and Elizabeth had very few interests in common and yet, being sisters, were often comfortable in their mutual silence. But as they struck balls and laughed, Elizabeth inquired about Mary's friendship with Lady Anne. Mary said only that she had not seen Anne for several days and neither of them had attempted communication.

"I am glad. It would seem too..." Elizabeth searched for words that would express the problem delicately.

"... complicated," Mary offered.

"Yes. At the very least. Try this shot from the hillock. See how one must get it to roll just so?"

Mary stepped up to the position indicated, swung and missed. "I did not speak to her for your sake, Elizabeth. I did it because I told her the truth."

"Of course." Elizabeth set her ball and measured the weight of her swing and knocked the ball through the iron hoop. "*Voila*. I knew the shot was possible."

By late morning, Elizabeth returned to find a maid packing her belongings. Quite shocked, Elizabeth asked what meaning could be attributed to this unforeseen circumstance, and the maid knew nothing but that she was following instructions. Elizabeth went across the way to Mary's room and found a parallel situation.

She sought the butler, knowing she must not arrive unannounced to any private room, and asked about Mr. Darcy's whereabouts.

"Please follow me. Mr. Darcy is waiting for you in his study."

He ushered Elizabeth into rooms she had never seen and it struck her as an irony that in her last hour at Rosings, she might finally visit the private chambers of her betrothed. It was much like her father's study in character, with books, and odds and ends and art, only vastly more opulent with several windows, an enormous writing desk placed at an angle and a beautiful divan and armchairs arranged before the hearth. She assumed that the bedroom was beyond through the opening which was hidden by a thick curtain.

"Come in," Darcy bowed. "Please sit."

"No thank you," she replied.

"As you wish."

She stood, waiting, while he seemed to pace and study her. She was already so close to fury that she schooled herself to be careful with her words.

"Lady Catherine has asked that you leave Rosings immediately with no explanation. I have written Bingley and asked that he meet you at the L- Inn and I have arranged for a carriage to take you that far."

"I am to leave. Now."

"Yes."

"And this is all you will say to me."

"I am afraid I have little to say that I would be pleased to remember at a later date, so I would prefer to say nothing."

"How can you?" She heard her voice become more shrill and she sought to control her temper. "How can you make love to me and seek my comfort one day and then send me away in this coldly calculated way? You might have sent the butler to dispatch this news, for he would have done it quite as well," she scolded.

"I preferred to do it myself."

"Well, that is *good* of you. Darcy, will you absolutely speak nothing more on this subject? Has it something to do with my trotting around her precious castle in my stockinged feet? Or was it for refusing to be inspected by the doctor yesterday? I cannot believe you would have agreed to such a thing!"

His surprise was answer enough. "Doctor? Yesterday? No, I have no knowledge of that."

But he did not ask or pursue, did not give any sign that he wanted to care about what a terrible shock she had suffered.

"I will see you off in a half an hour."

"Or Lady Anne? Don't look at me like that. I saw the doctor arrive this morning. When my family went through a terrible calamity, you were able to generously assist us in the matter, and to give comfort to us. But now, when it is you facing a trial, I am expected to ignore my care for you and your family."

"The two situations are quite incomparable. Please say no more for there is nothing you can do now except to keep silent."

"Yes, I see," she said, quite stunned and left.

In no time, she and Mary were handed off into the carriage by Darcy. Neither Lady Catherine, nor Anne, nor Georgiana were in attendance to say their goodbyes. He was demure and gracious and entirely formal in his address. As the eldest of the two women, it was incumbent on Elizabeth to offer the formalities of appreciation and good wishes to their hosts and she took the liberty to send her condolences to Lady Anne. Though, knowing Darcy as she did, in his many variegated features, the public face and the private, Elizabeth could see in him, of a sudden, a terrible confusion and grief.

"I will communicate with you when I can." Darcy helped her up into the carriage, closed the door and said no more.

They were barely out of the gate when Elizabeth started to cry, at first quite softly, hiding her emotions from Mary, and then sobbing and shaking. Mary pretended not to notice except to offer a handkerchief after Elizabeth had used up her own. Elizabeth calmed finally, and then, catching sight of Rosings over a rise, began to cry again.

"Elizabeth, you will be unfit to be seen at the next exchange."

"If you have nothing sympathetic to say, I advise you to say nothing," Elizabeth spat at her sister.

"He is an arrogant insufferable man," Mary continued. "He has said nothing to me since the carriage ride but hello Miss Bennet as if

I am of absolutely no interest or worth. A servant and not the sister of his intended. I do not understand why you waste your comfort on him. That you should marry into a circumstance of such opulence is understandable. Not only your children, but your great grandchildren will be cared for; however, that he should produce such ruin as this..." she nodded at Elizabeth's red eyes, blotchy face and runny nose. "Such devotion he does not merit."

"Oh, would you be Jane in this moment, Mary? Could you not, for one minute, take even a little of her tenderness into your being and see that I am quite devastated by this shocking turn and how I am to understand this sudden exile?" At which words she began again to sob.

The word exile expressed completely the feeling that the separation from Darcy had produced. Although lasting a mere half an hour, in her mind it stretched into a future which did not contain him at all, in which he was quite forever lost to her. That she should never again receive an embrace from him, or feel the warmth of his gaze, tender and loving, or sleep curled into his back, or smell the cedar sweetness of his neck. These details caused grief and shock. But she, furious at his behaviour, was also decided that she could not spend her life with a man who could treat her thus, dismiss her coldly at the merest hint of a problem. Locked in this exasperating confrontation, she was grieved and furious in combative refrains, at times feeling a deep sadness for them both and at others wanting to turn her back on him completely.

"No, I cannot," Mary replied. "Jane is kind, I will grant, but she gives allowance to people who are underserving of it and her innocence of people's ill intentions exposes her to danger. That house," she argued, tossing her head contemptuously back the way they had come, "that house is a pit of ill will and hate. You do not know the half of it. And how Anne is imprisoned there, it is horrible. Horrible Lizzy. And Mr. Darcy should never have brought you into his aunt's influence. She wants nothing but to destroy you...Anne told me so. None of it merits your bawling."

"Yes. I see that you would rather condemn than understand. Would rather be insipid and dour than expose yourself to the possibilities of caring for me."

"Elizabeth Bennet, don't you dare assume that because I choose to be reasonable and to see the reality..." Mary spat, but cut herself off and sat shaking. Elizabeth kept her own silence from the other side of the carriage bench. "You should not assume I have no…no stake in this," Mary accused, her words clipped with emotion. "And what of your regard for me? What do you know of what happened…" And unable to control herself, Mary began to sob.

"Oh dear, now what?" Elizabeth asked, but Mary was too upset and sobbed uncontrollably. The handkerchiefs were already well used, so Mary reached down and blew into her petticoat. As she explained what she had seen that morning in Anne's room, Elizabeth was quite horrified and interjected with sounds of astonishment and comfort as she listened. "Oh my! Oh, poor Miss Anne! Oh Mary. Poor you. How terrible. You do know you cannot be held accountable for any of that?" Elizabeth said tenderly. "It is not your fault at all, not at all." Her words had the effect of heightening Mary's distress rather than relieve it.

"I know you cannot absolve yourself now," Elizabeth continued, "but you must, for I will not allow you to believe that you were wrong in any way. She was already fragile, and you simply told her you did not love her the same way she loved you. People are rejected in love all the time and don't take such outrageous action. Do you think she did it to make you feel guilty? Oh sorry, no, stop. I'm sorry. You must, you must remember that she was unwell when you met. If anything, you have helped her by being her friend. I cannot believe that Lady Catherine is so rude that she sends us into the world without preparation, to travel over terrible terrain in late November, cold and quite shocked by this news. And to think that she blames you for her daughter's own terrible decision, berates you with vicious accusation, and does not see how Anne is also to blame..."

"Enough Elizabeth. I cannot stand thinking nor talking about any of it."

"They should have sent us out tomorrow morning when we might have a good day's travel. We will be in the pitch black soon enough. I do not like it, Mary. It feels wrong."

"We are rid of them. For that I am grateful," was Mary's only answer.

Elizabeth gathered her thoughts, but they fragmented under the strain of the restless sound of wheels and springs aching over the uneven road, the sudden jolts which catapulted them from one side of the seat to the other. When the road was washed out, it was a relief to walk as the drivers pushed and maneuvered over the crevasse. On her feet, her mind cleared and the disturbance in her stomach settled. And thus, they travelled.

The day's light fell to glow against the hills, deepening shadows and highlighting silhouettes. Lines of trees, catching the sun's last passage, were gilded gold and otherworldly.

She watched the sun in its methodical descent, the angled line of incremental change beckoning salmon hues to the wispy clouds, elongating the beauty in languid lines. She watched until, after ages of teasing at the horizon, the sun suddenly dropped as if speeding to visit its neighbours. A scene fit for an angel choir or small miracles, full of fairy dust and wonder.

Elizabeth stared at it, seeing its extraordinary beauty, but felt nothing of its invitation to joy.

Mary shifted suddenly in her seat. "Look, Elizabeth. A rider."

"Where?"

"At three o'clock but riding fast."

She squinted slightly, leaning into Mary to look out the window. A great horse was coming over the far hill at terrible speed. If not for the sound of the carriage, she would be sure to think the sound of its hooves would have warned of its approach. Although she did not recognize the horse or rider immediately, she identified the rider's style, the way his back angled, the set of his legs, and the way he shortened his reins and leaned into the horse's neck. She watched the two as one, moving in muscled grace and power as the sun came through them, shining a light around their movements.

"Darcy," she whispered, simultaneously furious and relieved.

As he gained on them, she dropped the window. He pulled the horse up and trotted in, nodding to her and moving to the front to speak to the man there.

"Harris, I am sorry to come to you like this..." and because of horses stomping and perhaps a little more distance, or hushed voices, she heard no more of Darcy's speech. When Darcy failed to re-appear, she feared that he had not ridden out to see her, but to bring news of great importance to this man.

She slid the window closed and sat back, furious with a man she loved more than she could have imagined possible, who ignored her as if she were a casual acquaintance, someone to be dismissed with

84

his cold public face. And just as she was ready for the carriage to move again, he appeared at the door, opened it, bowed to Mary and addressed Elizabeth.

"Miss Bennet. I would be most honoured if you would step out."

She glared at him. He did not flinch.

"Please Lizzy. I will not argue with you here."

"You will argue with me wherever I choose to be furious, Mr. Darcy."

Mary, uncharacteristically, giggled.

"I have not ridden over all manner of country, killing my horse with speed in order to gain on you so that we might argue."

He stood, still sweating with the exertion of the ride, tired, drawn, and haggard.

"Then you have wasted horse and breath."

"I see that you are upset and not merely angry, but also hurt. Please. Come, Lizzy." He held out his hand.

She was too furious to speak, but she gave him her hand and stepped down. They stood a little away, out of earshot but not out of sight.

"I could not let you go like that," he apologized. "I felt miserable afterwards. And it was wrong of me."

"I want to accept your apology, but I must remind you that I am not indifferent to your welfare. I cannot be tossed in and out of your inner circle like a rag doll which you choose to pick up whenever it suits and put down when it does not."

"Yes. I understand."

"I understand that you prefer to keep a public face, a perfect calm, but that is not how it will be between us. Between us there are emotions, good or bad."

He was crestfallen. Beaten. And she hated to see him thus. "I understand and I fail entirely to understand. It is quite a mystery what you ask of me."

"It is not a trip to the moon!" Elizabeth practically shook with exasperation. "I am asking you to communicate with me, to treat me as your partner, as someone you trust. We must share our decisions, our lives."

His eyes opened and his mouth closed and he shook with a deeply controlled anger. She thought he would climb back on the horse and ride away immediately. He dragged his hand through his hair and took a deep breath. "How is it that you are making it seem as if I am to blame!" he whispered as if yelling. "I too am furious. You know that I am. Not with you of course, but with your sister. And with Anne. And my aunt also. I do not want all this dissention and acrimony to occupy us. I want us to maintain our home as we see fit, to manage our own affairs without the invasion of such terrible eccentricities…"

"… you call Anne's act eccentric?!" She paced a little back and forth. "Darcy, how could you say such a thing? Yes, yes. Of course, I know what has happened. And I am very sorry for your aunt and Miss Anne. It is so very sad. Mary went to Anne to say goodbye and was confronted with her mother and she is quite destroyed by it."

"She is the cause of this tragedy. How could you tell me that she is to be pitied?"

"How dare you act as if she was the agent of Anne's self-molestation?" Elizabeth retorted equally aggressively. "How dare you? Did she hold the knife? Did Mary make Anne hate herself? Did she make Anne fall in love with her? Was it her fault she would not pretend to reciprocate those sentiments and that this honesty has caused calamitous grief?"

Their voices, begun in low tones, had increased in increments until Darcy shook his head and made sign to her that they were making a spectacle of themselves. He took her elbow and escorted her further away.

"What are you saying?" Darcy asked, confused.

"I suppose Lady Catherine told you nothing."

Elizabeth would like to have said your aunt is a great manipulator and you are one of her puppets, but she held her tongue knowing it would be better that his aunt bury herself by her own actions. Being right is rarely appreciated by those who are in the wrong. Elizabeth then explained, quite calmly, what she knew of the girls' friendship, of the kiss she had witnessed, of Mary's confession to her and later withdrawal from Anne's attentions. Darcy listened attentively, paced a little. Shook his head.

"But you told me none of this?" he accused her.

No, I told you nothing, she thought, realizing that he was asking her to communicate with him as she had requested minutes before. "It was not mine to share," she mumbled.

He took one of those deep breaths again, the ones in which he controlled his emotions. Like a porcelain statue at a gate, his face was set in a serious neutrality that she had noticed on so many occasions, but his fingers played on his watch fob and she could see the ridge of his jaw working as he set his teeth. Oh, she thought, I wish I could harness all that energy! What will you do, my love? When he spoke, Darcy's voice was charged with calm, as if he was breathing an agitated voice through a straw.

"Harris is a good man. He is one of my men and he is charged with your safety. I want you to know that I did not send you away without care. He will answer anything you need and will answer to me if he does not. Lizzy: you must continue. It is far until the exchange and almost dark already."

"And what of Anne? Will she live?"

Darcy nodded. "Yes, if we can prevent another occurrence. But I am dismayed by what you have intimated. It is common enough for men to seek the comfort of their equals, other men to whom they feel a deeper kinship, but women..." he shuddered and did not finish the thought.

The ensuing silence felt like a cocoon which magnified the overwhelming intensity of longing spiraling throughout her body.

"I cannot begin to understand the complexities of this situation," Darcy continued more calmly, "My aunt told me that Mary seduced Anne, that she made love to her and corrupted her passions, and then spurned her...but I am mollified in my condemnation of your sister for I see that it is not entirely of her making. As to the fact of Anne's being in love, I am quite dismayed and disturbed by it."

"It is not entirely possible to control one's sentiments. One falls in love with inappropriate people. I believe you are familiar with this human failing," Elizabeth said. "Perhaps social mores are not meant to interfere in matters of the heart?"

He smiled ruefully. "Yes, when you put it that way, I understand. But loving another woman is an illness, an aberration, and Lady Catherine is quite beside herself to understand how to dispel it from her daughter. Previously she sought only medical interventions for a kind of apathy and listlessness, but now she discovers there is also a mental aberration. You might confer with your parents about Mary."

Elizabeth's ire started to rise again, but she decided she would not fight him at the present on the subject for, truthfully, she was exhausted.

"Yes, I see it all quite clearly," he turned, and picked up her hands again, squeezed them gently, "Lizzy, I came to beg a kiss from you despite my rage. I could not bear that we parted with such formality. But I have gained a great deal more than a kiss."

"If you had only talked to me before..."

"I did not. I could not. 'If only' is not useful Elizabeth. And now I must send you off, for we both have some distance to go in the dark."

"We must promise one another that we will not end the day without reconciling, for we will fight."

He bent and kissed her on the cheek, "It is a good suggestion, but I do not offer promises lightly, nor unless I believe I can keep them, and I will do my best not to keep secrets from you," but as he spoke, a shadow crossed his face.

"What is it?" she asked.

He composed himself immediately. "Nothing. We have had enough for today." He offered his arm to escort her back to the carriage.

She did not take it. "I will not leave you with such a dry and uneventful offering if I am not to see you for many weeks. Please kiss me properly."

"Before these witnesses? Are you sure you want your reputation sullied in such an overt way?"

She nodded. To be sullied by a public kiss from Darcy seemed like the best kind of corruption. She leaned up to him and they kissed, properly, and hugged deeply.

As Darcy rode to Rosings in the dark, in the chill of the night, he thought of his mother. She had died when he was between being a boy and man, had left a little baby in her stead. He recalled his confusion. He had merely returned from his Aunt Catherine's to be told that his mother was gone and would not return, as if she had moved to another country or villa and had abandoned him and was elsewhere caring for other children, loving them as she had loved him. He recalled how angry he was even though he knew she was dead. Although he had been raised by Mrs. Reynolds, now his housekeeper and still something of a confidante in some matters, it was his mother who understood his quiet side, the way he felt things deeply and the way he must, to be a man, arm himself against sentimentality.

These thoughts gave rise to a longing to be called Will with his mother's tender voice and a determination to request that Elizabeth use his first name. He rode slowly in the dark and arrived late under a crescent moon. His anticipation of Yuletide festivities was gone. His anticipation of being in Georgiana's company with Elizabeth at his side, his excitement at a house full of people in warmth and humour, gone. As he came down the lane, the house was in complete darkness. Not a light showed anywhere. His toes were so entirely frozen that they hurt excruciatingly as they warmed. He sat at the fire alone and determined to leave for London as soon as possible, taking his sister and Anne with him.

.

LONGBOURN

MR COLLINS
IS THE WRONG MESSENGER

It is unfortunate that a good life does not make a good story. A good life cannot compete with a narrative of compelling violent tensions, love's sorrows, accidents and horrors, parades of that which destroys, corrupts, and kills. We are anaesthetized by fiction to the pretty pauses in life in which nothing happens. What engaging story portrays that we breathe easily, notice the flowers and the butterflies, think nothing of our lives but that we are content because nothing obstructs our happy days? In a good life, there is no conflict so visceral as a war, serial killer, or monster to entertain. No terrible mystery, no engaging terror. The best life floats in a kind of generosity which requires merely a mention for it does not create plot tension. Snow White plays in the forest with the animals and lives with the dwarves. Hansel and Gretel's childhoods are unremarkable until they are led into the forest. Bluebeard's bride lives in luxury until she investigates the locked closet (and it is a good thing for her that she does).

The simple narrative is the life most of us lead most of the time, and it is certainly the one most of us seek, for isn't it a pretty life? The ending of a romantic tale cannot come too soon for there is nothing so terrible as a love story that has not been tested to satisfy the greedy reader who, unwittingly, seeks pain and loneliness for the lovers. It is the glory of fiction that we can do our protagonists harm, put sorrow in their way in order to entertain the monstrous appetite of narrative plot.

Yet, fear not. Miss Elizabeth Bennet was only mildly concerned about how her own romance would conclude. She had received letters from Darcy since her return. These contained expressions of love. He many times promised to resolve the issues at Rosings Park and return to Netherfield with Georgiana, and possibly Anne as well.

She studied her own parents who had over many years of questionable marital bliss produced five daughters, not a single heir, and a way of interacting which entertained most of their progeny for they were dear to each other in ways of respect and care but were as different from one another as a social butterfly and a studious monk. She listened to their chatter with a new ear, discerning in their public conversation hints of intimacy and teasing which before she had heard only as patient formality.

"I am very happy for my girls, Mr. Bennet, but I cannot imagine how they will spend all their money," Mrs. Bennet remarked as if it were the first and not the seventeenth time she had said something similar.

"Perhaps they will not spend it," her husband replied, loading his fork with eggs and sausage, believing that frugality, even when one is wealthy, has merit.

"They will have a hundred servants where we do very well with five," she continued.

"Perhaps you would be better to worry how they shall spend their time?"

"And I am much relieved of my worry that, should you die Mr. Bennet, I shall not be turned out to live in the streets, for with great houses at their disposal, I do not doubt that one of my two daughters of importance shall see to my care."

"It is good of you to imagine so consistently that I shall die ahead of you."

"Oh Mr. Bennet, it is easy for you. You are a man."

"It is true, Mrs. Bennet, I am."

The sound of a carriage in the yard interrupted this dialogue and brought Kitty to the high window. When she announced the arrival of Mr. Collins, she begged to go upstairs and was told to stay. After the formalities of greeting and sharing news and other pleasantries, Mr. Collins asked to have a private audience with Mr. Bennet to deliver some very important correspondence from Lady Catherine de Bourgh.

"Her esteem of me has given me this most arduous responsibility to which I feel most ignobly honoured. And for which reason I have been delivered in one of her most excellent of coaches."

Not one of them laughed at his misuse of the word 'ignoble', pronounced with his usual flourishes, but Kitty rolled her eyes, and Mary and Elizabeth shared a quick glance in which they each wondered which of them was the subject of the message.

"To think that you might have had *him* for a husband," Kitty whispered to Elizabeth.

Mr. Collins frowned at Kitty's whispering. "It is to advocate on a critical issue on the great Lady's behalf that I am forwarded to this place and at liberty to express my condolences and the displeasure my superior benefactress feels in the matter of Mr. Darcy's engagement with your daughter, Elizabeth Bennet."

Mrs. Bennet suggested that Mr. Collins' condolences were not necessary while Mr. Bennet ushered him from the room. As the drawing room door closed, Kitty jumped to the divan, sat, and broke into a peal of uncontrollable laughter. "Imagine that he might have become our brother-in-law!"

The bell announcing the mail rang.

"Hill. Hill."

Mrs. Bennet yelled, wanting her housekeeper to be like a footman or a butler who would arrange her household like a large estate, but it was Kitty who ran out and returned with several letters. They each took up their comfortable chairs and activities. Elizabeth scanned Darcy's letter. She brought her chair near the window to read more carefully. Finally, Kitty, who was tired of waiting for news, asked about its contents and Elizabeth merely answered that Mr. Darcy says but a little, except to put in a kind word of love as always. Kitty sighed and peeked over Elizabeth's shoulder as if to read it, but Elizabeth tucked it against herself and smiled at her sister indulgently.

"I wish you would all get fiancées so I must not have the burden of sharing mine!" Elizabeth laughed.

Mrs. Bennet turned to Mary who had also received a letter. "Mary: do read it aloud."

"Anne is kept well enough, but she is kept in a hospital room, and even her letters are monitored so she must be careful what she writes."

"Oh, that is ill. Hospitals are not places one would wish to be. People in hospitals are unwell and unwell travels."

"Melancholia is not generally contagious, Mama," Mary corrected.

"So, they say, but I do not believe it."

"I should not want to be in one of *those* hospitals," Kitty interrupted. "Even with an imagination, a pen, and a good deal of paper. They say that anyone who is once admitted is never released."

"I don't believe she is anywhere but with her mama who will

never let her out of her sight," Elizabeth looked up from her own letter. "Darcy writes that Anne is home and that they all tend to her needs faithfully. I believe she is well kept."

"I am convinced that the illness is fictitious," Mary insisted, putting down the letter. "She is highly intelligent in many ways, but is uncomfortable in society, cannot understand the subtle gestures of interaction. She looks to her mother for advice, but her mother cannot serve but to inhibit her own unique nature. Anne turns between what she wants for herself and what her mother insists she must want, and the two are in opposition."

"She writes all this?" Elizabeth asked.

"Of course not. She writes about the fairies in the hospital gargoyles where the ice drips and imagines that an icicle will drop and pierce a young nurse's heart so that she will die a dramatic death... It is all fiction."

"From what you've told me, that girl needs time away from her mother who dominates her terribly with sitting and agreeing," Jane noted as if they did not all spend many hours sitting prettily in the drawing room doing various activities and agreeing with their mother.

"That aunt of Mr. Darcy's is quite an ogre, despite her title," Mrs. Bennet complained. "How she came into our house and sat without invitation and criticized that the drawing room faced the wrong direction."

"Mama, you should not speak thus of a soon to be relation," Jane suggested.

"I am sure your Mr. Bingley does not have an aunt who will be harassing you, Jane. He is far too amiable a man to have such a relation."

"Mama!" they all objected.

"I have proposed a strange idea to Mr. Bingley," Jane said changing the subject. "Elizabeth, we should marry together, travel side by side to the church and to say *I do* together."

Elizabeth couldn't imagine what might be endearing about sharing one's matrimonial ceremony. "I will consider it," she replied cautiously.

Jane had many plans already for the wedding which seemed like a fairy tale and Elizabeth was swept up in visions of flowers and beauty and choirs singing in an incomparable splendour. Only royalty had weddings of such complex grandeur and it went entirely against Elizabeth's initial plan to marry in a simple style in a church near Pemberley with a few people as witness, perhaps her family, and that would be the end of it. But Jane's enthusiasm was met with approval by both Kitty and Mrs. Bennet, and so Elizabeth said she would consider the idea and write to Darcy asking his opinion.

Soon, Elizabeth was asked to join Mr. Collins in her father's study. As she crossed into the hallway, she braced herself against the weight of Mr. Collins' ornamental speeches. True to form, he popped from his chair but popped back down as Mr. Bennet directed the conversation and explained that Lady Catherine was offering an annuity in exchange for a promise not to marry Mr. Darcy.

"A bribe?"

"I do believe, Elizabeth, that you would do quite well with five thousand in your possession," Mr. Bennet mused. "I have no idea what it is in the world that you might want to do with such a sum, but no doubt there are dresses and perhaps travel and then, you might try living on the remainder."

At which point Mr. Collins bounced back up again and began his formal address to Elizabeth, a speech which she thought had been rehearsed all the way from Rosings to her doorstep, and for which every mile he travelled had been an occasion to compose an additional sentence. He repeated the essential information, that she was to desist from marrying, added to which a cart load of unnecessary flourishes, taking pains to remind his dear cousin Elizabeth of the Lady's exceptional generosity of five thousand as well as taking great pains to recite the lineage to which Darcy owed his allegiance, stumbling over a few particulars to which he coughed as if to sweep them under a proverbial carpet. "I am bound to report that it is with a great deal of pain to both myself and Mrs. Collins that we are asked to sever your contact with the Darcy family, for your associations with me, as we share the bond of filial relations and tenderness of long acquaintance via my dear wife, which because of this association might compromise our livelihood at Rosings Park if you are to continue in this most unsettling engagement."

Elizabeth kept her hands in her lap and a rigidity to her face as Mr. Collins delivered his missive, which she thought made no sense and try as she might she could only guess that she was being told that his livelihood depended on her giving up her engagement. When Mr. Collins was finished his long and laborious speech, he read the entire contract out loud and Elizabeth worried for her father who must hear it all for the second time.

"Well Lizzy?" Mr. Bennet asked once Mr. Collins was finished. "Five thousand is quite a sum to refuse."

"It pains me, Mr. Collins, that you should have been chosen for this unpleasant task and I wonder that you should have agreed to it."

Mr. Collins, looking quite surprised at this rejoinder, sputtered.

"But of course, you must know that when a heart is taken, money is not an object," she continued. "And since I have once already refused Mr. Darcy's proposal of marriage some months ago, I believe I have proven to him that it is not money which directs my interest."

"He proposed twice?" Mr. Bennet asked.

"I believe I told you he had affection for me some time before I was able to return it; but return it I do and I fully believe he is the man with whom I would spend my life, whether or not he has property."

MR. COLLINS
PURSUES HIS DUTY TO PROPAGATE

Elizabeth retreated from her father's study more bemused than horrified by Grendel's proposal and agreed to walk with Jane. She shared the details of her interview and said that Mr. Collins was not the right messenger for the job. Jane commiserated with her, agreed that the bribe should be refused and Elizabeth promptly dismissed any further thought of it.

When they returned home, Kitty ran up to the garden gate flushed and laughing so hysterically that she could barely speak. She danced around them, gasping and blurring her words and, between sobs of derision, described how she had escaped the society of Mr. Collins who only just departed the house.

"He has been here all this time?" Elizabeth asked.

"After you left to walk, I ran upstairs to get away. Into your room, Jane, as you see." And she curtsied dramatically by way of displaying the proof, the fact that she was wearing Jane's new evening gown with a coat thrown over it. "I believed myself to be quite safe, but some time later, I heard them on the stairs!"

"They were going upstairs, together?"

"Father must have thought I was away with mother and Mary because he and Mr. Collins came into your room, Jane," Kitty added dramatically. "Father cleared his throat many times. And Mr. Collins was silent, which was shocking. And there was nothing said, but father, finally, in that voice when he must speak seriously and does not like to, said Look here. You blow out the lights, see, make it dark. Take off all of your clothing. All of it. Ask permission to enter the bed and ask that your wife remove her clothing before you do so."

"He didn't!" Jane shook her head, refusing to believe Kitty.

Kitty barely took a breath and continued. "Mr. Collins asked whether her bedclothes must also be removed? Quite shocked it seemed. Yes! yes! That was father. It helps, he said. Our father! Once you engage, the skin touching makes you forget that you are nervous. It helps. You know. It helps."

Kitty could barely get the words out and she was dancing around them in short bursts of energy as she spoke, her face alit and her eyes shining and the dress dragging a little on the ground where she forgot to lift it. Jane was now dancing a little as well in an attempt to protect her dress.

"That was all. Father said something to the effect that he was unable to continue, and they left! I did not move for fear he would know I was upstairs! Can you imagine? I had to remain *silent* - and *not laugh*. I thought I would explode."

"But why did they bother to go upstairs?" Elizabeth asked. "They could very well have had that conversation in the study."

Kitty shrugged her shoulders. "Perhaps Father would not corrupt his study with such an awful situation! Or, he had planned a demonstration...oh! oh! it is too painful to imagine," Kitty added. "Perhaps some of your small clothes would be removed from the dresser and shown as demonstration for anatomical placement!!"

"Oh, Kitty," Jane chided. "You are far too knowledgeable. Be careful or you will be in trouble with a boy who will not marry you and you will end up alone and impoverished in the streets of London."

They laughed, for their mother was fond of saying such things.

That same evening, Jane knocked on Elizabeth's door and entered, taking up the hairbrush to do Elizabeth's hair. She admitted that, upon preparing to sleep, she found herself very much distressed at the thought of Mr. Collins in her bedroom earlier in the day.

"Is it certain that he is in need of a matrimonial education?" Jane asked.

"Well just imagine it, Jane. Mr. Collins entering *your* bedchambers to do *that!*"

Jane gave Elizabeth a slight push. "You're not helping in the least! I am trying *not* to imagine such a thing!"

"Neither can he. He has not!" Elizabeth proclaimed.

"He has ...?" Jane began.

"Not," Elizabeth re-iterated.

"And Charlotte is...?"

"A virgin. Yes."

"Oh dear. It has been a year."

"A year of Mr. Collins arriving at her bedchambers attempting to do the right thing. Imagine you are Charlotte, yes? And he arrives at your door..."

"No. Too terrible."

"Knock. Knock. We will do our duty and propagate, he announces. He is seductively decorated in a long nightshirt, his socks still trailing around his ankles, a book – a large Biblical book – is gathered like armour under his arm, and perhaps even his jacket..."

"And his cross," Jane added, giggling.

"Not to be forgotten," Elizabeth nodded. "And thus, dressed as the man of her dreams, he will be ready to proceed with the necessary evil: the procurement of little Mr. Collins's...."

"I can see them now, the little men in their black frock coats all serious and pontificating."

"He'll stand by her bed arguing for admittance. Please move over, for I will lie beside you (with my book and socks and other protection) so that I might inspect ways to proceed..."

They were both laughing quite hysterically and sobbing between words. "Do stop. I shall have to pee!" Jane gasped.

"...And she would say, Mr. Collins please remove your socks. And this would be too much for the poor man. My socks! Never! For that is too intimate and our feet might touch. And he would excuse himself from the room insisting that his wife was not sufficiently ready for the full wealth of his passionate embraces. And so, for a year now Charlotte is still a virgin."

"Did Charlotte speak of this?"

"Of course not. Well yes. Only that he has not mounted her..."

"Oh stop, Lizzy. That is so rude. She said nothing of the sort. But seriously, Lizzy, I am sure I will be relieved when my first matrimonial evening is over. It might be a pleasant thing to be left alone."

Elizabeth disagreed, arguing that she could barely wait to be naked with Mr. Darcy. But Jane covered Elizabeth's mouth with her hand. Blushing red. Elizabeth grabbed it away, wrestled Jane onto the bed and stared down at her.

"Do you not desire Mr. Bingley? Do you not feel excited in his presence, or dizzy by his smell?"

"His smell! Elizabeth Bennet, you're not an animal."

Elizabeth pinched Jane in her side, under her ribs as if to say, that is not the right answer.

"I'm so nervous, Lizzy, that I can't imagine ..."

Elizabeth dropped onto her pillow. "Oh, your nerves will clear when you let your yearnings rise beyond them. When your body goes all sparkly because he has touched your lips…"

"Lizzy!"

"I quite fell over from the warmth permeating my arm when Darcy first held my hand. And now that he has touched other places, it is unbearable to be apart."

Jane considered this, and nodded as if she understood, but then added, "I'm worried that I'll not please Charles."

"But what is there not to please? You're such a wonderful pair together. Why would that not be so in…in other ways? Surely it will be quite easy and natural if there is great affection."

"Enough of this Lizzy. I can't stand this talk."

"Well, if we don't share these things together, then with whom will we have intimate conversation?"

"Well, it is clear there will be no help from Charlotte," Jane grinned. "Mother will instruct us."

"Indeed, we will be as educated as Mr. Collins when she does."

Elizabeth pulled the cover out from under Jane and spread it over them both so they were side by side in her little bed. "She was once a Gardiner, Jane. Do you ever think of that? Our mother before she became Mrs. Bennet?"

"Of course not."

"But she was once as we are. A Miss. She has a Christian name, a life before us, Jane. A life before father. Don't you see? How strange to think of it?"

"No. Of course she did."

"But what did she think of her future, of her life as a woman, as a mother, when she was a girl? Who was she before she was a wife and a mother?"

"Elizabeth, you forget of whom you refer. Our mother would not have thought."

Elizabeth laughed. "Quite true. It is I who think, Jane. One day I'll be more a 'Mrs. Darcy' and a 'mama' than an Elizabeth Bennet. In fact, soon, I'll not be a Bennet at all. But I like being Elizabeth Bennet. I don't want to lose her."

"I wonder if Mama talked with Auntie about her love of Mr. Bennet," Jane giggled. "It's funny to think of them, Mrs. Bennet and Mrs. Philips as young girls, talking as we are…wondering how father will manage their first night together…"

JANE AND ELIZABETH
TALK ABOUT SEX

On the Sixth day of December, the Bennet family gave modest gifts to one another to open the season, offering rough tribute to Saint-Nicholas whose habit it had been to distribute secret gifts for charity. Mrs. Bennet's sister, Mrs. Philips and her little family who lived nearby, were always about. Mrs. Bennet's brother, Mr. Gardiner, arrived with Mrs. Gardiner, their children, as well as a governess, Amanda Webster, filling the house with a noisy and cheery crowd.

The days grew dark, with the shortest day arriving in but a fortnight. The sun rose from the horizon, gained an altitude of several hands' width, rode along the horizon for a few hours then dove back again peeking into the world for less than eight hours. The days were cold, wet, often with a deep frost overnight, especially higher in the hills, and the nights very long. The dullness of these dark days was counterpoised by a flurry of festivities and customs, gathering of family and friends, of charity and gift giving, all in an atmosphere of a mini fairy tale in which some magic lit the night and made the spirits soar.

On Christmas Eve, the family collected and laid out their decorations, filling the house with the smell of rosemary and evergreens, holly especially, but also hellebore and hawthorn, as they could find it, and made circlets of these. Mrs. Bennet, tasting the air with appreciation, said it was almost as good as opening the doors and bringing in summer. A small party went out to collect a yule log, pulling it home with the help of a horse and lighting it with the coal from last year's log which had been carefully protected in a little tin box in the larder. This was a tradition in Mrs. Bennet's childhood home and the ceremonial lighting of the log made her sentimental and weepy.

On Christmas day they feasted on goose, hare, and partridge, a figgy pudding (as Mrs. Hill called her plum pudding), mince pies and a Yorkshire Christmas Pie which stood a foot tall and looked like a feat of well-crafted architecture. There was such an abundance of food that every time Hill delivered another plate, she said, "There'll be much forbye for suppin' later, even after we eats whot we can." They played games with the children, filling the house with squealing and delight. On boxing day, all the men went out fox hunting (even Mr. Bennet who was not a hunter but rode around following and enjoying a turn in the air for the delight of being with a crowd of men for a change). The girls went around Meryton delivering little boxed gifts to the butcher and the baker, the candlestick maker, and others who had provided good service during the year and for whom they had sewn useful little items, such as a hanky or little collar of lace, or knitted socks or, for some more celebrated, a good shirt made with a fine cotton. Mrs. Hill and cook, as well as the stable hand, the gardener and the scullery maid were all equally presented with their own little boxes.

Elizabeth wrote consoling letters to Darcy, for his were of a Rosings in gloom, of Lady Catherine's increased severity, of a house without decorations, of an oppressive silence. His aunt had banned Christmas from the premises and reduced it to a single evening at church. There was no company as the Earl and his wife had moved off immediately while Anne's terrible misery invaded all corners of the house. He wrote that he and Georgiana spent a great deal of time sharing the burden of reading to her and trying to keep her spirits from complete despondency.

A new single man had occasion to spend a great deal of time with them. Mr. Nathan Bingley, who was Charles Bingley's cousin and who, having finished his degree, was moping about wondering what to do next while procrastinating at Netherfield.

Elizabeth had heard about him through Jane and Kitty's letters in which both emphasized how absolutely gorgeous and charming he was. Yet when she finally met him and saw for herself, she had to admit that they had not exaggerated. Nathan Bingley was endowed with a compelling beauty which Elizabeth found too pretty, even too perfect, if such a thing was possible.

He was so entirely attentive to all the young girls over the holidays that Jane and Elizabeth spent some time discussing which of them might be his love interest. At first, they presumed the Gardiner's governess, Miss Amanda, as she shared Nathan's love of dramatics. Elizabeth once caught him on his knees holding one of Amanda's hands. He placed a kiss as she curtsied and stroked his head tenderly knighting him in word and gesture; but when he stood, she stuck her tongue at him and pranced away mocking horse riding. His attentions to Mrs. Hill, for whom he carried heavy baskets of laundry, were similarly dramatic. He bowed to her deeply as if she were a queen while she blushed and grinned and said, No Mr. Nathan, You Must Not! It was obvious that Kitty favoured him for she stammered and stuttered and seemed not at all like Kitty when he spoke to her; yet, he paid as much attention to Mary as anyone, sitting with her for many long minutes, discussing her book or her ideas regarding the welfare of the poor, equal rights for women and the source of the soul, which seemed to be as compelling to him as Mrs. Bennet's ideas about hat design. She and Jane decided that he was attentive to everyone in the household and that none of these attentions were signs of a man in love. He seemed, in fact, to be interested in whatever interested his friends.

Because of Nathan's special love for dramatics, he often read out loud in the evenings. His witty impersonations of beloved characters from children's stories and fairy tales became a favourite entertainment. Once he chose a play for them all to read out loud. Mr. Bennet played a young girl and Mrs. Bennet a travelling peddler. Kitty was the romantic prince and he, Nathan, the princess. Elizabeth was a talking horse and Jane the peddler's angry sister. Finally, Bingley, who had not yet been assigned a part, complained, and was asked to read the stage directions in urgent tones. Mary offered to play piano interludes between each scene. As the play progressed, they realized no one had taken the part of the gnome, and everyone was hysterical as Mary performed her part on her knees as if she had a bad head cold. The Philips and Gardiners all performed the part of audience and clapped loudly and gave a standing ovation more because they were tired of sitting than that the drama was so exceptional.

"They will be married by next year," Mrs. Bennet whispered to Elizabeth as they watched the final meeting of the lovelorn lovers. "Just you wait. He is very, very fond of our Kitty. I have been paying attention. You must stay out of the way, Miss Lizzy."

"Me? Mama, I am not a puppy in love following him about!" Elizabeth whispered back. "She is disgusting in her attentions to him. Have you not noticed that his friendly demeanour is not especially directed to her ..."

"But he chose her for his love interest in this performance!"

"Mama, it hardly qualifies when she was the *prince* and he the princess. In any case, I am not interested in him, and did you see the way he keeps glancing at Mary?"

Nathan was receiving Kitty's prostrations as she kneeled before him to ask for his hand. Everyone was rather amused and twittered and giggled, and one of the Gardiner boys laughed and approved of Nathan in a dress! How could anyone not want to marry him!

"Mary?!" Mrs. Bennet practically yelled, "She will stay and care for your father and myself in our dotage."

Elizabeth, noting how her mother often contradicted herself, did not mention an earlier conversation about finding Mary a husband.

"As I study him," Mrs. Bennet leaned in to whisper, "how often he returns to you whenever he is otherwise unoccupied, how often he takes your arm as you move from room to room, it seems more and more likely that he's devoted to *you*, Lizzy. You are betrothed. You must allow him to love Kitty."

Elizabeth had formed a brotherly-like bond with Nathan. They had fun together, teasing, being silly, mocking others in a friendly, spirited way. He knew nothing about the books she preferred, nor her dreams, and she nothing of his, but they regularly laughed hard enough that their kidneys hurt. They were such cheery companions that Jane eventually asked whether he had said any words of adoration to her.

"Oh, no. He's not spoken a word and I think it isn't true. Perhaps," Elizabeth chided gently, "you're jealous? And I see him following *you* about, asking to see your sketches. But really Jane, I don't have any of that excruciating desire for him which I have for Darcy who – need I remind you - I miss terribly." Elizabeth cocked her head to one side, clasped her hands at her heart and mocked a lyrical sincerity. "When the debris of daily distractions settle like silt in a river, revealing beams of striated colours and sparkling pebbles at its bottom, the important things of one's life rise. It's Darcy who comes to me in these moments, Darcy who interrupts even my busy thoughts, Darcy who reciprocates these attentions. No, I don't love Nathan Bingley. Do you?"

"You quote some poet."

"Probably, though I don't know which one. But surely you have desire for Charles. That longing that rises through one's body. Draws one person to the other."

Jane nodded. "I was very despondent when he severed our relationship last year. It was as if a part of me was torn away. And when we are together, it is his tender smile and constant easiness which delights me. But it is not visceral Elizabeth, as you say. I don't feel it in my body that way."

"Not his smell, his touch?"

They were squeezed into Elizabeth's bed after brushing each other's hair. Elizabeth shared a few details of her intimacies with Darcy. But when she described how he had pulled her into the garderobe for a kiss, Jane, having heard that he had some reputation with women, asked whether he had coerced Elizabeth.

"You are repeating words you hear in drawing rooms, behind covered mouths, whispered by people who have nothing better to do than to defame others." Elizabeth referred to Caroline without having to name her. She dared not mention the secret tunnels and the passionate embrace in which his desire was palpable through her thin nightdress, the way he had slept with her, on the covers. Jane, she doubted it not, would filter the information through the lens of this gossip and blemish something which was, for Elizabeth, joyous and beautiful.

And it was in that moment that she truly understood Anne de Bourgh, that although her love was unacceptable by society's values, it was nevertheless a visceral love, directed toward the one loved, the one adored, the one wanted. There was no repairing that love. There was no deciding who one loved. This little thing, this spontaneous combustion of feeling, came unbidden out of something mysterious and grand, and it was miraculous. To love like that was rare. One did not, after all, walk the streets and fall in love. One could love strangers with a kindness and compassion, but to desire a close circle of intimacy was precious. In some mysterious world, they had chosen each other. And everything had changed with that decision. Darcy's past reputation was still a topic of gossip, but the rest of their society would have to catch up to the present. Darcy had grown up. Darcy had picked.

"There are boundaries, Elizabeth. Charles and I respect them."

"Do you not trespass a little?" she asked, hopefully.

"He is very proper," Jane responded. "He respects me terribly and takes very good care with me, that I remain pristine and uncorrupted by the debasing of improper intimacy."

He would have you be the Virgin Mary *and* mother of your children and he will seek other women with whom he might get pleasure, Elizabeth almost said, for she had learned too much in her studies of the Earl and his wife, and from Darcy who had revealed something of his knowledge of those married men who stray often from their wives. Too many men today prize their women as vessels of purity, which prevents them from enjoying intimacy because they must keep the pretense of purity, he had said one day. They then seek true gratification elsewhere. Which is everywhere to be found if you know where to look. They may enact their true mind's desires with strangers to whom they pay for the promise of discretion. The Madonna figure, their wives, are bright and virginal keepers of sanctimony and should never want to descend into that bristling fire of hellish bodily desire. Their wives, who are also frustrated, survive on no gratification or, in a few cases, seek it elsewhere. Either way, everyone maintains the delusion that they are pure and unsullied. I tell you these things, my dear, because I want you to know that I have no intention of being one of those men, nor do I want you to be one of those women. It seems, I am the kind of man who listens, and apparently you are the kind of woman to whom I tell everything. Now, sew up my lips, for you are already completely corrupted!

"But do you think Charles has desire for you?" Elizabeth asked Jane.

"Lizzy, how could you ask such a thing. We will have children," Jane answered, as if that was the answer.

"But what of his needs, and yours?"

The more Elizabeth probed the more contracted Jane seemed to become. "Well, surely you will not have a hundred children, but will you not want to have marital relations more than the few times required to conceive?"

Jane relaxed a little and giggled. "I had not thought about it. First you speak of not wanting children, and now you speak as if you will be so intimate with Mr. Darcy that you will not stop having children."

"Yes, that is the problem, is it not?" Elizabeth laughed.

"Charles loves talking with me, and being gay, and we have so many wonderful conversations about everything Lizzy, but until we're married, I don't believe he wants to speak to me about those things." She kissed Elizabeth on the forehead and got out of bed. "I'm not so sure I would like to know if he has made love to another woman. As long as I know he is with me now, I should be happy not to worry about his past. For he must have one, don't you think? Most men do, do they not?"

"Well, I'm quite sure he's not a Mr. Collins!" Elizabeth laughed.

"But I'm quite sure you aren't a moll!" Jane replied. Elizabeth winced a little, aware how fine a line there was for women. One was perceived as perfectly pure, or else was immediately categorized as wanton, with little wiggle room between. "Like Miss Amanda. I'm surprised they agree to associate with her, for she's rude and outspoken, and she is shamelessly coquettish with Mr. Bingley," Jane pronounced seriously.

"She flirts as much with father as Mr. Bingley," Elizabeth countered, thinking Amanda's actions were nothing compared to the Countess of Somewhere and her overt attentions to Darcy. Amanda was as at ease with people in the same way as Nathan, but in a woman, this was seen as flirtatious and rude. "Many people have accused me of being rude and outspoken because I'm intelligent and independent. Miss Amanda is an active, happy, boisterous girl, Jane, and why shouldn't she be?"

Jane was silent a minute. "I worry how my Charles and Miss Bingley will receive her. How she reflects on me, do you see? The company we now keep, Elizabeth, will reflect on our husbands, and we must be mindful of who we choose as our associates. She is crass and opinionated. She touches Charles on every occasion as if he were her brother. I even saw her once pinch his bottom."

"And Bingley? Does he respond?" Elizabeth asked.

"He blushes and asks her to refrain. But it's Miss Bingley who really disapproves. It's written on her face."

"I believe you give too much credit to Miss Bingley's opinions, Jane. And care too much what she thinks of you."

Elizabeth thought that Jane was beginning to speak too much like Miss Bingley and to lose her honest tolerance of everyone, but she held back those thoughts and felt grief that she might be losing her dearest sister in an inevitable, slow crawl towards their separate lives. "Besides, she came with family. We can't control that."

"No Elizabeth. That is precisely what makes it more damaging."

INAPPROPRIATE
FOR THE DRAWING ROOM

When Elizabeth read Charlotte's letter, she could not help but gasp. Kitty hurried to peer over her shoulder as the entire household begged to be included, but Elizabeth delicately placed the letter in her bosom by way of response. There was a general conversation in which they speculated on the reason for the sequestering of the letter, speculation which continued for almost a quarter of an hour as many hilarious propositions were given and a lovely parade of bantering ensued. All in all, they were having such fun imagining the contents of the letter that Elizabeth hoped they might have forgotten about the reality of it. But not Kitty who decided she could obtain an answer by wrestling her sister and ignored her mother's admonishments. Kitty's success in obtaining the letter from its fleshy envelope was assured as Elizabeth could not control her laughter. A race ensued in which a chair became an obstacle. Hearing the commotion from across the hallway, Mr. Bennet peeked in and said "Oh, it is just you girls," and returned to the library not in the least curious about the uprising in his drawing room. Kitty, who was not stronger but more determined, overwhelmed Elizabeth who convulsed with the mere mention of being tickled, but Mary snatched it from Kitty's hand at her moment of triumph. Kitty, snatching it back, lorded over Elizabeth with it in her hand. "Now that I have it, will you permit me to read it?'

"No. Charlotte would be horrified if she knew."

"But she will not know. We will swear to secrecy."

"You may not. It is not the sort of thing one should even put to paper."

"For fear it will get in the wrong hands!" Kitty sang waving the letter with emphasis.

"It is Mrs. Collins' letter. It cannot be so entirely inappropriate," Mrs. Bennet concluded, quite reasonably.

"No, mam," Elizabeth replied. "This is not the Mrs. Collins nor the Mr. Collins that we know and love," Elizabeth corrected, stalking her sister slowly as if no longer interested in the letter, but of gaining the window, the desk, the door. "I have no idea what I shall write in reply. I do not want to even acknowledge having received this correspondence. Yes: perhaps that is what I shall do. I shall not answer and she will assume it lost."

Of course, curiosity is not an easy thing to tolerate when one is confined to the dark and winter season, and even Elizabeth, who had had a lot of fun playing her part in protecting it, decided she would simply leave the room and abdicate all responsibility for the letter's further care. It is not so very terrible really, she thought as she gained the front entrance, turned and poked her head back into the room and, hoping to dampen interest, suggested that it was, after all, just about books.

"That does not bode well for entertainment as promised. You have exaggerated the thing, Lizzy, if it is about books."

Kitty read out loud. "*Dear Blah and blah blah blah.*" As she scanned the letter, her eyes became large. She gasped. She giggled. Mrs. Bennet leaned forward and snatched it from Kitty and handed it to Mary.

"Mary: please read the letter. You have a nice loud voice."

"*Dear Elizabeth,*" Mary read, "*I am terribly sorry to be writing this letter, but I have no other close friends with whom I might confide. I will begin however by saying that there are rumours about why you and Mary left Rosings suddenly which I will not believe until they come from your own mouth...*"

"Which you girls have still not revealed even to your mother!"

Mary read on.

"*It is lonely without you and I wish you might have stayed longer and that we might have spent more time together. After your departure, Lady de B chastised my Mr. Collins quite harshly for having brought you into her acquaintance, and she then chastised me for being your very good friend. I am very happy to say that although he did not stand up for you Lizzy, Mr. Collins did delicately ask her ladyship to refrain from speaking of the future mother of his children in a disparaging way- meaning me, though I cannot imagine how he expects to have children as there are no... Oh Elizabeth! There are some strange advancements in this regard but I'm afraid I find them rather horrifying. Mr. Collins behaves increasingly strange. He leaves for his private chambers every night and returns to me more pale. Sometimes he peeks at me and giggles, his hand before his mouth. He raises his eyebrows at me. Then I find him, in his room, before the mirror doing something unspeakable. I will not describe. I will not corrupt your young mind. But instead of embarrassment he turns to face me*" *and invites me to watch. To watch!!!!!!!!!!!"*

Mary looked up from her reading. "I should note that there are no less than eleven exclamation marks. That does seem extravagant." She turned back to the letter.

"I believe we have heard enough," Mrs. Bennet squawked. "That is too… too…too..."

But Mary did not pause.

"He then runs after me and says it is natural. He brings me a book. Shows me (shows me!!!!!!!!)" Mary addressed the room again. "More exclamation marks." She shook her head like a grade schoolteacher commenting on the grammar and not the content of the letter.

"He insists how natural it is, and more," she read. *"He brings me another book, ostensibly claimed from a secret library at Rosings. Brings it to my room..."*

Mrs. Bennet pulled the letter from her daughter's hands and tucked it in her bosom.

"Mother: it is my letter. Please return it."

"You did not protect it very well, Miss Elizabeth. I believe I will take it into custody at this point and deliberate as to what shall be done with it."

"You will not share it with father!" Elizabeth asked horrified at the possibility.

"Of course not. But what is this secret library she speaks of?" to which she received no answer. "I see, yes. Well, perhaps Lady Catherine de Bourgh is not as civil as we have been led to believe."

How this became the subject of their supper conversation requires some explanation as well, for the Bennets were neither in the habit of discussing their friends' intimacies nor of exposing their private letters to companions at the table; but there are exceptions to every rule and exceptions should be written into every rule so that rules might be reasonably accommodated. It was Mr. Bennet who provoked the subject by describing the uproar in the drawing room to Jane and the Bingleys who had been away all day, and he suggested his daughters needed more exercise and better diversions. Kitty objected saying that she was merely stealing a letter from her sister. Mrs. Bennet, who normally ploughed into delicate conversations with a stampede of words, actually refrained and tried to moderate a change of topic by asking if they had seen any badgers on their ride, which did not raise any interest, for when one has not seen a badger one has nothing to say, and when one has indeed seen a badger one has little more to say, except of course, that one had seen a badger.

Jane asked why Kitty felt compelled to steal the letter; Bingley delighted at the fun he had missed; Nathan grinned; and Caroline Bingley remained upright and rigid and showed no emotion at all. Elizabeth, observing her style, felt that she had been sent to a finishing school much like the one Lady Catherine had designed for her, except that Miss Bingley had not perfected the art of being in control while appearing to be delightful and casual. Miss Bingley had got stuck on rigidity in order to avoid the excess of emotion Lady Catherine had so often warned against.

Mr. Bennet suggested that since half the room knew and half the room did not know the contents of the letter, their family might be more balanced if they were all to know its contents since it was impossible to reverse the order and make half the room forget the contents, which logic seemed fair to him, as he laughed at it, knowing how silly he was being; but Mrs. Bennet, who thought him quite ingenious, wanted to contradict him, for she was wisely sedate on this subject and would not wish the letter exposed.

"Hill. Hill," she yelled, creating a diversion. As she called, she searched about the room for an excuse in calling Hill before Hill presented herself expecting one, and one which would make her stay in the room and prevent the letter from being read. Elizabeth, smiling at her mother's transparent attempts to arrest further conversation about the letter, had already resigned herself to the fact that the letter had gained too much notoriety to be silenced. Hill arrived from her own supper to find that there was no excuse for her being called and, vociferous with annoyance, returned to eat.

"Would you like me to install a bell for you?" Bingley asked. "You could ring for her instead of call out."

Mrs. Bennet seized on the topic. "Yes yes, that would be lovely," but Mr. Bennet stood and picked up a bell from the sideboard, dusted it off and put it beside his wife's left hand. "No need, Bingley. We have got a bell, but we prefer to yell. It keeps our lungs fresh and vibrant. You should try it."

Jane chastised her father quietly. Elizabeth and Mrs. Bennet hoped the letter forgotten, but Kitty would not allow diversions, as the letter's content was a prize for which she had fought bravely and for which she had been greatly rewarded. "It is about Mr. Collins. He has found a secret library at Rosings."

This statement led to questions about why it was secret. Jane, quite innocent as yet as to the delicacy of the proceedings asked Bingley to explain, to which he of course refused. And Caroline pursued so that he must answer that he knew of the library but had not actually visited it. Mary, who was the only person in the room to have perused its delights, spoke up.

"It explores human nature as a sexual being in our many differing tastes. It has scientific pamphlets about diseases as well as historical and colourful material relating to physical intimacy. There are novels and pictures, pamphlets and posters." She listed these attributes in a deadpan voice as if naming the horses which had run good races at the fair. Most of the diners stopped eating and looked at one another and then to Mr. Bennet. Finally, he laughed uncontrollably while Mrs. Bennet looked embarrassed for them all and clucked. Mr. Bennet wiped his eyes with a napkin and exclaimed that he would never in his wildest dreams have imagined such a statement arriving at his dinner table, and that it should be introduced by his most sober daughter was absurd.

"Reality is more hilarious than fiction," he finally sputtered. "Do you not all agree?"

Bingley provided a few sensible words, and Elizabeth, refusing to read the letter again, merely described her friend's difficulties in having a spouse who, in a few brief months, had transposed himself from celibate to wanton. The conversation did not proceed much further than this because Nathan introduced the topic of art, and the fact that nudity was prevalent and acceptable and that there were many naked women hanging in the best houses across the land.

"There is nothing so beautiful as the human figure. Michelangelo's David, for instance, in which he stands unselfconsciously, with every vein and muscled line perfectly carved, rendering the stone soft looking. And the incredible serenity of his face draws one from the nudity, from the prevalence of his body to the spirit of his visage, his countenance, the glow of presence in all of him, uniting the two. It is remarkable."

"I have not seen this David nor know of this Michelangelo," Mrs. Bennet remarked.

"We intend to see it when we are on our bridal tour, do we not, darling?"

"We will chase all the masters, my dear," Bingley replied.

"But are you not concerned that your wife will be viewing a male body while you stand beside her? Is that not uncomfortable?" Mrs. Bennet asked, not realizing that the question itself might be more uncomfortable than the act.

Jane blushed a little. "Mama. That is not your business."

"I believe it is impossible to explore great art without occasionally being confronted by the human body," Bingley answered sensibly.

Nathan added that nudity in art is acceptable. One looks beyond the body to the art as one looks beyond the religious ritual to the sacred within it. Both seek to reveal what is hidden. The better the artist, the more successful they are in exposing the mystery. But Jane had been strangely quiet.

"I do hope it is true that art and nudity are understood to be agreeably matched." Elizabeth noted a quick look between Jane and Nathan.

"But that is sacrilegious! For you suggest that the sacred is caught in any religious ceremony and that all religions are therefore equal and it is the person bringing the ceremony to manifestation who controls whether god emerges in it."

This sober comment was of course from Mary's mouth.

"I do," Nathan answered, glowing. "Religious wars are stupid wars for no one can have monopoly over the infinite."

"But we are not talking about war, we are merely talking about the enactment of our beliefs in ceremony and lifestyle," she answered.

"The Irish for instance? Who believe differently from us and against whom we continue to fight on the pretext that our religious beliefs are superior?"

"How did we evolve from discussing nudity to religion?" Elizabeth laughed, thinking that Nathan and Mary's conversation would be better had in the corner of the drawing room where their philosophical sobriety might be less tedious to the diners. "I for one would be happy if we abandoned both subjects so that I might enjoy my pudding."

"Hear, hear!" Mrs. Bennet gushed, raising her glass.

"To changing the subject. A few times," Elizabeth mumbled.

The subject was changed, for there was no badger seen that day on their ride, but they had heard talk of a wolf.

"Wolves have been extinct for hundreds of years and it must have been a wild dog," Bingley said.

THE ASSEMBLY FAUX PAS

The end of the yuletide season arrived as always with Sir Lewis' Twelfth Night Ball. Elizabeth, upon entering the hall, became immediately nostalgic, remembering how she had first seen Darcy in this same place but a little over a year ago, as he stood and glared about the room, challenged by the apparent lack of refinement and sophistication.

Sir Lewis was a man to whom any excuse for gathering the neighbours for an assembly was a good one, and he had always been the local proprietor of the Christmas season finale, keeping the usual traditions of a Twelfth Night cake with a bean and a pea to name the king and queen for the evening. The mummers, well informed and well organized, arrived to deliver their play and went away with pockets of shillings and guineas, and the Wassail Bowl was more than twenty times refilled with mulled wine. They all danced and played games as this was a family event as entertaining for the children as the adults.

The Bingley sisters were of course in attendance and Elizabeth noted their disdain for all the rural pleasantries. They did not often seem to be in London, but they did often seem to speak about it as if they were integral to its social elite. On this evening, they talked of a recent fashion begun some years ago with the Queen. She insisted on keeping her German tradition of erecting an evergreen to celebrate Christmastide, decorated with ribbons and such (imagine!) and it was becoming quite the fashion among the finer families in London.

Elizabeth did not linger with them as there were many other guests less refined and more fun. She danced with the Gardiner children and her father, talked at length with Charlotte's mother about Charlotte (who of course could not be with them for her husband, a parson, must be very busy at Christmas time in his own parish), sat with Nathan and Mary who were discussing the rich convergence of pagan and Christian traditions at work in the village. She noted Jane and Bingley happy as they danced together, Mrs. Hurst laughing gaily as she danced with Mr. Bennet while Mr. Hurst slept in an armchair in the corner (Was he not well? She had never thought to pry, but his reserve was beyond what one might expect from a quiet person and more like a practiced coma). But no sooner did she sit by herself to ponder her sudden grief of missing Darcy than she was pulled again to dance in a line led by Kitty.

Somewhat late into the evening, there was a sort of hush as Mrs. Bennet exploded into a loud outrage, chiding her sister-in-law, Mrs. Gardiner, with uncivil words. Mr. Bennet looked about the room in a confused panic as Mr. Gardiner hushed his sister and insisted they speak in private, then led her to another room to calm. Elizabeth, standing with Jane and Caroline Bingley, learned that Mrs. Hurst had recognized their young governess, Amanda, and had told Mrs. Bennet that she should not allow such a one to be in their presence. Mrs. Bennet, not caring about the cause for this, was horrified at her family being disgraced, and insisted that the girl be immediately removed to London before she might defile their home further. The whole disruption lasted but a quarter of an hour and the music and games recommenced easily as no one knew exactly what this young woman had done to deserve the verbal lashing. Except of course Mrs. Hurst who whispered it to Caroline Bingley who then whispered it to Jane who then passed it on to Elizabeth.

Miss Amanda, who she very much liked, had had relations with her betrothed only to be shunned by him for having no sense of propriety. Elizabeth, who had heard of such a thing too often, felt sorry for the girl and determined to talk to her mother and convince her that she was not such a bad influence, really, for wasn't she quite the opposite? A model of what one must not do and the example of what happens when one does not respect the prejudices of the time? In fact, she argued, Mrs. Gardiner was showing a great deal of charity in providing shelter for this girl (her sister's husband's sister's niece) and was this not a time for charity?

For several days after this schism in the Bennet household, there were many conversations in twos and threes. It was a kind of internal family gossiping session as each sorted their own attitudes about the matter. Jane was most concerned about her visibility with the Bingleys and how the whole might tarnish her reputation with them. Kitty went about the house perplexed, gathering bits and pieces of what happened without anyone spelling out exactly what the governess had done wrong. Mrs. Gardiner could be heard whispering loudly to her husband from within their chamber rooms.

Miss Amanda was overheard telling the children why she must leave in words most discreet and proper, and this became proof to support her staying. Mary, who Elizabeth had decided was becoming one of the most clear headed and sensible people she knew, unmarked by the opinions of other people, reminded anyone who would listen that once again there was an unacceptable double standard, that the man's reputation suffered not at all, for was he not also participant and benefactor of their pre-conjugal relations? Mr. Bennet repeated often that it was not their business to run another person's household and that Mrs. Bennet must speak with her brother and make peace. Which she attempted, but with so many undertones of disapproval that Mrs. Gardiner was no more than civil afterwards. Mr. Gardiner, who had not been informed of Amanda's disgrace, was clearly annoyed with his wife.

Elizabeth took pains to further ingratiate herself with Amanda before her departure. It took almost no time and no effort to acquire the information she sought, for Amanda was not a shy girl, nor an unhappy one, but confident and spirited, bold and funny. While the children tobogganed down the hill, Elizabeth gave her little speech, asked her little question, and got her answer with a simple nod, a great wide smile, and useful details. All to the effect that Elizabeth was now in possession of the means by which a young lady might protect herself from getting with child should she wish to, and that although the techniques were not foolproof and required some cooperation from the man, could nevertheless aid in the delay of having children. And these methods were not the commonly known hexes or stupidities such as superstitions that a girl cannot become with child the first time, or that jumping up and down will rid one of the seed, or drinking lots of blueberry juice will prevent anything unwanted. Amanda's method did not involve a violent expelling of any little bit of something that might have been caught. No, it was simple medical information by which a person will study one's rhythms and add to the protection a sponge doused in something somewhat accessible, brandy, the French way, and all very civilized really.

MR. COLLINS IS REDEEMED

Not long after the close of the holiday season, a cold fell over the landscape that was unusually bitter. For the first time in recent memory, the Thames froze solid and people skated. Communication was slowed or arrested and even a trip from Netherfield to Longbourn was undertaken with some difficulty in a deep snow. The Gardiners, who left just prior to the worst of it, barely made it home. Darcy apologized in a letter now seven days old that he could not leave Rosings because of both the weather conditions and Anne's terrible health. Elizabeth, missing him now with a terrible ache, felt a tantrum rise inside her and she would have liked to be a four-year-old and scream and rage.

As the cold confined everyone to the house for many consecutive days, the entire household was affected by boredom, bad humour, and temporary disenchantment with everything and everybody. Hill popped in and handed letters to Mrs. Bennet and all heads turned. Even a single letter would break the dull routines.

"You'll sup soon, cook says. She's havin' a bit of a fight with the cook stove. 'Tis not pulling as it ought and 'tis not the air, cause a cold clear day like this ought to dispense the smoke from the house as easy as a goose will its droppings. The way we're burning it and the coal already almost used. You might talk to John 'bout getting' more before the rest of the village is out looking."

"Thank you, Hill," Mrs. Bennet said, flipping through the letters. Hill, who never curtseyed or bowed or scraped as Lady Catherine's servants did, turned and left the room. "Charlotte and Darcy for you Lizzy. Caroline Bingley for you Jane. And Mary, another note from Lady Anne. Oh, and here is one from Lydia for you Kitty. No doubt she merely complains and begs you to visit her. Let us hear from Charlotte then," Mrs. Bennet proposed.

Elizabeth, who had not yet read the letter, scanned it quickly. "Oh, Charlotte is with child."

"Finally," Kitty giggled.

"Read it. It is not enough that you summarize her news. It is in the details that there is interest," Mrs. Bennet sang, apparently forgetting the details of Charlotte's previous letter.

"Dearest Lizzy, (and hello to Mrs. Bennet and Jane and Kitty and Mary dear)," Elizabeth read, "You may have already been made aware of the greatest news by other channels. Yes, I am expecting my first child and will make you the god mother if Mr. Collins accepts. I have little to tell about how it has affected me as my confinement is in a distant future. Nevertheless, Mr. Collins pecks around me like a hen, clucking and propping pillows and acting as if I were wounded. It is a remarkable thing and we are both delighted.

I must admit that I find the process was not as interesting nor as traumatic as one might imagine. I would like to reassure you that at the worst you will find this service dull. I reassure you because I know your mother will tell you nothing of this. I know mine did not."

"Tut," Mrs. Bennet interrupted. "Of course, Lady Lucas would speak nothing of this to her daughter for she is not as enlightened or progressive as I am. Mr. Bennet and I, in our decisions regarding your education, were quite together in our wanting you to be raised in a happy family in which your mother and father were your closest companions, so that you might speak frankly when you want. Charlotte was kept by a governess, or seven, who shifted as often as they stayed. But I, I will educate you all when the time comes. I will share with you all I know because if we have nothing to commend us, we have intimacy between us, do we not?"

Elizabeth did not contradict her mother but continued out loud. "It is not dull, however, to receive the cares of a husband in a new way and for his manner to increase in affection and care as a result. He is quite more familiar with me and seeks my attention more than I would wish, so I have reminded him of our former habits, he of walking to the village and me of doing my work as I please in solitude. He fretted at first, expecting me to need him every minute, but I have disabused him of this belief with some carefully chosen words which he ignored regardless of the care with which I chose them. I finally had to say, quite simply, 'No Mr. Collins, you may not remain by my side one minute longer'. Yes, I practically chased him from the room. As he left, quite cowed, I mollified him by saying 'in a little I will need your help.' 'Yes yes,' he exclaimed. 'When you are quite affected by the growth.' Yes, he said growth. I can hear you laughing as I write this dear Lizzy.

"I cannot answer your questions about the current events at Rosings for we are kept away. The house seems to be in mourning although no one has died, and I have seen not a single one of its inhabitants since your departure. Mr. Collins, who sees Lady Catherine, will not put any questions to her. There is only she who comes to church, so I believe they may not be at Rosings at all."

She finished reading and Mrs. Bennet began talking about Charlotte's baby, that they should sew a little crib quilt, or smock a dress for her christening.

"I quite believe she sends advice which should not be kept," Elizabeth whispered to Jane while her mother chatted to no one in particular.

"Oh?"

"She says that physical relations with a spouse are dull," Elizabeth added, with a little grin on her face.

"She did?" Jane asked not looking up from her drawing.

"I do not think that Mr. Collins could be compared to a Mr. Bingley or a Mr. Darcy, do you? I find kissing Darcy not in the least dull and can barely imagine what it might be like to have the freedom of marriage."

"You shock me, Elizabeth. I said we should speak of such things, but I did not mean to suggest we would do so in a public room."

"Your ears are too large, Mother," Elizabeth reprimanded. "I whispered those words to Jane."

"It would be dull with Mr. Collins. Imagine? It makes my ears go all squiggly to think of it."

"Your ears, Kitty? But that is too funny," Mary remarked soberly.

"Girls! Girls!" Mrs. Bennet reprimanded as if she was the only person allowed indiscretions.

"But I will say," Mary began in her usual pedantic voice, "speaking to everyone, that I think the pleasure of companionship has not so much to do with the abilities of the individuals; I believe that it is love which makes these interactions happy. That we should be beholden to one another in a way that is different from any other relations, both familial and amicable. It marries both and adds another element..."

"Mary, you do tangle your words," complained Mrs. Bennet.

"I was trying to be obtuse. I am saying that marital relations and desire have little to do with a person's ability and more to do with how they love one another," Mary specified.

"For most people in this room, this subject is foreign. By what authority do you speak?"

"Love is not foreign," Elizabeth argued.

"Yes, but the intimacies of husband and wife are to be kept entirely in private. You see, Mr. Bennet does not ever address me by my first name, even at home before our children. You witness our public aspect, but you do not know it all. That is how it ought to be."

"Mother!" Jane scolded, shocked at the mention of her parent's having a private life. Kitty giggled and Mary actually put down her book.

"Well, where do you suppose you girls arrived from? And do you suppose that your father is a Mr. Collins?" She laughed out loud, as if she had been dying for years to remind the girls that Mr. and Mrs. Bennet had once been, and perhaps still were, in love despite an entirely absent display of public affection. "And what should happen to our private lives if they were brought into the open? They would no longer be private!"

NATHAN'S PREJUDICE

Because of the cold, the boredom, and the need to break a dull routine, the entire Bennet family spent several days at Netherfield. They each took turns organizing games in the afternoons, and they read *A Sicilian Romance* by the fire in the evenings. Nathan gave great impersonations and he could make his audience jump with fright at the right moments.

One afternoon, Elizabeth was reading alone in one of the smaller drawing rooms. She did not notice Nathan's arrival in the room until he was at her side. When she looked up, he seemed unusually pensive. She teased him with a remark which might have normally made him smile, but he merely acknowledged the attempt and went directly to what was on his mind, pulling the chair up to hers so that he might lean close to her and speak in a hushed voice.

He said he must broach a difficult subject, adding apologies for the presumption of probing into her personal life, but, as you see, we have become good friends and I believe it is my duty to say what is on my mind, etcetera, etcetera, with all the proper preambles. And she accepted his kind offer of friendship, agreeing that they were friends and that if he felt compelled to say something then he must.

"It is about Mr. Darcy," he began.

"Indeed. You know him?"

"I have met him, briefly, on several occasions. I cannot say that I know him, personally."

"Then? What might you say?" her curiosity was piqued.

"He is not the right man for you, Liz, and I am horrified at the thought of you spending your life with him. There are rumours of all kinds about his dalliances. Secrets which have not been kept."

It was not the first time he trespassed beyond conventional propriety with such an informal address. She had allowed it on several occasions, but now she told him she was Miss Elizabeth. She controlled her temper a little, for she would hear what he had to say, and why he might say it with such extreme vehemence.

"You are upset," he noted gently. "I am sorry. I did not know how to broach the subject. I must admit, I did not want to speak of this at all, not for all the world. But Lizzy, don't you see? Under the circumstance?"

"No. I fail to see anything, Mr. Nathan."

"I know of him. A great deal. From reliable sources, including my cousin who knows him well."

"Mr. Bingley does not think we should marry?"

"Oh, dear, no. Don't accuse him of that: he would have my head."

"I might also have your head," she said half seriously.

"Please don't," he laughed. "I rather like having it, though it serves me less than I would wish and too often I am dragged around by some other thing, a spontaneous combustion of impulses which direct my actions. Such as now with you. Bingley told me things about Darcy over the years, some made me dislike the man. For instance, Charles admires his ability to befriend women. Darcy attracts them like flies, he once said to me, as if something to be desired, and he has a knack for …." And here Nathan changed what he was intending to say. "He has a propensity to enjoy them. I think that quite awful. Imagine, a man to whom every woman is drawn. And to whom he responds without discrimination and... I know what that is like. To draw women, but I have not accepted these invitations as he has."

Elizabeth had dropped her arm from his and controlled her voice as she spoke, "I think you should remember that you are speaking of a man I love dearly and who has asked me to be his lifelong companion."

"But you should know what kind of man he is. He is not for you. You don't want to be married to a man who will engage with all manner of women."

"You know nothing of who he is. You admit yourself that you have not met."

"He is known to be proud and disdainful. He is generally seen as a lady's man. And he... well. I will stop. I have said what I have had to say. And I say it so that you may be informed. I care for your wellbeing. You know I do. Please, take it with this caveat: that it is for you I speak. For you I risk our friendship."

"Your words do nothing to change my opinions of Darcy for there is nothing in them that is new to me..."

"And yet you proceed? That is the kind of man you want?"

"A libertine? No. No, of course not. But you are mistaken in your assessment. Have you asked yourself when these events occurred? How long ago these rumours were forged? What perpetuates them?"

Nathan shook his head. "It is not rumour. Miss Elizabeth, it is fact."

He squeezed her arm encouragingly. And then, as if as an afterthought, he asked "When was the last time you saw or heard from him?" And then, a few minutes later, "I understand you haven't set a wedding date."

"It is not your business, Mr. Nathan. Please desist from this. I do know Mr. Darcy." She paused and thought how kind he was to care about her wellbeing, no matter how misguided, and mollified him a little by thanking him.

"He will break your heart."

"But I also could break his heart. We are locked that way now. Our hearts are woven together, and we weave more every day and the more we are woven the more it is possible for us each to ruin the other with loss. If he should die, I would cloister myself in a nunnery. I would never love again this way, would never accept another man, for how could I, after having lived with such a tender care that exists between myself and Darcy."

She leaned away from him, to indicate the end of the conversation, and he leaned forward and took both her hands in his. "Oh, please, don't be vexed with me."

There was a noise like a croaking frog and Elizabeth looked up to Miss Bingley standing in the doorway staring at them. She could not have heard their close intimacies, but she could clearly see the way they were bent to each other as they talked.

"May I come in?" she asked.

Of course," Elizabeth said, pulling back from Nathan and sitting up much straighter. "I believe our conversation is finished. Have you passed a pleasant day? We have not seen you at all. What have you done to amuse yourself, dear Caroline?"

JANE'S SORROWS

The leaves of the ivy entwining Elizabeth's favourite hawthorn were budding, but the old tree would not bloom until May and its branches were yet bare. Its crooked trunk and ragged exterior were part of its charm for she could imagine generations of people having visited it on the rise of the hill overlooking the river, and yet, standing as it did alone in an isolated spot, could be for her a solitary sanctuary. Since leaving Rosings Park, she had had no satisfaction in her own romance. She missed Darcy with a sudden pang. The severe cold had kept him away through February when even the mail was stopped for over a week. The last letter she had sent, a silly one with tear stains and a big heart drawn onto it, a childish communication which embarrassed her a little now to think of it, had not received any reply.

She worried that he had found it so incredibly silly as to dismiss her and not knowing how to tell her that she was just a silly girl and that he had no time for silly girls and would not marry a silly girl, he instead remained silent pondering how to break their engagement. She doubted him and then hated herself for it. She trusted him and then didn't. Missed him then hated him. Was furious for his absence and his silence, then made excuses, then worried, then ignored it as if she did not care, and then thought perhaps she had better write to him again and ask why he would not reply, and then didn't because surely his reply would soon come. And then, after she had these thoughts circling like turkey vultures, she decided to ask Charlotte to probe a little more, but that too seemed like the sort of silly thing a girl would do.

She realized that loving someone was one of the hardest things she had ever done. As she lay, gazing into the tree and beyond it to the marvellous sky, she began to weep. She ached for her beloved Darcy, yearned for a single word of contact and marvelled that there should be such a cataclysmic silence between them after having such tender and deep communion. While she trusted that there would be an explanation, she also worried about Lady Catherine's meddling nature, and how Caroline Bingley might have sent a missive to Darcy misrepresenting Elizabeth's relationship with Nathan. She imagined how misinformation and the deliberate capsizing of truth could ruin even the most beautiful trust. She imagined worse things than these. She imagined a woman who stole his favour or that he might decide to marry Anne in order to save her. She imagined that he was upset about Mary's proclivities and did not know how to speak of them. But finally, she quieted the diatribes of her heart, resting on the simplicity of how they felt, the many moments she had understood how deeply they cared for each other.

She stood and walked home. Lambs, early born and shaking their tails everywhere, were a fascinating subject for both Jane, who drew them, and Elizabeth, who merely watched. The lambs leapt and bound in sudden expressions of ecstasy as their feet left the ground more than they touched, providing moments of delight in which any other thought was entirely erased as irrelevant.

The generally happy mood at home changed dramatically when Jane returned unexpectedly early from Netherfield and went directly to her room. One look at her face and Elizabeth knew that her sister was terribly distressed. The last time she had seen Jane express such a violent reaction was when, as an eleven-year-old, she had watched a horse being beaten. Remembering this, and how Jane had recovered very slowly from this trauma, Elizabeth knew something terrible must have happened.

"You must go up to her, Lizzy," her mother requested. "Sit with her even if she sends you away."

Jane was silent when Elizabeth knocked at her door. She made no response at all and, when Elizabeth entered, she found Jane sitting in her little corner armchair staring out the window. She was so still that, except for the straight and upright nature of her stance, Elizabeth might have thought her asleep. Jane did not turn, did not respond to her words, did not agree or disagree when Elizabeth offered to sit with her. She stared blankly to a distant horizon. Elizabeth pulled a chair beside her sister and put her hand on Jane's and stayed that way some hours.

Eventually, as she was very hungry, she went downstairs and obtained a small plate of fruit and bread and cheese, as well as a bit of watered wine, and brought it upstairs. Jane ate little and refused to get ready for bed. The vacant stare terrified Elizabeth both by its depth of sorrow and her own powerlessness to affect any improvement. When she was relieved of her duties by her mother, she went to her own room and sobbed. When she woke later in the night, she went to Jane's room to find her mother sitting in the chair overseeing Jane's sleep, and Elizabeth crept back to her bed and slept soundly.

The next morning Bingley arrived and Jane refused to see him. He was received in the drawing room and no one spoke. They all had questions which they would not dare ask; yet they did not want answers to the questions permitted to them. Bingley, on two occasions, broke the silence to make a casual remark about a triviality and no one encouraged his civility.

Finally, Mr. Bennet arrived home from somewhere and Mrs. Bennet caught him in the hallway as he took off his coat and whispered violently into his ear. He immediately went to the office with Bingley. Almost an hour passed and the drawing room remained oppressive. Once they heard a loud incensed voice which was not Bingley's. They all looked at each other with astonishment for never once had Mr. Bennet raised his voice except one occasion, many years earlier, when he yelled at his brother on the very last occasion they had had contact. Soon after, Bingley bid them adieu in the drawing room and, as soon as he was out the door, Mr. Bennet was bombarded with a cacophony of questions from all corners and he put his hands to his ears and said that he could not speak if they would not listen.

"But you pause overly long!" Mrs. Bennet scolded.

"I was merely composing myself and determining how best to proceed," he defended himself.

"Yes, but we don't want a composition. We want the situation. Tell us the unabridged edition!" she replied.

"I will not. There are elements which I will keep to myself to be sure. And no amount of prying from you, Mrs. Bennet, will change my mind." He stared over his glasses at his wife with a seriousness that kept her quiet. "I will start by saying that Mr. Nathan has left Netherfield and we will not be in his company again, not so long as Mr. Bingley is in our attendance."

"Oh, but he is a delightful boy and beyond reproach, I am sure of it," Mrs. Bennet objected.

"I do not think that he did anything particularly wrong," Mr. Bennet agreed, "But he apparently agreed to stand for Jane as a model for her drawings. Bingley had been filling her head with all the ways of artists and how they often sketched from a live model."

"Quite so," Mrs. Bennet agreed.

"And Mr. Bingley, late yesterday morning, found one of Jane's sketchbooks and picked it up to see what work she was doing and found these sketches of Nathan, these multiple sketches of him."

"And for this, the trauma? For this the exile?" Mrs. Bennet probed.

"Mr. Nathan was partially unclothed in the sketches. He wore but an untucked shirt and open at his chest, and breeches with bare feet. Bingley is scandalized."

The entire room gasped with a single voice.

"But Papa," Mary spoke. "You yelled. Why should you yell at Mr. Bingley? It seems to me Jane has done something quite unlooked for."

"It is downright rude!" Mrs. Bennet agreed.

"He told me I gave you girls too many liberties. That I could better manage my household by making a decision or two."

"Well, that is a side of Bingley we haven't seen before," Elizabeth exclaimed.

"He came for the express purpose of telling me so."

On the third day on which Jane refused to speak, Bingley arrived midday with her gelding and a note asking that she ride out with him. Elizabeth, who was alone in the house with her, returned it to him saying that Jane refused to read it. He did not leave immediately, but stood and sat and paced, and then asked her if he might smoke. "Mama does not like it in here," she answered and so he put his pipe away. Hill arrived with tea and scones, but glared at Bingley, then slammed the door. Elizabeth apologized for her.

"Jane is in a very bad state and Hill is displeased with you for it."

"Hill is furious."

"Well, maybe a little furious."

He laughed, yet there was a trace of bitterness in it. "There is no such thing as a little furious," he remarked. "Caroline is furious also. For different reasons," reasons he did not speak. Elizabeth did not like this Bingley, this serious and contrite and miserable Bingley, any better than she liked the sad and aggrieved Jane.

"Did she say anything to you?" he asked.

Elizabeth assumed he was referring to Jane, not his sister.

"Nothing."

"That is not good. She confides everything to you. What does it mean that she keeps all this to herself and will not come out? What does it mean that she will not forgive? How can she believe that it is only me who is in the wrong?" Elizabeth remained silent and did not look up as he paced. "I was furious, Elizabeth. I yelled at her and I have never seen anyone go so stony, so absolutely shocked."

"We have many faults in this household. My sister Lydia is silly, self-absorbed; my mother is loud and lacks propriety, my father shrinks from problems and would rather let things manage on their own and come out the other end without his working overly hard to attain it. Jane trusts overly much in people, and I suppose I am somewhat forthright with my opinions. But we do not shout. Ever. No one has ever yelled at Jane. Not once."

Bingley blanched. "It is a part of my heritage."

"Then if she is to reside with you, you must unlearn it, for she is sweet, as you know, and will shrivel and die if you think that she can survive regular doses of fury."

He paced and asked again about the pipe and she tried the window for him, but it was seized shut. He tried and managed to get it open an inch. He puffed, the pipe went out, and he changed his mind about it and closed the window.

"I don't really like this thing. Your father introduced me to it and now I am rather used to it, but I don't actually enjoy it." She had no answer. "Nathan wrote to me from town where he is staying as he refuses to go far until we are happy again," he continued. "He told me to be wrong in all things to do with loving a woman, that it was a safe route to a good marriage."

"He said no such thing."

"I think he was joking a little and was trying to get me to calm down."

"Well, judging by your behaviour just now, it did not work."

It was almost a week before Jane came out of her room. She did not disclose anything beyond replying that yes, she wanted the jam or no she would prefer to walk a little later, and her deep silence suffused the walls and corners of the house and even Kitty seemed to find it hard to be silly and to laugh. It was as if there had been a death in the family and Mr. Bennet joked (out of Jane's earshot) that they might all get out their black dress and really make a show of it, but not one person thought it was funny.

One evening Jane entered Elizabeth's bedroom and went about picking up and putting down things in a strangely agitated state. She finally confessed to Elizabeth that she had suffered under the terrible strain of shame, vexation, betrayal, sadness and grief. She did not know if she could marry a man who would display such a rise of temper, who would trespass into her book, who would assume that she was unfaithful merely because of a few drawings.

"His sisters and Mr. Hurst were in the room while I drew the studies. And Nathan was discreet. It was good fun, really, and Caroline encouraged me saying Charles would not mind."

"I wouldn't be surprised if she told him to look in the sketch books..."

"That is terrible. How could you say such a thing? Elizabeth, that is pure maliciousness. Since when did you become such an enemy to my future sister-in-law? Now I cannot trust any of you. I hate this. I hate it."

Jane began to sob. It was as if a glass which had been slightly smeared and hiding some of the worst in people had been cleared of obstruction and she, only just seeing what most of them had taken for granted, was shocked and unprepared.

"You may forgive them all," Elizabeth said. "Myself included. But that does not mean you shouldn't protect yourself and be aware how their interests may collide with your own. She may not want you to marry her brother. You are a country girl and beneath his station. That is not incidental for her."

"But I don't want to surround myself with that kind of nastiness,"

"I don't think any of them are nasty, but they – well Miss Bingley in any case – puts her interests in front of anyone else's. And Charles does not always see it, and will not always protect you from it, for he is accustomed to her. It is not malicious, Jane. It is human nature. Her human nature."

"I think you are quite wrong in your assessment of her. Yes, her conversation is not 'meaningful' the way you want, she talks of fashion and station in life, but that is her world. And she is very sweet to me."

Elizabeth changed the topic for she could see that to malign

Caroline Bingley would not serve either of them. "Were you so surprised that those pictures bothered Mr. Bingley?"

"No. I was surprised by the vehemence and the violence of his reaction. I have never seen anyone so angry. And so unwilling to reason. He said terrible things to me, Elizabeth. Things I will not repeat. I've never seen Mother and Father violently angry with one another. I have no idea how to feel about this."

"Nor have we seen them passionate, or even companionable in a way that you and I are with Bingley and Darcy. Perhaps in having a greater degree of companionship we will have an equally greater possibility for hurting one another."

"I am terribly confused, Elizabeth. Shall I marry him? I think it would be dreadful to not have him in my life, but can I spend a lifetime with him furiously attacking me? I doubt I can moderate my actions sufficiently to accommodate his every wish. I doubt I should wish to. What did he say to you the morning he came?"

"He wondered at your not seeing sense."

"Yes, that's what he said to me. That I should have asked his permission."

"And you did not because...?"

"He encourages me to be serious about my art and then is upset that I take my art seriously."

"I suppose he didn't expect you to take it seriously as if you were a man. And you hid the drawings."

"No. I returned the sketchbook to the drawer he provided."

"Have you drawn Charles? A portrait?"

Jane shook her head.

"So, you have seen Nathan without his shirt, but not the man who will be your husband?" Jane shook her head again. "He's hurt, Jane. You can imagine why, even if you don't agree."

Jane threw a towel at her which she had lately picked up and was folding and unfolding. "Unfair." Elizabeth, catching it, threw it back at her.

"Unfair indeed. At least you are fighting with your intended. Mine is entirely silent and absent these weeks. I am not even sure I am still engaged. I would much prefer a good and dramatic argument to this terrible unknowing."

Within the week two letters arrived at the Bennet household from

134

Rosings Park. Jane flipped through them. "Only this from Georgiana."

Elizabeth tore open the note. "Three lines. Darcy misses me but is indisposed. She regrets that she cannot write more."

"You must be terribly worried. Indisposed could mean all manner of things."

"That he does not want to be with me is one of them," Elizabeth noted. "There are too many – far too many – translations."

"He does not come he does not come," Mrs. Bennet chanted as if an incantation might change things for her daughter. "Your man is absent now almost three months, Elizabeth, and now he does not write. I am very glad to see that you are safe home and that you seem to have avoided the pitfalls of so many young girls who, once betrothed, feel they can safely allow their fiancé access to their womb."

"One might think your Mr. Darcy doesn't exist," Kitty muttered.

"He might not come for many reasons, all of them reasonable," Elizabeth argued. "There was Anne's illness to attend to, then the terrible weather – even the Gardiners found it difficult to travel. Now he is indisposed. I really am not worried. I will see him again soon."

But she was perplexed and, comparing the signature on this note and the little congratulatory card she had received from Georgiana earlier in the autumn, she found them to be alike but not the same. Lady Catherine's letter arrived soon afterward. It was blunt and rude and it did not mollify any of its sentiments with pretty phrases of greeting or goodbyes. It merely stated that she had been informed that the two Bennet girls were – for different reasons – entirely unsuitable companions for men of distinction and noble birth and that she was glad the engagements to both girls had been severed.

As Elizabeth re-read this missive, astonished and filled with disbelief, Charles Bingley strode into the house unannounced, walked past all onlookers to Jane who sat in a chair. He bent on one knee before her and said, Please dearest, I hope that you may forgive me. And Elizabeth wished again that she had heard from Darcy.

LONDON

ANNE'S CURE

Anne de Bourgh is not a model princess. It is believed that her lack of beauty will produce no handsome prince, which is a relief to her since she does not want one; her natural inclination leads her to a woman's love. Her ostensibly weak heart has kept her confined to her mother's obstructive attentions and removed her from normal social venues, but this has entirely suited her reclusive nature. We do seek for her a happy ending, though we may have to redefine the terms and seek neither Prince nor Princess, but peace and contentment, safety and calm.

She has been rescued from Lady Catherine by her cousin Darcy who was once intended for her in marriage, though Anne, seeing quite clearly that he is a man of great independence of mind and attractive princely-ness, recognizes that he would never have her.

Lady Catherine sent Anne to the hospital when Anne, sufficiently recovered from her despondency, declared quite vehemently to her mother that she had fallen in love with Mary, that it had not been Mary's fault at all, and that it was she Anne who had corrupted Mary and not the other way around, and would Lady Catherine please send for her friend. I was happy mother. Do you know how good that is for the heart? Darcy heard from each of them. For Lady Catherine, Anne's vehemence in the matter was proof that she must send Anne to the hospital for a cure, and from Anne, that her despair was a testimony to her deep love for Mary. However much Darcy wanted to reconcile mother and daughter, he fell so terribly ill that he could do nothing to prevent his aunt's decisions. Anne was delivered against her will to a confinement where doctors were instructed to re-educate her.

With a terrible fever and a burdensome schedule of bloodletting which did little to improve his strength, Darcy was at times bordering between life and death. For the latter part of his illness, he failed to notice the absence of letters from Elizabeth. When he later investigated, Georgiana claimed to know nothing at all, had not communicated to Elizabeth as instructed by Lady Catherine who said she would take care of it. When he questioned his aunt, she told him that Elizabeth had sent no letters, no messages of care and condolence, had not offered to care for him in his hour of need. At the time, he was puzzled, but would in time realize that his aunt was lying to him and that she had not only hidden Elizabeth's letters to him but had not informed her of his illness. She told him she had instead received a letter from Mrs. Bennet most terrible in its contents, horrified that her daughters had been welcome into a home housing literature of the most lewd and foul kind.

"I informed her that I would go to all ends and means to eradicate her and her family from my sphere of society," Lady Catherine told Darcy. "Such threats of slander I have never once received! I would advise you to do the same."

He could not bear to divest his aunt of the illusion that her dear husband was unimpeachable in the matter of the library most lewd and foul, or the other matters of mistress tunnels and poke holes that were once active within her home and of which she knew nothing. He sent a letter to the Bennet household in general apologizing for his absence and secured a promise from Mr. Bennet that he would let a house in London, that all explanations and apologies would be forthcoming in person upon their reunion.

The moment he was well enough to travel, he left the gloom of Rosings Park with Georgiana and The Dog, determined to remedy any and all mischief which had been perpetrated. He immediately fetched Anne from the hospital, the place she might have spent her entire life locked away if not for his uncle Sherwood who found a way to have her released. On what charge do you confine her! Was his refrain up and down its halls. He went about and found an attorney who knew how to make administrators loosen their principles. He convinced her ladyship to sign the necessary letter in which Darcy became custodian to her. A London home was rented nearby where she was provided with a new companion, Mrs. Jenkinson having already departed from their service to commune with those other members of her sect who believed the world would fall in 1815. She said, as she went, it is already almost 1813. There is much to do to prepare.

The new caregiver was a smart, sensible, cheery soul, Mrs. Markham, who joined Anne as a fairy godmother in a fairy-tale where her charge might wake from a stupor, perhaps not to be a beauty queen, lips red as berries and hair jet black (and we must remember that these are not the only provisions required to be happy), but nevertheless to recover from a poisonous curse and to wake to the prince who, in this case, may happen to be her own personal guidance, self-care, courage, and more than a smattering of self-esteem.

Darcy, concerned for Anne's future, met with a doctor who specialized in sexual deviancy who claimed that in cases where marriage was not possible, or where, despite it, the proclivity for unnatural behaviour was nevertheless maintained by the patient, it was customary to confine the subject in an institution so that other cures might be attempted. When pushed for details concerning these cures, the doctor claimed that medical interventions to train the subject in the proper reception of male attention would cure them. Sitting comfortably in the doctor's office, Darcy was both horrified and skeptical. It sounded to his ears that a male would force himself on the patient in order to mature the woman's sexual tastes.

"And does it produce results?" Darcy asked not even trying to hide his contempt.

"The subject is passive and receptive afterward and sometimes does return home to live a successfully married life."

He left the doctor's office determined that "cure" was not what he sought for Anne. He coached Anne to try harder, to flirt a little. But how, she asked, when one is not interested and one does not want? But you must marry, he told Anne, not quite knowing why she must marry. Anne merely cried, like a child who was lost. And he felt that it might take ten years for her to develop enough character to attract a man. She thinks me vile, Anne wailed. She will never see me again! And he was not sure to whom she referred, her mother or Mary.

Darcy thought about what a woman must do to attract a husband, the pretty poses and the sweetness and the demure agreeability which was generally assumed to be the natural state of a gentlewoman (and perhaps was not) and suggested she practice these arts a little so as to seem interested. You know, be twittery and silly. Then, really not knowing what a woman must do to attract a man, he said, Ask Elizabeth. No do not, he changed his mind, for she does not know any more than you and she will quote Wollstonecraft to you. To which Anne asked, Who? And Darcy said Never mind, Wollstonecraft will not save you. Did you learn nothing from the

Countess?

Such was Darcy's week preceding the Bennett's arrival in London. Exhausted and overwhelmed, he sat before a small fire wrapped in a coverlet like an old lady with his quilt, his slippers, and a cup of a herbal concoction beside him. Sherwood, who stood at the mantelpiece, tapped the bowl of his pipe against the marble. He pulled out his leather pouch and tamped tobacco into it, then lit the pipe with a long stick he put to the coals. The two men were both deep in thought, but each considered the same problem, the one in which Anne was now Darcy's responsibility. They had not yet landed on the ultimate solution, which would come in time and with Mary's encouragement, which was that Anne should be responsible for herself and had no need of a husband she did not want.

"I'll be heading back to Pemberley in a day or two if ye 'ave no further need of me," Sherwood mumbled as he puffed at his pipe to get it going, smoke and words drifting from his mouth in alternating sequence.

"Yes go." Darcy put his head back and closed his eyes. "I could sleep three days." He reached to stroke The Dog who was lying beside his chair in a perfect position to receive affection.

"Ye shouldna ridden to the hospital. A carriage, a barouche even, would 'ave been better." Sherwood took the wingback near the window to take advantage of the last of the day's light to read his Morning Chronicle, reading headlines and conversing while puffing.

"I didn't realize how weak I was."

"I shoulda gone with ye."

"Thank you for the offer, but it comes late."

"Ah, look," he held up his paper again. "T' Americas re-elected Madison. And how did ye find Anne? That place, I mean. I saw nowt but the grand gardens and brassy offices."

"Don't ask. Now I understand how it came about, that word 'bedlam'. A good corruption of Bethlem Royal. There are places, Timothy, where no human should live. The smell and – well I don't know what I was thinking. There are places everywhere in London, people living seventeen to a house, with no good access to water, who toss their filth out the door and call that cleaning because it is the best they have. But even those conditions are better than what I saw at the hospital. The stables at Pemberley were more appropriate for human habitation. Yet, I was fascinated. Even as I could do nothing to aid its inhabitants, their screaming at invisible demons, their aimless wandering and picking at their skin in repeated and frantic ways, I could not turn away. I can tell you that one day in that place as a sane man would drive me quickly to insanity. There is nothing wrong with her that such a hospital could fix, despite the administrator's attempts to convince me. The place is lovely from the exterior, but the staff could not hide how it crumbles on the inside. The water gets in, Timothy, and putrefies everything. She would be dead in a year."

Sherwood snapped his newspaper. "See here! Napoleon is about to fall. He must – how does that bastard do it?" He looked up again. "And Anne? Her mother's quite the ogre to put 'er in 'at place. And now, how will ye find 'er a groom?"

"I whispered into a few select ears – and three men stepped forward, each worse than the last. Baron de Hallowell – you know him? Lost his wife in mysterious circumstances and spent his entire fortune – which had been hers originally. He actually said to me 'I will get to the mark quickly: I believe you're in a bit of a fix and I'm your man.'"

"Damned good of t' fella. Not t' keep ye with a lot of rubbish."

"Then he said 'I'll propose to her if that's what you want. Bring flowers and go down on my knees. You know, the usual stuff to make a woman happy.'"

"Quite."

"'She wants rescuing, I've heard.'"

"He said that?"

Darcy nodded. "He was the best of the lot. The second one said 'I'll give it to her and she'll be fixed alright. I'll give it to her so she'll never forget a wife's role.'"

"Not sure what ye expected…Per'aps ye must seek a molly who will hide in plain sight beside 'er? Hide his proclivities by marrying?"

"That's not a bad idea, old man. But it is not easy to advertise."

"Bad luck 'am too old," Sherwood raised his eyebrows, laughing. "Please, Miss Anne, I will be most delighted if you would take me as your dearest and sweetest."

"Where's the ring?" Darcy asked. "You propose without a ring. How rude."

"Ye really should marry 'er!" Sherwood replied. "Keep Miss Bennet as a mistress. You'd 'ave more brass and less kerfuffle."

"Oh, we might yet marry you to her, old man. I have no doubt that a tough bachelor like you would be the perfect match for dearest cousin Anne. You could easily say to her 'Anne, it is merely a convenience. I will live in this wing a mile from you; and you in that wing a mile from me. We will live happily ever after!'"

Sherwood chuckled and snapped his paper up in front of his face. "Imagine our wedding."

"Would rather not."

"T'would be late, hobble with me cane…"

"…and she would be dragged down to the front of the church by Lady Terror who hates you."

"'I' virgin would cry t' entire service and I would 'ang 'er on t' wall with my stuffed lion and tiger heads. A trophy."

Darcy chuckled. "That is cruel."

"Ah, 'ere is a sign of changin' times." His tone was clearly facetious. He folded his paper to show Darcy an image. "'ave you noticed? There's a new style of standin' for a portrait. It's not just a silly new trend with the trousers. That friend of Byron's. That clod. B – somewhat. Brummell. Some of them think t'is good form t' stand with their 'ands in a vest like Napoleon. Encourage a tyrant, why don' ye."

"I am simply glad that the trend towards powder and white wigs has left us to our own hair. I remember father loading his own pate in the powder room (aptly named, what?) and would emerge from it sneezing profusely. But I am needing a husband, Timothy. Not curious about where to put my hand while posing for a portrait. Nor who is ruling that former colony. Perhaps, for our marriage portrait, I will suggest it to Elizabeth. She will create a new trend for the modern woman with her own hand trespassing her pelisse buttons, the strong, independent, tyrannical type…And I'm sure it isn't Brummell; he does something cocky with his hand over a walking stick."

Despite all the ways in which he worked to sort Anne, establish her in some way satisfactory to her mother, interviewing suitors and seeking medical advice, all of which he found distasteful, he failed miserably. He arrived home one day and found Mrs. Markham waiting for him. She confided that she must leave at once and that she would accept no less than twenty pounds to keep her secret, the one in which Miss Anne is found with a maid kissing. Cheery Mrs.

Markham was apparently also a prude and opportunistic.

And then he received a short but distraught note from the Earl Evan Montpetit. Apparently, having located the mistress tunnels and the secret library, Lady Catherine removed the exquisite and scandalous collection to the front yard and burned it.

BONNIE STATELY

It was with deep relish that Darcy climbed the stairs to his dear Bonnie Stately's home, an elegant house in Mayfair not far from one only slightly larger, Lansdowne House, near Berkeley Square and not very old and still quite modern to the current tastes, with the appropriate number of galleries and drawing rooms and a back court and terraces, not to mention a room fit for a gala of a hundred persons and a table to fit half that. The butler received him saying It has been such a long time, Mr. Darcy, sir, I am very glad to see you. And even though it was not common for a butler to be casual with a guest, Darcy smiled and nodded, and handed over his hat and coat. Bonnie stood and approached him as he entered the drawing room and greeted him with her frank openness and a kiss on both cheeks, *comme les francais*, she was fond of saying. Without any preambles, she remarked that he looked wan and skinny. Darcy laughed as he sat in his favourite chair.

"I am so glad to see you well again. Your fevers were well known to us and I am terribly sorry for your pains. You are haggard with illness, yet you shine with mirth. And engaged to be married! But, before we speak of your betrothal, tell me of the rumours about Lady Anne and the Countess of Something. There has been a veritable parade of astonishing 'facts' with regards to Rosings. I believe none of them."

"Elizabeth called her the Countess of Somewhere, you know. I thought it quite funny since they seem to be landless gentry these days. She's wife to Evan Montpetit. Do you know him?"

"Wish I didn't."

"They are gone now, thankfully. And Anne is here in London, living near me."

"And her mama does not come?"

He shook his head. "I don't know what circulates, and I'll beg you not to tell me, but there is probably some truth in some of the stories. The Montpetits were 'hired' by Grendel – oh, that is Elizabeth's name for my aunt – to help 'train' Anne in finding a husband. I believe Aunt Cate had held out hopes that I would resolve to marry her since there was such a fortune in it. That I should not want more wealth confounds her. But tell me about yourself. You seem very well, and I am glad of it."

"Chamberlain will be here soon. I told him you were coming and he is trying to return early from parliament. We are well Darcy. I do love him. The children are growing strong and are happy. And I have everything I should desire except that passion I see in your eyes when you speak of your beloved."

"And your brother?" he asked.

"I would rather not talk about him!" she grimaced. "Mother is here daily asking what might be done. Get him married she says as if I could enact miracles."

"We are in the same boat as I must help Anne similarly. Perhaps we should introduce them?"

They chuckled, imagining it.

"Yes. My tomcat brother marrying a tribade…. Oh yes, Fitzy. I see from your look that it is true! Oh dear, poor you! Who will marry her? The rumours are all over town!"

Barns delivered a tray of tea and little cakes and jellies, and some plates of meat slices and cheese. "Thank you Barns. Isn't it fine to see our Mr. Darcy in our midst after a year's absence?"

Darcy adored this woman who did everything her way, and the habit he had found most shocking, but had learned to appreciate, was her habit to discourse with her servants. She liked them, as people, would not have any about her whom she did not like. That was her rule. And they were astonishingly loyal. He had once mistakenly broached the topic with his aunt to no avail; she would not imagine a servant as a person, for if they are perceived as people then they would want to act as if they were people and then one must treat them as people and that confusion would cause an uproar of expectations gone wrong. He had mentioned Bonnie's casual manner to Mrs. Reynolds, his housekeeper with whom he had great attachment and care, and she had mumbled, It is a wonder that her estate holds.

"And what brings you to London?" Bonnie asked after Barns left the room and Darcy explained about his intentions to settle Anne and to spend time with Elizabeth.

Bonnie nodded. "There is nothing like London in the spring when the light returns after winter and the parks become glorious with crocuses and tree buds. Certainly, the enchantment is buoyed when one anticipates a reunion with one's true companion and love. How perfect for you. And you have been separated all these winter months. There is nothing like finding the person with whom you would wish to spend your life, and to later be separated from them. Yet, separation is not the same as loss, and the loneliness of missing your lifelong partner is not the same as the loneliness of being single and waiting for a special person to appear in your life," she mused. "And neither are like the kind of bereft emptiness which accompanies marriage to a person with whom there is nothing but hatred, or worse, indifference."

"Yes, indeed."

Bonnie chuckled as she poured their tea. "You have not listened to a word."

"Barely. Spring?"

"I said one must be careful about who one marries."

He nodded. "Indeed."

"Have you considered that Miss Bennet marries you for money?"

He laughed. "I am listening now."

Bonnie smiled endearingly, her eyes winking a little, and her teeth showing. She dropped her shoes and curled her feet up under her, leaning into the armrest of the chesterfield like a cat curled to sleep. He could not remember a time when this was not her favourite pose for all but the most formal situations.

"I have not seen you in a year and in that year you have fallen in love, become engaged and almost died. There were wagers throughout the land as to who would carry you off into fairy land, but Miss Elizabeth Bennet was not one of the contenders."

"I think you'll like her very much."

"I do believe I will. I have my spies, you know."

"They bring news that she is worthy?"

"They do."

"I see her tomorrow." He looked away, out the window where a dog barked and a horse neighed and the smell of hyacinth in the vase wafted across the room. He returned his gaze to Bonnie who was observing him in her quiet way, waiting for him to speak, knowing how to draw him out. He felt a strange agitation, and his leg bounced unsatisfactorily beside him with a will of its own.

"I believe you are nervous, Mr. Darcy!" she exclaimed.

He laughed and shifted his weight in his chair so as to appear more relaxed. She laughed at him as he did so. She knew him entirely too well.

"But I am terribly excited. I am nervous! It is unlike me is it not? I feel like a boy again."

"It is adorable."

"I'm glad you think so. I think it is ugly and unmanly. I know this sounds arrogant, but I could visit her home and dominate the drawing room with my London society knowledge and my brilliant mind and her family would be thrilled to see me and fawn over me; instead, I feel as if I am going to buy my first horse with my father beside me watching how I handle the transaction."

"So adorable."

"Can I tell you something which I barely admit to myself?" She raised her eyebrows. "I am terrified by how much I love this girl."

"The great Darcy is terrified of a country girl?"

"Unbelievable."

"And you do not believe her sincere?"

He did not answer directly but gave her a brief history of all that had happened, his aunt's obstructions, his separation from Elizabeth, and rumours of her courtship with Nathan Bingley.

"Nathan! That boy is a charmer! That your betrothed should turn his head is quite a testament to her beauty and her intelligence. Perhaps you have caught a surprising little fish, then."

"She is young, and inexperienced. And she has never been in love. Has never experienced loss. She thinks she knows her mind, but impetuous youth has that propensity of certainty which can be overruled by experience. There is a sudden shift of attention which happens to girls who flutter about and do not know their mind."

"And you worry that she will be charmed into other arms?"

He shrugged. "Truthfully, I do believe she is committed. But we have been separated for some time now and she does not write. I receive nothing from her since my illness. Did I tell you that I proposed to her soon after we met and she refused?"

Bonnie laughed. "Oh, I wish I had seen *that*...Oh, my poor dear Fitzy!" She laughed and laughed, though it should not have been so entirely funny as that. "And how did you manage the wrath of Lady Catherine? She must surely have objected? Another sporting event I have missed! Everything I have heard about your girl is that she is brash and bold and opinionated. She does not strike me as a girl easily intimidated."

"I have just learned from my sister that Elizabeth was not informed of my illness."

"Oh. But everyone in London knew of it…"

"She is not among those circles. And has been isolated by the cold winter we've had. She has not received any correspondence from me since just after Christmas."

"And why was she not informed?"

"I believe it was Lady Catherine meddling again. She convinced my sister that she must not disturb Elizabeth with worry."

"I see it already. This girl, your beloved, has changed you. You are softer. You are kinder. To yourself, even. You seemed haunted before, and now, I see none of that."

"It was the fever, it burnt it out of me."

"Ha! Do not renounce its true source. It is love. It is nothing but love. But may I remind you that you are betrothed, which is an agreement of some weight. Not to worry, you'll soon find she is by your side, happily ensconced with the best man." Bonnie paused and considered him, allowing the silence to change the tone of the conversation. "We have been close friends many years now, Fitzwilliam. If things had gone differently, do you think we would have been good as husband and wife?" she asked.

"My dear Bonnie. I do love you."

She laughed. "That is not an answer, but it is sweet to hear."

"I am dull at Pemberley and I love only to be there."

"You are wrong. It would not be dull in your company, even in India. But alas, neither of us will have the chance to find out as it is clear to me that you are quite changed by her. Congratulations."

He nodded.

"But I shall ask that most difficult of questions, dear, the one your father would ask you if he were about. You know which one of course."

"Indeed not," he replied, genuinely confused and caught by surprise.

"The one in which we discuss whether or not you have informed your bride to be about your daughter. Rose, is it?"

REUNION

In the London shops, Mrs. Bennet moved from luscious cloth to floral arrangements to spices in bins. She was trailed by her three daughters who indulged her enthusiasm as parents might a child in a candy store, amusing themselves, but Mrs. Bennet was all too conscious of being dressed in a manner less obviously fashionable than the high fashion clientele and went about trying to rectify the problem with a bit of lace or ribbon. It was clear that their own pelisses were longer than the style, their bonnets of a previous year's design, too forward in the hood and less elaborate in the décor. A new colour was the refrain, a blue to which Mrs. Bennet was constantly drawn saying, That is the colour for Jane!

Hearing the clock bells chime eleven, Elizabeth took her mother's elbow. "Mama. We are quite late. It would be ill to keep Mr. Darcy waiting."

"There is time. There is time yet. Oh, look Kitty how well this sage ribbon would do for your bonnet. And here Jane, there is a lavender in this paisley which would pick up the tones of your wedding dress. See how we could make a pretty shawl for you in case you are cold."

"Mama. You may return for more items if we believe it necessary. We must leave now."

"But look here…"

"Mama," Elizabeth argued, her voice rising slightly, "I have not seen him in three months and in that time I've… well, Mama. You know! … and yet you insist I shop!"

"It is good for you. Take your mind off your worries, my dear. Look here. This tawny brown would do so well on you."

"It is a terrible colour."

Darcy, overeager to rejoin his Miss Elizabeth Bennet, arrived early at the Bennet's house which they let near Cheapside not far from the Gardiners (and he mused, looking up and down the street, perhaps also the Earl). Darcy joined Mr. Bennet in the office where he declined tea, asking instead for a coffee. He spun his hat which he had forgotten to leave at the door and twice started to stand. He asked a few polite questions, received polite answers. He apologized for being early and Mr. Bennet apologized that the family had not yet returned from their excursion. Mr. Bennet asked if he was well, Darcy said that he was. Mr. Bennet asked about his health, noting that he did not seem well. Darcy replied that he was much improved, but that yes, he was yet very weak.

"We have seen very little of you," Mr. Bennet said. "It seems to me, the last time we had an audience together, you asked for Elizabeth's hand."

"Not all circumstances are within my control. This is a fine room," Darcy added, changing the subject.

"You are being polite. It is small and stuffy."

"It is constricted by the presence of too many books," Darcy remarked.

"Which lends itself to me. Do you have a library Mr. Darcy?" Mr. Bennet asked.

The Pemberley library had an excellent reputation especially, but not exclusively, for its architectural and scientific books, as well as an exceptionally rare collection of Medieval manuscripts. Darcy wondered if Bennet was being polite, conversational or was ignorant of his library's reputation. "I do. It is an extensive library. You will have to visit us and enjoy it."

He considered, perhaps for the first time, that he would also have to entertain Mrs. Bennet whose voice, character, and values he found so base that he was often gritting his teeth.

"Thank you. I should be glad to see the home where Elizabeth will live."

And Darcy, perceiving his mistake, for of course Mr. Bennet would come, laughed. "I apologize. I am anxious to see Lizzy... I should say Miss Bennet."

Mr. Bennet waved away the indiscretion. There was a sound in the hall and Darcy stood, expectantly. His desire to simply hold Elizabeth in his arms, to cradle her, to smell her, to hear her voice, these things were stronger than any other. To laugh with her. He could not remember laughing since she left, not the way he did with her, open and fully. The maid entered and he found himself awkwardly standing for a maid who curtsied, and she, embarrassed by the attentions, delivered a message and fled.

He threw his hat on a side table. Mr. Bennet's face was quite alive with amusement and Darcy felt he was the object of ridicule. He stiffened. His mind became alert, as if there was a danger lurking, and he prepared to attack if necessary. His dignity would not be challenged by a man of Mr. Bennet's stature. "Perhaps you would like me to wait elsewhere. In the drawing room," he offered. "I am in your way."

"Indeed not. Please, Mr. Darcy, do sit down. She will arrive soon."

Darcy was disarmed by Mr. Bennet's gentle serenity, but he could not sit.

"I believe neither of us are particularly good at making small talk, Mr. Darcy. May I speak frankly? Mrs. Bennet insisted I speak with you."

"Indeed."

Darcy sat finally and Mr. Bennet considered him.

"Mrs. Bennet has been quite distressed at your absence. It did not seem genteel to her, but Elizabeth was rather stalwart in her confidence in you." Mr. Bennet paused overly long, as if gauging his reaction, but Darcy gave none, his face still and expectant. "I am not good at these conversations, Mr. Darcy. I do not like to interfere, but I must consider my daughter's well-being. Here are the correspondences we have received since shortly after Christmas."

The first, in Georgiana's hand, apologized of his being indisposed. The second in Lady Catherine's hand, announced the severed engagements, and the third in his hand, which he had sent a few weeks previously, asking that she see him in London.

He wrote many letters to Elizabeth after his illness in which he explained, apologized, asked for her apology, asked for her forgiveness and, not knowing what was true or not true, had thrown them all away in favour of a tête-à-tête. Mr. Bennet spoke again.

"Elizabeth wrote to you many unanswered letters and received but these from you, or your family. I do not consider this a reasonable treatment of your betrothed, to leave her in this exile. But I see you have not been well."

Darcy picked up his hat again, wanting to leave. The door at his back called to him, while Mr. Bennet, his small little face, his little tidy hands, the wear in his jacket cuff, the chipped tea pot on the desk with the cup and a small bowl of sugar, the four books open face up and face down lent a calm against his urge to leave. Mr. Bennet's glasses were jammed in the leaves of one book and behind him was a small pile of books climbing the window ledge. The window was cracked open and let in the spring breeze. "I believe I will sit in the drawing room and wait for Elizabeth and I will speak with her about these matters, Mr. Bennet. I understand your concern, but I would prefer to speak with Elizabeth."

Mr. Bennet nodded and laid his hand on his volumes lying on the desk as if he would rather be reading them.

"But I will share something with you also, Mr. Bennet, that I have received no correspondence from Elizabeth in many weeks of illness, yet I have been told that Jane and Elizabeth's behaviour with Nathan Bingley has been without propriety."

Mr. Bennet nodded. "I am merely interested that my daughters are respected and treated well. Neither have done any wrong, as you might find out if you asked the particulars of the events."

"I repeat, Mr. Bennet, that I would prefer to discuss these matters with Elizabeth."

"She speaks very favourably of you and I believe that she has sound judgement. She did, after all, refuse Lady Catherine's bribe."

Darcy, disarmed by Mr. Bennet's easy frankness, replied "She does not favour anything with casualness." He returned the hat to the table. He knew nothing of a bribe, but the depth to which his aunt had meddled was beginning to take its full shape.

"I believe it took you almost a year to gain her favour," Mr. Bennet probed.

"I was far from graceful in my first proposal. I am quite loath to remember it. I believe I suggested the match was beneath me but that I would have her for a wife despite it."

Mr. Bennet laughed. "Yes. That would not do."

"I quite expected her to accept."

"Ah, indeed. There were others who sought your favour, I imagine."

"There were."

"Do you still feel that way? That we are beneath you?" Mr. Bennet asked sincerely. "Our station remains unchanged, as you see."

Darcy suddenly saw himself in Mr. Bennet's situation sitting across the table from his daughter's groom. He imagined an upstart, a viscount's son, arriving to marry his own daughter and finding her dowry unsuitably small, but proclaiming his favour. He sat again.

"I will admit to you, Mr. Bennet, that I still find my situation surprising. I never once imagined that I would find such a wonderful partner in a small rural town where dining with four and twenty families comprises the totality of society."

"And yet, you are here, in my humble house, let for a month so that my daughters may become more accustomed to London ways. You wear a fine jacket, boots which are the price of a year's worth of feed for a horse. You keep many horses, I have no doubt. I have two, for which I am most privileged, and which I rent to various farmers when they are needed for light work."

"I am aware what you seek from me."

Mr. Bennet's face did not change from its very kind expression, but Darcy noted a glimmer of curiosity in his eyes. He smiled.

"You want to know if I can respect her family as much as I respect her," Darcy agreed. "You want to see how much I realize that she is loved here, and that she comes with all of you as a part of the package. You want to know that I do not intend to pick her up into my fairy tale mansion and turn her into a lady of distinction who will never see her family..."

"You are wrong. I know Lizzy would not want or allow that. But I do want to make sure that *you* know that she is not interested in your fairy tale. She will be Lizzy in a hovel and Lizzy in a palace."

"I for one am glad that she does not come with me to a hovel, Mr. Bennet. And I am fairly sure that you would have denied me permission to marry her if that is what I offered. So, you see, we are not so entirely different."

"You are not a simple man, Mr. Darcy."

"Unfortunately, Mr. Bennet, that is true. You will not find a delightful Charles Bingley in me."

"Mr. Bingley is not entirely simple either, Mr. Darcy," Mr. Bennet noted with a sad smile.

A hall clock struck the hour and Mr. Bennet remarked that the women were quite late from their return. Darcy suddenly hated his chair and popped up. "I am sorry, but where are they? I do hope nothing has happened to them," Darcy said, despite himself, pacing in front of the desk.

"No doubt they have been caught by the lure of storefront

windows and excessive purchasing needs."

"Ah."

"You do not know my dearest wife. She can be distracted by a shiny ribbon in a storefront and she has gone where there are thousands."

"Am I to understand from this that we may dine alone?"

"It is possible."

Darcy realized Mr. Bennet was being facetious. He looked out the window, eager to see Elizabeth on the front walkway, eager to catch sight of her before she arrived. But the street was quiet and only a cab passed, and so he again took his seat and handed the letters to Mr. Bennet. "Thank you for bringing this to my attention. I will deal with it. I will apologize to Lizzy."

They smiled convivially at one another and spoke of men's clubs and a few mutual acquaintances and then the weather and eventually there was the unmistakable chatter of several female voices, all speaking at once. Mr. Bennet rose with Darcy, stepped from behind the desk and tapped Darcy on the shoulder. "I will seek our Lizzy and send her here before you are found out."

Darcy bowed, infinitely grateful for the man's consideration. He would have a moment alone with Elizabeth. He heard Mr. Bennet in the hall answering questions and chatting as they entered, and then he asked for Elizabeth to come with him.

"Oh, is Mr. Darcy here?" Mrs. Bennet exclaimed from beyond the door as if she were a hound and could smell him there. "You keep him hidden in your study for your own amusement," and opening the study door, she entered.

"Mama, let me by," he heard Elizabeth say from behind the door, which her mother held quite firmly. "Mr. Darcy, so sorry we have kept you waiting. You and Mr. Bennet have no doubt had a conversation about what we should expect in your provisions of our dear Miss Lizzy?"

Darcy bowed. "Mrs. Bennet."

"Will you come in the drawing room? There is little space and not nearly sufficient air for us here. Wait here – I'll organize the matter."

She turned and scurried ahead of him, clucking. "Girls! Girls! Elizabeth. Come here. Now. Settle yourselves in the drawing room. Hill. Hill. Where are you Hill? Oh, there you are, right by my side as

I want you. Now you must announce Mr. Darcy when we are all in the drawing room... Lizzy, there, there. No, you must go in the drawing room. Yes. Just sit and wait, he will come when we are ready."

Hill, who arrived at the library door to fetch him, curtsied, and said, "Please to follow me, Mr. Darcy." He entered the drawing room behind Hill, mystified by Mrs. Bennet's elaborate rituals.

"May I please announce the very welcomed Mr. Fitzwilliam Darcy of Pemberley Estate in Derbyshire." Hill would have continued according to her mistresses' instructions but Elizabeth stood and gave her a look. Her sisters also stood and Mr. Bennet, lingering at the window, smiled benevolently. Darcy bowed to Mrs. Bennet with a flourish and before he was quite straight again, he bowed to Jane, to Kitty and turned to face Elizabeth, and bowed to her, but before he could complete his formal greeting, Elizabeth stepped up to him, tears welled in her eyes, her hand on his cheek.

"Darcy. Oh no. Oh no." She would not stop crying.

"Elizabeth Bennet. Your manner is quite unacceptable," Mrs. Bennet hissed. "Mr. Darcy will be quite shocked by such familiar behaviour in our drawing room no less. In front of all your sisters! He will abandon you."

But Darcy took both Elizabeth hands in his. "Hush dear. I am fine now. I *will* be fine. It will not show in a few more weeks of good food and your company."

"What is the meaning...?" Mrs. Bennet asked.

"Mama," Jane stepped up to her, "Hush. He has been ill. Can you not see how much weight he has lost?"

Darcy led Elizabeth to her chair and had her sit, for she was visibly shaking. He stood beside her with one hand lightly touching her shoulder and faced the rest of her family. "I must apologize for not having alerted Elizabeth of my condition. I have been quite a bit more ill than Georgiana suggested in her letter. She did not want to alarm you. By the time I understood that you had not been fully apprised of the situation, it was too late to rectify, for it was but only several days ago that Georgiana admitted it to me that you have been ill informed."

"We are very glad that you come to us much better, Mr. Darcy," Jane said.

"Perhaps it would be time to set a date for the wedding, Mr.

Darcy," Mrs. Bennet scolded. "Had something happened to you, my Eliza would have been almost quite compromised by your devotions and without any protection of a will to moderate the possibility of your ill health causing an interruption in your life..." a speech the entire Bennet family hushed. "And I am very displeased that you brought her into the circle of your aunt's ill will."

Elizabeth began to cry again and turned to speak to Darcy. "I could not have born it..." she whispered. "You must have thought ill of me that I did not come or send best wishes and doctor you with love notes. Oh Darcy, how dare they keep this from me?"

"I do believe, Mrs. Bennet, that you are correct," Darcy said, hoping to answer Elizabeth's complaints and her mother's in the same breath. "I had the same thought myself when I was recovering and I will tell you all that I have resolved that we secure a date for the wedding and shall no longer seek my aunt's approbation in the matter."

Elizabeth stood suddenly, practically baring her teeth at him. "But, Mr. Darcy, it is not your money I want and it is most insensitive to be speaking of fortunes when it is clear that you almost died." She curtsied and left the room.

"As I thought, Mrs. Bennet. It might have been better had we given them a few minutes alone in the study," Mr. Bennet suggested.

"But then I would not have had the opportunity to witness the reaction of their re-acquaintance," she replied quite without blushing.

"In that case, you have done remarkably well."

Darcy smiled. Apparently, Elizabeth was still rather fond of him.

"Mr. Darcy," Mrs. Bennet said from across the room, "I do believe we were very wrong about you. You are a quiet man, a man of few words who we misinterpret, seeming to snub present company with your silence going on ahead of you like lion, but it is we who have misjudged. You are a quiet man to be sure, but I think what you keep to yourself is probably not as horrible as we have imagined. Not so terrible at all."

Darcy, not knowing how to respond for he had no clue what she had just told him, merely nodded his head.

"Mr. Darcy," Mr. Bennet said, "I do believe you have just received the most generous acceptance that you could hope to receive from my dear Mrs. Bennet who, I might add, does not often admit to being wrong despite the fact that she is most of the time..."

"Mr. Bennet, you quite play on my nerves," was her reply and Darcy, again uncertain about these remarks, nodded, smiling.

RISKY ON THE SOFA

Dinner was pleasant with the conversation of travelers who had spent most of the morning exploring London streets. Although more animated and less mannerly and formal than the dinners to which he was accustomed, Darcy was surprised by the way their conviviality made him feel relaxed. He added little to their chatter and noticed that Elizabeth was likewise quiet, but he smiled and laughed and found that he and Mr. Bennet could have a great deal of conversations about books.

They retired to play cards and to read. The family occupied one end of the drawing room talking rather too loudly while leaving the other end for Darcy and Elizabeth to spend time alone. They sat side by side on a settee and he allowed himself the freedom to put one arm around the back of her without touching. Leaning in very close, he spoke into her ear.

"I am madly in love with you, Miss Elizabeth Bennet. I hope you know how much my life is enfolded in yours. I hope you know that I have wished to be with you every day since you left me in December." She put her hand up to his, and held it there, and would not let him move again. "I suppose we should talk about what we have each lived in our separation and to re-acquaint ourselves. I apologize for my aunt's obstructive activities. And my silences, which were not intended. My family did us no good service, I'm afraid, and I will in future protect us from Lady Catherine's interference. But to tell you the truth, being in your presence again makes me want a singular thing and all else is entirely gone from my head."

He squeezed her hand by way of suggestion. She blushed and her eyes widened as if to say, Oh yes, me also, and she ran a finger onto his wrist. He closed his eyes as he received her touch, how it travelled into and through him, igniting urgent appetites so that he could not think. When he opened his eyes, she was staring into his, smiling, her lips slightly open, her tongue perched just inside her teeth. He sighed. He sighed! He touched her lip quickly, just a little, with a finger and pulled away again.

He continued whispering. "You must pretend that what I am

about to say concerns the many weird dreams I had while I was terribly sick and it is true that I did have strange dreams and that I should like to tell you of them one of these days; but not tonight. Tonight, I should like to shock you, Miss Elizabeth Bennet, for I will say that the only thing I want tonight is to undo each one of your buttons, to kiss you as each button is released and to relieve you of every scrap of clothing you wear."

But while there was a little surprise when he first spoke, there was also then a little jerk in her body, a little trembling, and then a deep breath in which she mastered herself. "Indeed," she spoke loudly, "that is a strange dream. Pray, continue."

"Once you are completely undone from the constraints and protection of clothing and having kissed you in many places I have only dreamt of kissing you, for instance, the blade of your shoulder which is sometimes revealed when you wear that particularly fetching blue dress with the silver back. When you wear that dress, there is a place I wish to kiss, Miss Elizabeth Bennet, and I quite forget the words I would like to speak when you turn and that shoulder blade faces me. Yes. Once I have you like that, with all those places kissed, I would ask you to unbutton me. I should like particularly that you unbutton my trousers so that ..." He struggled for the words. Erection, he could not use. Penis. Desire. Sex. Hard-on. Bone. Tool. All banned. "Remember, when I quite lost myself, in the cupboard... you had me in the cupboard... you remember? And how I pushed into you... that..."

He stopped. His entire body strove with a heavy weighted longing, remembering that stolen opportunity. And now, frustrated by her inexperience, the words he could not use with her, and having no means even to describe his own anatomy without an unacceptable crassness. It was all he could do not to pick her up and steal her away that very minute to show her what was in his mind. To elope. To be married suddenly and to then have his way with her.

"You must not stop, Mr. Darcy. It is fascinating."

"The problem is that I must stop, Miss Bennet. For fear of losing my position here on the settee."

"But your story is only half complete."

"Perhaps that is where we shall leave it."

"I would unbutton you Mr. Darcy. And I believe that whatever you have managed to do to me, I will learn also to do to you?"

He closed his eyes and took a very deep breath as she whispered these words in his ear. He dared not look at her, nor move. He breathed in order to control himself, and he thought of shooting pigeons from a tree, and of finding a decent doctor for Anne, and he thought of Mrs. Bennet's hat, which she had recently purchased and a lengthy and not particularly interesting story of the shop, its location and how she had found it, and the other hats she had seen there and how this one just seemed more perfect than the others, even though it was quite a bit more expensive, but would be worn at the wedding which justified the expense.

"When you are close, Darcy, your smell, and the sound of your voice, and your laughter, and the way I feel you as if your moods are pushed through mine, how even the way your hands move in the air when you speak, these all make me feel as if I want to absorb all of you into me, to take you somehow and become merged. This heightens to a tingling that lights a passageway all the way from my throat to that place between my legs. Darcy, it is so with you also. Do you think this way with other women even now?"

"No Lizzy. Never."

"There have been terrible rumours. Everyone would have me believe you will be unfaithful."

"I will not. I cannot even imagine another woman in my bed, not even my mind will be unfaithful to you."

She smiled. "I believe that. The winter was especially hard and I know what you've been told about Nathan, or that I suspect it. Your aunt's letter… You must know he is not a lover. Nathan. Please believe it. Believe that I love you entirely… Oh, I am so sorry I was not with you to help you through that terrible suffering. You were horribly ill."

"They thought I might die."

"And they did not send for me."

"It was unpardonable. But you change the topic."

"Yes, yes." She paused and was so incredibly full of attention that he felt her eyes spill down into him, causing him to vibrate with longing.

"So," she whispered with a wide-eyed smile. "Tell me now: what would I do once I was released of my clothing and everywhere kissed?"

"You would unbutton my trousers, and you would set me free.

And you would kiss me. There."

Elizabeth paled. He had said too much, had offended her.

"Really?" she finally gasped. He could barely move. The idea of her lips on him, and the feeling of standing over her, her head in his hands, holding her face against him; it was too much to bear.

"Yes. If you would like to. And when I do it to you..."

"Kissing me there?"

"Yes. You will be so far gone, Lizzy, that it will make you..."

She put up her hand to stop him. Then she smiled and told him she thought it would feel like a kind of tightness and loss, or a space that needs to be filled, and a desperate ache. He thought a minute, and decided Yes, one could describe physical arousal with those words, and then, because she had the words to describe the experience, he realized she had experienced it.

"Elizabeth! You touched yourself."

She nodded shyly. "It is so wrong, Darcy. Yet feels..."

"No, no. It makes me... no, I am glad for you. Here, lean into me, my darling. Put your head on my shoulder." She did as he asked, and his arm behind her back moved in a little closer and rested on her shoulder, while his other hand rested on her lap.

"Oh, Fitzwilliam, you are not Mr. Collins."

Darcy laughed loudly. "No, my dear. Neither are you! I don't think even Mr. Collins is Mr. Collins anymore."

And Darcy leaned into her and kissed her once. Then again. Lingering. In public. Then a third time. Lingering more.

Mrs. Bennet, from the other end of the room, called "Mind yourselves. Mr. Darcy, mind yourself."

But Mr. Bennet, peering up from his book and saw only that they were holding hands and quite close together, their heads leaning into one another a little, dismissed her. They stayed leaning into one another for some time until Darcy could restrain no longer. Checking that every person in the room seemed occupied, he leaned forward slightly, rousing Elizabeth's head from his shoulder, and with his back turned to the room, he kissed her again, tracing his tongue along her lips and down into her mouth, and into her mouth and lightly slipping in and out along the lines of her tender care and eager reception of his affection, into her mouth, into wanting her and saying it all with his tongue, and meeting hers, and her wanting him. His hand slid up her legs and pressed firmly, solidly, for the briefest of seconds, through the cloth of her dress, and then slid back down again, and he waited as he kissed her longer and more, thinking soon someone would notice and he would be forced to break away from her, and yet it did not come and he continued to kiss her and she to kiss him and it seemed that they were now alone, and quite alone, they would kiss...

Mr. Bennet stood beside them. Startled, Darcy and Elizabeth broke away from each other and, without turning to Mr. Bennet, Darcy took her hands and kissed them both. "It is late, and except for the temptation to kidnap you now, I have no other business here."

He stood, bowed to Mr. Bennet, and bade Mrs. Bennet and the Miss Bennets a goodnight. Elizabeth and Mr. Bennet walked him to the front door and he wasted no time with long goodbyes. He intended to be there the next day. And the one after that.

In the carriage, Darcy thought of his young self who would have, at this very minute, gone to a particular section of town and wandered the ale houses and found a lightskirt; but now the idea was abhorrent. It just would not do. He would simply have to wait. It was not merely sex that he wanted. It was not merely the pleasure of a night, an embrace, of rising against the inside of a woman and taking his pleasure. He wanted to give Elizabeth Bennet pleasure and nothing else would satisfy.

Elizabeth, at the end of her father's arm, watched the carriage pull away amazed at the potential that married life offered in the way of passion. Darcy had quite sparked her imagination. Her father, however, was frowning.

"I like your Mr. Darcy very much, but he shows signs of being a man accustomed to having his way. Be careful, Lizzy, you are not yet married."

GOOD SOCIETY

The memory of Darcy's lips, his tongue, his inspired suggestions about love plagued Elizabeth as a tyranny of social engagements prevented intimate contact between them. Everywhere, she was on display as his fortune and stature made her the belle to be inspected, the subject of gossip and examination and, occasionally, interrogation. She became advisor to young girls seeking methods for attracting eligible men. She advised honesty, which puzzled them, and she felt foolish trying to explain what seemed obvious to her. It certainly has nothing to do with the dress I was wearing the night I met Mr. Darcy, for it was not exceptional, nor the way I behaved, for I think I was curt and unwelcoming, and I cannot play well or recite lines of poetry, nor am I more than tolerably handsome.

It did not take long for the circle of girls to seek advice elsewhere.

Darcy's friend, Bonnie Stately, had befriended her immediately and had advised her in ways to avoid and quell the inevitable gossip. They would forge a friendship which would last their lifetimes. "You must realize that there will always be people who talk and there is nothing you might do to stop it. They have been talking about you since the marriage was announced. You are an unknown quantity and an invader."

"I the invader? A girl of no consequence – just a young girl?"

"Who will acquire a great deal of influence once you marry. You do not yet realize what power money has. You will learn if you pay attention to what it is doing for you and who will listen when before they did not. It is a corrupting influence – or can be – if you let it rule you or let those who think too highly of it dominate you. Remember, Miss Bennet, who you are."

"I care nothing for money."

"Perhaps not, but that is irrelevant. 'They' (the great and glorious 'They' who are interested in running the world and making sure it is to their liking) they *do* care. That you do not care about money and power is unbelievable to them, for they cannot imagine that it is an option."

Elizabeth accepted a glass of punch, saying "Thank you" to the young lad in livery who delivered it. Bonnie arched her eyebrows. "It is better not to acknowledge the servants," she suggested quietly putting a hand on Elizabeth's arm, as she too thanked the servant. Elizabeth, whose Mrs. Hill was a beloved member of her home, could not imagine such a scheme in which the existence of another sentient being should be objectified into mere property. "I'm not sure I can actually change that habit," she admitted. "Lady Catherine quite went mad trying."

"It is believed that our social positions are so entirely separate that their sentience, once acknowledged, makes it difficult for both of us to fulfill our roles, theirs as servants and ours as lords and ladies. That is the common refrain. But mine do their jobs quite well despite my breaking those rules."

Elizabeth spoke of Mary Wollstonecraft's arguments against the entitlement of men and saw in it the same argument that could be made for the respect and care of servants. "I do not believe we should be casual about the existence of another living being, quite simply," Elizabeth ended her argument. "There is nothing short of miraculous in all this living, flowers and mountains and streams as much of you and me."

Darcy was watching the entire room, but especially Elizabeth who was in conversation with Bonnie. As he watched, there was a slight change in the tone of conversations generally. He watched as a young man entered the room with a bright blond head of hair and a god-like smile. Recognizing Bingley's cousin, Darcy noticed that old men and women, just as often as young girls, sought his hand and fawned over him with some enthusiasm. But the young man eagerly moved on and bent his head in search of something. He found what he was looking for, it seemed, for he stopped in front of Elizabeth and stayed with her.

Darcy, fascinated, watched as Nathan kissed her hand and bowed, and she – not blushing at all – smiled and greeted him. He said something, which seemed very funny, for she laughed very loudly and then covered her mouth and shook as she suppressed her laughter. She then introduced Nathan to her companions.

Darcy suddenly knew from a particular smell that Miss Bingley had snuck up behind him and he waited for her inevitable comment. She would point and say, I told you so! They have a special relationship. But she did not speak of Nathan Bingley and instead asked if he had seen Charles, and had they found an artist to paint the girls' cameos, and would he prefer it in a leather frame or a small brass one, and did he notice how the Viscount had aged since the last time they had seen him, for Chamberlain seems of poor colouring and she suspected his liver was not functioning well.

La boulangère was called, a dance which Darcy knew was an especial favourite of Elizabeth's and she, looking up, smiled directly at him as if she knew exactly where he had been all that time. He excused himself from Caroline, and Elizabeth touched Nathan's arm to bid him adieu and turned to Darcy as he crossed the room. He bowed and she curtsied, and she blushed as if they had just met, and he led her into the circle with other dancers.

"They are all jealous of you," he observed as they skipped and hopped. They pulled and parted, swung and regained each other, slowed and spun, swung and circled, laughed when she bumped into him with a thud.

"They are jealous that I have the sweetest man," she batted her eyelashes with a exaggerated coy glance.

"No – I am a scrawny effigy and only you would have me now. No, the young debutantes who are dying to talk to Nathan Bingley are jealous. You should have heard the silence when he kissed your hand."

She frowned. "Did I do anything inappropriate?" she asked as they regained one another.

"I was furiously jealous."

"You were not," she scolded. He did not speak again and they fell into a sweet rhythm, moving easily, so entirely present to each other that he felt the room disappear. He was left with the lovely music reverberating through their hands and their feet. As they moved, he felt her breath on his cheeks and the warmth of her back through his kid gloves which he would rip off if permitted. He felt her relax into him and she whispered, "This is lovely, Darcy."

For weeks, Elizabeth had been trying to tell Jane about the passions which occurred in her body when Darcy kissed her, the way her heart pounded and a fire opened her, how he made her blush and love him more and how she wanted to give everything up for him and hand herself to him. She would say it is more like handing herself to herself (a sentiment enigmatic and confusing). This longing was a doorway into a new part of who she was, one that was opened by him. But Jane, having not been approached by Bingley in anything but a deliberately chaste way, was more confused every time Elizabeth spoke of desire. This frustrated Elizabeth as she would love to share these moments with her sister, to compare experiences and temper her own passions with Jane's wise thoughts, to giggle a little about the awakening of their bodies and compare kisses. But Jane's lips had not been touched, her inner thigh, her wrist, her tongue, had not been visited and she was mute on the subject of desire and sex.

One evening Elizabeth saw a painting in the Lord Edgewater gallery where there was a large party. She was arrested by a great tall painting framed in a heavily gilded frame because it portrayed physical love as she experienced it. A gorgeous man dressed in Roman armour (who reminded her of Nathan Bingley) held a great sword while a red velvet cape cascaded to his feet. Before him stood a woman whose luminescent skin shone like alabaster as if she were partly divine. She was loosely draped in a cloth of gold which hid almost nothing of her body. Her left hand was gently arresting the sword's hilt, a tender obstruction to its violence, while her right hand dangled an olive branch beneath his chin.

The composition was clear in its intent to suggest peace, but Elizabeth saw how they gazed at one another, meeting each other's eyes with a deep conversation which admitted to no other witness. An entire communion occurred, a whole meeting of souls, a whole understanding without words, with no witnesses, despite the many who would commune with the painting and see that they were alone together.

"There, Jane," she pointed to the lovers, to their gaze. "The lightning I try to explain when Darcy kisses me. My words are quite not up to the task. But in this… You must feel something of it!"

Jane thought the painting was quite spectacular. "But I cannot look at Charles that way, Elizabeth. I blush too deeply. My eyes fall. How could I hold such a gaze? Perhaps I will learn. However, it is not this passion which causes my anxiety, Elizabeth. It is this passion."

She reached into her little reticule and pulled from it a little book.

"Charles handed it to me just now and I sat with him looking at it not long ago. He found it at a little art bookstore and it is reprints from some French art. Most are of landscapes, but this one has made quite a stir. Or so it has for me."

Elizabeth studied the reproduction that Jane offered of lovers in a bedchamber from a French artist. "Fragonard," she read.

"It is the violence of this passion which concerns me, Lizzy. This woman does not look well."

"I believe she is swooning."

"He reaches to bolt the door – to capture her."

"I don't think so Jane."

"And why not?"

"Because she is fully dressed and he is not. She has come to his bedchamber. It is not to keep her in that he bolts the door…"

"It is to keep others out," Jane said, understanding. "She swoons in his arms."

"Yes. His masculinity overwhelms her. Look at him! Would you not want to be taken in those arms?"

"She swoons," Jane repeated, pensive. "And this is a physical emotion. It captures her…"

"Yes. It captures her body. It robs her of her legs. It makes her shaky and lightheaded. She wants him as he wants her."

Jane took back her little book and tucked it away again. They walked back towards the main hall.

"Elizabeth, you have been overly educated by Mr. Darcy."

"Yes Jane. And perhaps my own imagination. You should try it a little. It is quite safe."

The sun which stayed late in the spring sky was colouring the horizon. Darcy watched it quietly from the Edgewater's terrace. There was not a breeze in the air and, as he heard a light footstep come upon him from the French doors, he smiled expecting Elizabeth. She would make a comment and he would laugh, and they would share the quiet, long view out to the sky, beyond the whiffs of cloud catching a perfectly angled sun. Then they would find the first star as it appeared. When he turned, it was not Elizabeth.

"Hello Lady Lyttelton."

"How dare you use such formalities," she scolded. "You've been terribly ill. We were all so worried when we heard."

He bowed again. "You look ravishing. How is your dearest?"

"The young one or the old?" she laughed. "Oh, you know, Henry gets older by the minute and still no heir. He can barely perform to make one, is violently abusive when he cannot and blames me for the lack of a child despite the fact that I am two and thirty and he seven and sixty. Otherwise, I am fit and waiting patiently for him to decide that he has had enough of heirs, and of living, and I may go about my life more productively. Nothing has changed."

"That is sad. I am sorry things have not much improved for you."

"Regrets have a way of piling up if one is not careful, but I believe I have cured myself of it. I do everything openly and happily and do it even if I think I might regret it, for I will only live once, and I would rather regret a few actions than regret not having done many things for fear of regretting some of them. Have you met my new admirer? He trails and follows well enough, but he is not you, William. No, indeed not. And he does not receive his lessons very well either, so I fear he will not last long. And you have been ensnared by a nymph of mystical charms who will never again release you from her talons."

"A nymph with talons. You exaggerate," Darcy laughed.

"But I believe that is what you need, my dear. A nymph with talons. I suppose I am to understand from this that you will not be following me into the darker corners of the garden nor into my private chambers ever again."

"You are correct. I am no longer a free man."

"By your own choosing." He nodded. "She made quite the impression tonight. Until this evening, I believe everyone thought you a fool. But she has charmed Nathan Bingley. What is it you men see in her that we women fail to notice?"

"Ah, well that is a secret for the men I am not about to reveal," he answered coyly. They turned as another person came through to the terrace.

"Ah, here she is. My nymph. Miss Elizabeth Bennet."

Elizabeth curtsied. "Miss Bennet, may I introduce you to a good friend of mine, our hostess, the Viscount of Edgewater's bride and treasure, Margaret Lyttelton."

Elizabeth curtsied again "Delighted," but Margaret said, "None of that, give us a kiss, here both sides the way the French do. *Ecoute, nous sommes déjà de bonnes amies.*"

They exchanged pleasantries for a moment and the Lady excused herself. Darcy and Elizabeth stood alone on the terrace. The clouds were translucent and gave the sky a hint of mystery. A few stars were out and more arriving each minute the longer they stared. She squeezed his arm. "I like your friends, Mr. Darcy. Your Bonnie as you like to call her... so wonderfully kind to me. And this Margaret seems lovely. So intelligent earlier when we spoke of the ballet."

"Her husband is a brute."

"I have danced with him twice. He is a charming brute, in that case."

"Yes, charming enough when the world watches."

"You were lovers," Elizabeth said frankly. "She is very sad. I can see it in her eyes. And you love her."

"No. I cared for her, but I loved no one for a long time, Lizzy. I was in love once. And now again." He kissed her forehead gently. "And you have some fine friends as well. Nathan warned me not to break your heart. That it was precious and deserved all the care and consideration which a man like me did not have."

"He didn't!"

Darcy nodded. "He was almost rude, but my patience must be improving for I ignored him. Well, not exactly ignored. I merely said that I agreed. That you deserved only the best."

"Oh, Lord." Elizabeth exclaimed. "Was that the extent of your conversation? Men. I can't believe two of the finest men I know can't behave better than that."

"Oh, we'll get on in a few years when his prejudice for me wanes a little and my terrible jealousy is sated from years of having you deliciously by my side."

"How can you be jealous?"

"Actually, he spoke to me as your brother might. He cares a great deal about you Lizzy, and I was remarkably touched by his affection for you."

He took her in his arms and they stayed like that, in a close embrace, watching the stars arrive. "I am very sorry dearest for all the complications."

"Yes. I am sorry for them also. But they are ours together, aren't they? We share them, whatever happens."

"I do," was all he replied, pulling her into him.

He could see tears in her eyes and he kissed them away.
"I do," she whispered. "I do."

DARCY'S SECRET IS REVEALED

Darcy and Elizabeth spent many lovely hours together at various social gatherings, the races, attendings ballets and operas, and accepting invitations to dine in smaller and larger parties. They became reasonable dancing companions and Elizabeth was a success in his favourite circles. But they were everywhere also companions to Anne who they introduced to society with the impossible dream that she would encounter another person, a man, who might be somewhat like Anne, and who might be delighted by the prospects of marrying her. Unfortunately, at the large galas and balls, she preferred to sit with older women where she received no men's advances to spurn. Mary (who remained at home) suggested that a small, cozy party, with a few people playing easy games might delight Anne and bring out her sweetness and intelligence, so they devised a series of afternoon events at Darcy's home in which a dozen people were invited to play cribbage, the game he, Georgiana and Anne had frequently played during Anne's convalescence. They invited a mix of people well known and a few men who were eligible older men, widowers mostly, somewhat late in their marrying years, or generally considered awkward.

Due to unforeseeable circumstances, Elizabeth arrived early and found herself alone with Anne waiting for the rest of the party. She asked Anne various innocuous questions about her evenings, her morning walks, her ponies, her choice of dress for the party, her conversation with Mrs. So and So, gaining in these questions short and direct answers leading to silence. Elizabeth smiled and nodded and did her best to be interested.

Anne picked at her fingers, gently pulling them one by one, providing her own stock phrases, How Good Darcy Is To Me or Georgiana Is Too Very Talented. And her most often How Is Mary? You Know I Love Her.

Elizabeth found herself worrying her gloves and tapping her foot as she looked occasionally out the window for signs of relief. But then Anne spoke without looking up.

"My mother writes to me daily. She asks me questions for which

I do not know the answers. She wants to know what plans you have made for Darcy's daughter, but I wrote to say that you are wonderful and will be a wonderful mother. My mother wanted to know," Anne mumbled, head down, almost apologetically. "She asked me, you see, to assuage her mind that Lettice Rose would be well cared for."

Enraged by Lady Catherine, that she should use Anne this way, and wanting to protect Anne, Elizabeth merely told Anne not to worry about Darcy's daughter and that she must tell her mother to mind her own business. She stood and begged Anne's forgiveness, that she had a headache and would leave. She called for her coat and hat and met Darcy at the door as he arrived. She excused herself as having a headache, to which he replied that she had never had a headache and would she please tell him what had occurred to cause the headache, but she replied that if she chose to have a headache then he must accept it. To which, if he did not understand that she was quite angry about something, he might have laughed. But he dared not. And she, furious, could not. He was entirely unsure how to handle the situation as she wanted only to rage and cry, which was the thing she hated most about herself, that when she was furious, she cried.

"Oh, my darling. What can I do for you?" he asked sympathetically. Which was the reaction she wanted least when she was outraged.

"You may leave me. Now," she added coldly through her tears so that he might understand her confusion and fury.

He stepped back, bowed. "As you wish."

As Elizabeth went out the door, Darcy saw Anne alone in the drawing room. He knew the look on her face, the tightness around the lips, the eyes wide and astounded, the agitation of fingers as she pulled on hers incessantly. He knew as he walked towards her that she would stammer a little. He was not angry, and he hated her fear.

"What has happened?" he asked. The door knocker clanged as the first guests arrived and Anne remained silent.

Elizabeth fumed silently for many hours. She was restless and after arriving home, she walked out to the park and circled it many times. It was Jane who finally calmed her by reminding her of the time she was furious with Bingley. Forgiving. It is the only way to be in a marriage, she said quite simply. Darcy sent her a little note of love by the evening post and said that the party was a success but that no men seemed interested in Anne, instead they fawned over Georgiana who was confused and hated them and refused to join in any other matchmaking parties. I hope you are well, he signed, and that your headache, in quotation marks, has cleared.

When Elizabeth returned from her walk the following morning, Darcy was with her father.

"I have told your father about Lettice Rose and her situation," Darcy said immediately as she entered the study, stepping towards her from where he stood at the window. "She is eleven. She lives happily with a family and knows nothing of her true origins. I have only just found out about her whereabouts myself."

"And you would tell me this when? Rather you let Anne do your dirty work? Or, you might say a few years after we have been married, We must prepare my daughter for her coming out... Oh don't you know. Oh yes, I have a daughter who is of age?" Elizabeth could hear the nasty sarcasm in her voice but could not constrain it. She wanted to hurt him a little.

"You may, if you wish, break our engagement."

"Now, now," Mr. Bennet beseeched. "Don't be hasty."

"I want to release her from the contract. I would not marry her if she felt under any obligation."

No sooner had he spoken these words, but Elizabeth spat her anger. "You say that because you would rather be released from having to explain yourself, Fitzwilliam. Why did you not tell me earlier?"

"You are unfair in your expectations. You cannot expect every man to come to you without a past, a virgin, and without a history."

"Now, now, I did not hear her asking you to be a virgin, Mr. Darcy. Now will you not both sit?"

Elizabeth could see Darcy gritting his teeth. She saw his hands clench and she felt the brute force of his body straining as he stayed immobile at the window. He turned, finally, facing Mr. Bennet, his full height, broad and imposing and statuesque, an Achilles towering over the desk. Elizabeth leaned a little further out of her chair astonished by his passion, and astonished that for a second, her body filled with an urge, a passion for him.

"I bring everything to this marriage. Wealth and position. I offer it to a girl who might – if lucky – find herself a Mr. Collins. I cannot accept that I should feel guilty about an event which happened when I was sixteen…"

But her father continued to lean comfortably in his chair. "Be still man," he said. "I am quite fond of each of you and wish only for you to be together and have my grandchildren." Her father's tender words, spoken calmly, gave her pause to admire him. And the idea of his being the grandfather of her children made her feel a warm rush of gratitude. Darcy spun and retreated, back to the window, not quite appeased.

"Father, is it appropriate to speak of grandchildren given the subject of the conversation?"

"I would have told you earlier…" Darcy defended himself. "I had intended to before you left Rosings, but we were having a delightful time, and I did not want to spoil it. And then the horse had the accident and I was distraught. And then…" he paused, looking at Mr. Bennet, and she thought of Mary's secret. "Then that other issue. I am sorry - I was ill and here I am, backed into a corner of my own making. But Elizabeth, you must see that I am not under any obligation to give you this information, that many men marry having similar circumstances which they keep secret until their death when a young man shows up at the funeral to claim some right to something. Surely it has been done before and…"

"It fills literature for its sudden unexpected turn of fortune. Yes, I am aware. But I do not want to have that kind of relationship with you. It is not that you have a daughter that is objectionable; it is that I may not trust you."

And Darcy mumbled, angrily, as if to the window. "I am worthy of your trust," while Mr. Bennet explained that it was not a matter of trust, but a matter of risk.

"There is nothing to be gained if you do not risk anything for one another. Now, is anyone else as hungry as I am?" but when he rang for Hill, she arrived with Mrs. Bennet who complained that they were all spending far too much time away from her and that they must all eat together for she could not bear another minute with only Kitty and Jane for company. Mr. Bennet left them alone, excusing himself by saying that he had offered all the advice he considered worthy in the moment.

Elizabeth grinned as the door closed. "Father… he quite believes he offered wonderful advice."

Darcy, still looking out the window, said "I believe it was for me."

"Is there nothing else I should know?" Elizabeth asked. "A crazy woman in the turret, already your wife? An uncle who will come and take all your money and title? A scientist in your basement building a monster?"

He shook his head, a smile growing on his face as he walked across the room to her. She stood and let him hold her as he whispered "No, but there is a slightly odd cousin who threatens to sleep between us."

"You might advise her to be careful about her mother's letters. They guide her in inappropriate ways."

They held one another for a few minutes, laughing together in the embrace. Then Elizabeth, who had also understood her father's meaning, asked "Is the mother of your daughter alive?" She felt a sudden nervousness in her belly and realized that it was neither the fact that Darcy had a daughter nor the absence of his communicating it which bothered her, but the fact that he might love another woman, that he might yet be beholden to someone else.

"Yes. She broke my heart, Lizzy." He was not forthcoming, and she waited patiently, hoping he would tell her something to relieve the terrible ache in her stomach. She waited far too long and what he said did not appease her. "She was older than I by four years. She believed my youth protected her from conceiving. Or so she said. There was a dramatic ending in which we eloped, giving up our inheritance; but her family caught us before we were married and kidnapped her away. They would not let us marry. I was not good enough for them. You see, she was an aristocrat of a very high order."

"And she is well? Your daughter?"

He shrugged. "We may talk of her again. She is not in my charge - and for now we will leave it that way."

She nodded, her mind racing. "I want children with you, Darcy, I want our children. You do know that. But in the moment, I cannot think of either of us as parents. I barely know myself," she answered. "And how will I be at Pemberley? A house so incredibly huge that I am afraid to wander in a dark corner and find skeletons of your ancestors mouldy and forgotten..." Darcy laughed. "And how to manage the housekeepers and the maids. It's a big job, is it not

Darcy? I will be expected to be a lady, to be a model... Will I go for walks? Might I run and skip as I love to do? Will I have to be dour and serious when I would rather laugh and tease? Your aunt's list was quite abominable. And now there is a girl who will need a London society launch and a husband in a few years. It is quite a lot to imagine."

"And we will have Anne's suitors coming to the door every day seeking her fortune," he added.

"And you will have basketfuls of puppies," she agreed, squeezing his hand, "and we shall name them all Mr. Collins, except for the males, who we will call Lady Catherine," to which they laughed again.

"We'll have one of those portraits drawn that all wealthy lords make, you know the ones, where they are presented on a far lawn in great armchairs and sofas, with the house in the distance so that its grandeur can be admired. We will have your new grey on parade, with all the puppies running about, and a dark-haired girl somewhere lurking in the background, skeletons coming from the windows and babies falling from the sky. Lady Catherine shouting from the rooftop and Miss Anne praying beneath a tree. And we will hang it in the..."

They heard Mrs. Bennet yelling from the dining room. "It is ill to keep us waiting..."

"No, we shall not hang it..."

"In our bedroom."

"I am forgiven then? I am sorry. You will come haunt Pemberley with me, and make children? And perhaps, when the time is right, introduce ourselves to my daughter?"

CARRIAGE PLAY

Every morning Elizabeth continued her habit of taking a walk alone. Her mother had insisted that she go with a chaperone, but Mr. Bennet had disagreed and asked what trouble she might get into in a public park walking but five blocks away, and so she was allowed her daily quiet, her time of peaceful contemplation. She circled the park a few times until she felt that she had cleared her head and loosened her spirits. No matter how pretty the park, she missed roaming about the hills and forests of home and became increasingly disenchanted with the demands of London's social life.

One day, a short man in a tweed jacket called to her from across the green. "Miss Bennet? There is a gentleman in the carriage beyond who would wish to talk, Miss. He seems smart enough but would not give his name."

Not puzzled, for she was certain she knew the man's name, she followed the cabby, and within the cab, hiding in its shadows, was Darcy.

"I see you knows one another. Are you climbing in miss?"

She shook her head. "No thank you sir. Good day to you."

It was hard, but she could not climb in. She turned and walked as quickly as she could without running.

"Miss! Miss!" the cabby came after her, puffing a little. "He would speak to you."

"I am sure he would not." Elizabeth refused, giggling, "Perhaps he should join me."

Darcy beckoned her from the cab door and she shook her head and walked away.

Darcy was determined and persistent. He showed up in the park and waited for her. She began to change her schedule slightly, and they made a game of whether or not he could find her. She was hoping to force him to leave the anonymity of the carriage; he to entice her into it. Later in the day, when they were inevitably together speaking privately in a public venue, they would laugh and tease one another about the morning's adventures.

Two situations tempered Elizabeth's resolve to stay away from a private audience with Darcy. The first that they chose a date for the wedding and it was now not far away. It was, more to the point, imminent, and Elizabeth became confident in its reality. Contracts were signed, banns were prepared, the whole was becoming quite established.

She was also mollified by his ability to find her in a quiet corner at some public event and to kiss her with such acute tenderness and passion that she forgot where she was, and wanted more and more to be with him. At night, alone, her body was an agony of restless energy and desire which even her own touch could not sate.

And of course, there was a little knowledge she had gleaned from Amanda some months earlier, knowledge which she had intended to use after her marriage, but which might serve before it as well. And so, against her better judgement, she accepted his invitation and sat opposite Darcy who, saying not a word nor showing any surprise, tapped the roof and the horses walked on slowly.

"Well, Mr. Darcy, you wanted to talk," she smiled coyly at him, her face welcoming, her body tucked back into its seat.

"Yes. I want to say to you that it is about time you know a man's body so that you might have something to think about when you are alone in bed."

He had had a week of chasing her to prepare this little speech. He was no longer interested in being subtle. He reached for her knee and peered into her eyes, and said Lizzy, you have no idea how much… and she took his hand and kissed it and said she did also.

"But I cannot. I will not," she repeated, almost in a whisper. His hand moved to raise her skirts and to kiss her there, and she moaned. And she arched as he pressed his face into her, and then she took his hand and slowly stroked his fingers with her mouth as he pressed his lips to the place she dared not name. And then, when it was too much, she gently pushed him away and hit the roof of the carriage to make it stop.

"Trust me, dear Lizzy." He looked at her provocatively, then hit the roof again urging the driver to move on. He lay back against the bench so she could examine his body, his desire for her, and he touched himself briefly while looking at her. Then he changed his attitude and sat quietly before her, holding her hands. "I'll do nothing that will compromise you. We shared a bed - if you remember- and I did not even remove my clothing." He arched an eyebrow at her, a look she found irresistible. "I think of our kiss a few weeks ago. Lizzy, it feels as if it were years ago. And our time at Rosings! A century. Come, let us take a moment to enjoy one another a little." And as he spoke, he slowly undid his cravat and laid it on her lap.

"Is this all you think of?" she teased, picking it up and waving it like a flag.

"With you? Yes. Now, you may proceed to undo my waist coat."

"I cannot because I want it too much..." she whispered again, as if the cabby might hear her over the sound of hooves in the cobbles.

His face became serious for a moment, but he shook his head. "Lizzy, you don't get to be cautious right now. Now you get to play. Now you get to be the Lizzy I know you are and the Lizzy I want for the rest of my life. Now you get to show me..." and he paused, smiling. He leaned back into the carriage bench and stretched his hands on the smooth leather on either side of his hips, opening himself to her. He was smiling so widely, she thought he would crack his face and she laughed, and jumped into his arms, and kissed him. Then she leaned back into his lap and began to undo each waist coat button. He did not move.

Soon she was stroking his fine chest, her face pressed into it, his hands caressing her neck and face and hair and his glorious smell infused her entire being. He hoisted her skirt a little with one hand and stroked her thigh and she shifted her skirts up and out of the way and she felt him beneath her, his power, his desire, his wanting her. Her body ached to accept him.

There was something in how much she trusted him, the way he held her and the way she felt their bond travel between their bodies that made her suddenly stop and look up to him.

"What is it?" he asked her.

"I feel so blessed to have you in my life that I can barely stand it."

His face became serious, and he said, "You cannot say something like that casually. Those are big words, Lizzy, solid words and words that make me feel so entirely grateful but also words that will destroy me if they are given as empty platitudes to flatter and appease."

She was confused for a minute, but then she said, "Darcy, you have been terribly hurt, haven't you?"

And he said, "Yes, by death, betrayals, and a terrible pain of guilt.

I didn't know how a person's heart could have lies which even they don't recognize."

And they kissed. They kissed lovingly, with tears and with pain and longing and with a terrible knowledge that they were bonded each to the other in a way that was mysterious and terrible, great and awful, terrifying and eternal. They held one another for a while until the carriage had made several rounds of the large park. And it was more an agony to separate than it was to refrain from making love.

One day, not long after she and Darcy had their first intimacy in the carriage, Elizabeth had the strange realization that she would soon be married. Of course, she had known, but on this day she understood the consequences. That there would be no chaperone. Her life would change. She would become Mrs. Darcy. It struck her as funny that she agreed to become his wife but hadn't exactly considered the implications of such a contract. She laughed and began imagining her wedding for the first time, of being led down the aisle by her father, straight and proud, and of receiving a kiss from Darcy before the witnesses. Would he kiss her as he had the night they were reunited in London, in the drawing room, uprooting her from all knowledge of the world? Would he make her body rise to such terrible ache in a church? Would he dance in her mouth rhythms of joy and wonder? Would she reciprocate the dance, follow, lead, and tell him that this desire was with her also? Could she do so in front of a congregation of her friends and family? She heard "You may kiss the bride" in her head, the permission granted and all that those words entailed.

Then their first night together. What it meant, though, the truth of what men and women do with one another so clearly portrayed by the animals in the fields, and yet inconceivable between men and women. Strange and horrifying; but also, after knowing how a kiss produced a tirade of longing, she could imagine falling under a spell that would be nothing less than wonderful. Darcy, she knew, had experience, and believed that she could enjoy her life with him and their bed. She was incredibly excited by the prospect, could not wait to have him beside her every night.

And this thought led to another: that she did not immediately want children. To prevent children, one must abstain from desire, sleep in opposite sides of the house, keep one's clothes on at all times, hold hands throughout the marriage as the only way to express love and care. Impossible, she thought. They would have forty children, like the Miller's in Meryton who stopped finally at fifteen when Mrs. Miller's brother threatened Mr. Miller if he were to make his wife with child one more time. It was reported that he said seven is quite sufficient, Sir, to prove your manhood capable. Ten is quite enough to be greedy. But fifteen is bestial. Desist from propagating or I shall remove her from you whether or not 'tis legal!

Yet how could she remain in a state of perpetual restraint? It was quite difficult enough now, when they were unmarried and endlessly supervised, unable to enjoy intimacy without the guilt of trespassing into prohibited actions, of hiding in a corner or broom closet or carriage hoping for another quick kiss and getting one's heart going with anticipation and nothing beyond it but polite conversation and pretty poses on a chair, pretending that one does not feel one's legs, that one's nipples do not harden, to smile prettily and nod one's head and accept an offer to dance with a slightly cocked hand when one's hand would rather play in his hair, snake into his shirt. One's hand would rather press firmly into that wonderfully rounded place which she once felt against her, hard and urgent. After marriage, what then?

One day she spoke of her concerns about having children as they walked in the park with the family, the Gardiners and their children and Jane and Bingley, and Mr. and Mrs. Bennet, all in a little parade spread out along the paths. Darcy agreed to delay having children then asked how she would choose a governess and she said she would have no one mind them but herself. Darcy said that she could spend as much time as she pleased with their children, but he would not have his wife beholden to them.

"But I do not want liberties from my children. That is why I do not want to have them immediately Darcy, don't you see? I want to be with my children, often."

"But what if we should want to go to London? Or for a walk?"

"They shall come with us."

He was beginning to understand the implications of this marriage. He had assumed that she would merely fold into his privilege and adopt it as the finer and best version. But now, the thing he admired terribly about her, that she had an independence of mind and spirit, was also the thing which caused conflicts between them. She did not assume the entitlement of money, the possibility of being served, the promise of living perpetually in leisure. Try saying yes Darcy, no Darcy, he suggested. She cocked her head.

"And do you like children?" she asked, ignoring him.

"They're noisy and dirty and speak with a lisp..." Elizabeth laughed so loudly he raised his voice a little. "That's why we have nannies. And governesses. So that they may bring the children to be viewed and then..." He tried to speak over her laughter.

"Don't sulk."

"I'm not sulking."

"You'll see. Children are like us, only small. They have personalities and they're very funny, some of them, and you'll see. They'll be *our* children, Darcy. Born of our love."

He looked at her and saw her again, and again, as if for the first time. She never ceased to surprise him. He had thought of children as heirs, as little things who must be raised properly. To finish them well so that, as adults, they might not embarrass one.

"You'll like our children, if you spend a little time with them, and not worry about whether or not they're dirty. For most children, being dirty is the sign of having a good day."

"How do you know so much about children?"

"Well, I am the eldest but one. We went off, all of us, young and old and had adventures. I remember being a child, it was almost yesterday."

"Yes, I forget sometimes, overwhelmed as I am by your extraordinary wisdom and maturity, how young you really are," he retorted sarcastically.

"It's true. I can only get younger as I have already reached maturity."

"I should like to know more about this childhood of yours. It sounds pleasant," he declared.

"I'll teach you to play this minute." She looked around as if someone might be watching and lifted her skirts and shook a leg at him.

"Just as long as we don't have to share the sandbox with other playmates," he raised an eyebrow. But of course, their little sandbox soon filled with the laughter of the Gardiners coming around a corner and Jane and Bingley advancing from a little fountain, arm in arm. Darcy turned and looked at Elizabeth as if they were alone in the carriage and he had just removed all her clothing. She practically could not breathe, and then he grinned at her and turned to greet their friends.

After many lovely intimacies in the carriage, of fondling and kissing and playing, discovering, and expanding their horizons together, and after following her menses for several months, Elizabeth arrived at the park with a pit in her stomach that was both excitement and nervousness. The reasons for restraint had become quite irrelevant and the desire churning in her body and mind had overwhelmed her. She had deliberated about her choice and had chosen. She weighed the force of the social contract which valued caution against the personal one which suggested that dancing freely and laughing and enjoying one's partner were the stuff of which life was made, its nourishment and joys.

She knocked on the carriage door, climbed in and sat opposite Darcy, and contemplated him sternly. She thought, in that moment, of Amanda who had been abandoned the minute she offered herself to her groom. But Elizabeth was convinced that Darcy was not a boy looking to con a woman just for the possibility of having some relief. Nor was his independence of mind constrained by the narrow puritan values of current society. They had some days ago agreed to refrain from having children immediately, and he had admitted to knowing how such a thing might be possible.

She lifted her skirt slightly to reveal her naked leg and, once she noted his change in countenance, from perplexed to expectant, she hitched it higher.

"I have left my undergarments at home, Mr. Darcy. I do hope you do not intend to discuss things like money and how to raise children for I am not interested in words at all today," she added.

"You are not yourself, Miss Bennet. Are you very well?" He grabbed her ankle and stroked her leg. She pushed him with her foot against the seatback and moved directly to his trouser buttons. "Once again, I understand why I was initially attracted to your impertinence, Miss Bennet. I certainly like the way it expresses itself today."

He leaned back, stroked her hair and face, and let her mouth fall into him. And when she saw that he was quite lost, she looked up at him with a charming smile and, climbing into his lap, her skirts bundled around her legs like a curtain, she let herself down slowly on top of him and perched at the very tip of him, her eyes open with incredible awe. He shook his head.

"Don't Lizzy, we'll be married in less than a fortnight."

"Don't," he said as she slowly moved around him.

"Don't," he said, throwing his head backwards as he felt her body's eagerness for him.

"Don't," he whispered as he drew her down and pushed further and further into her.

When the carriage came to a halt and they both sorted themselves, Darcy kissed her and asked if she was well.

"I have no legs with which to walk. I feel dizzy and strange. But I am well."

He kissed her lightly on the forehead and began to open the carriage door when he saw a look pass over her face. "What is it, darling?" He pulled the door closed again.

"I am suddenly worried that you will think less of me. I feel scared, a little, and it has just occurred to me that I will feel quite the hypocrite wearing a white wedding dress."

"I believe, Lizzy, that you are not the first, in that case. There are quite a number of hypocrites."

"Oh, you monster. That is of no help." He was trying to be funny but saw tears well in her eyes. Darcy would say, as many men have before and since, that he did not understand women.

"Please, tell me you love me," she begged. "That you do not disrespect me for what we have done today."

"I have told you every day for months. I am here. Always. My regard for you is entrenched and there is nothing to blame. We have done nothing I am ashamed of, my dear, nor should you be. You have given us a wonderful gift. You have shown me not only that you trust me, but that you also desire me. That you want me in your bed. Do you see? Do you know how many men complain of their wives, that they but tolerate their attentions and that it is more fun elsewhere? That is not a marriage for me, for I do not want to be that man. Go now. Go home. I will be there soon. We will pretend this did not happen."

Her eyebrows flew up. "Oh no. That I will not do!' She reached for the carriage door, and then stopped. "Oh dear! Jane will know. She will see right away that I have been unchaste with you. No, you must not come to lunch. I will blush all day."

"Apparently you did not deliberate overly long for it seems there are many consequences you have not considered."

"I thought only of pregnancy. It was the only consequence which worried me. But now, yes, it is true. There are others which seem to come racing in after the fact," and she started to cry. He pulled her into an embrace.

"Oh, Darcy, don't let me regret this. I rather enjoyed it."

"Then what is wrong?" he asked sincerely perplexed.

"I don't know. I feel strange, like I'm sad and happy and scared. Yes, scared. Not of something, but of everything. It sounds strange. I cannot say..."

"Hush, come here." He took her in his arms. He imagined that her reaction might have something to do with it being her first time engaging in sexual play, of receiving an orgasm from a man, of seeing a man's desire; but in the many years to come, he would be mystified by the many deep and intense ways she experienced love making.

When she seemed calm again, he soothed her. "Go Lizzy. In a few weeks we shall enjoy it more as we will have no more of these considerations about what so and so will think. In fact, I have an idea for our bridal tour. Will you permit me to surprise you?"

"And I'll not be able to answer when asked where I shall go? I shall have to say it is a surprise? Do I trust you? Is this a test?" she answered very scattered.

"No, no. Not at all. I could tell you, for I'm sure you'll be enchanted by the idea, but I believe you will be doubly enchanted if I surprise you."

For their last afternoon in the city, Kitty was begging to go to Vauxhall gardens while others insisted they visit St. Paul's Cathedral and Mrs. Bennet wanted to visit the London towers. Jane, referring to Kitty's second favourite novel, said But you don't wish to be like the Branghtons do you? They choose all sorts of gaudy places to go where one meets all the wrong people. But Kitty, looking up from her sausage said, Dear me, Jane, not you! Just because you will be marrying Mr. Bingley does not suggest you can get all hoity-toity. She threw a look at Bingley who was across the table from her. I must count on you and Lizzy for some of my entertainment. You must agree that the B- family know how to have a lot of fun. Besides, don't you think Evelina is quite a snob? Kitty put a helping of bread lavished with butter into her mouth and chewed in a rather satisfied manner.

"Well, no one has suggested it yet, but up on Drury Lane there is a little theater that, I am told, has a delightful puppet show," Bingley suggested, and Darcy agreed that he thought such a diversion would be excellent.

Elizabeth avoided Darcy, especially his eyes. She was hollow inside, as if a space had been extracted from her bones. Weak and strangely fragile, it was a wonder no one noticed that she had been corrupted that very morning. That she had been ruined. That she had compromised herself with the man she would soon marry. Not even Jane noticed that she was a changed woman.

MRS. BENNET'S SEX EDUCATION

As the Bennet girls had both time and money, Jane had become consumed by the activity of orchestrating their wedding. She had designed and sewn her own dress, but as soon as it was completed, she continued to dream of ways to enhance the event. Mrs. Bennet, who had been married in a quaint church with her family in attendance, dressed in a Sunday-best and holding a bouquet of flowers, was delighted by the prospect of a grand operatic-like production in which a choir was hired, flowers brought in from hothouses and the church decorated with garlands and ribbons.

Elizabeth agreed to most of the details as they were all quite enchanting, and although she herself would happily have married without all the magical touches and flourishes, neither did she object to a ceremony full of visual beauty. She had ordered a dress in a simple style, with a pretty neck of lace which elongated her high neck and strong jaw line. The lace flowed down her back to reveal, through it, her shoulder blades. The dress moved and flowed and did not need three little girls to carry its train and for this she was grateful. She refused the veil, and instead had Jane design a headdress styled of a pearled thread which wove in and out of her hair. Darcy had given her a delicate pearl bracelet which had belonged to his great grandmother and which he had presented her for her birthday. It was the only other embellishment she would wear.

Jane had envisioned this ostentatious wedding in the large town of W- near Meryton, with a little parade in a gilded carriage to transport them. Jane, who was usually modest and sensible, imagined such a grand event because of pressures from Mrs. Bennet and Caroline Bingley who wanted to make sure that they flaunt the grooms' wealth, and was subsequently carried away by her own creative imaginings. The other members of the wedding party, in other words Elizabeth, Darcy, Bingley, Mr. Bennet, and other interested people, agreed with all her plans because no one wanted to say no to Jane who was sincerely having a wonderful time imagining a wedding suitable for a queen. Fortunately, she saw reason and agreed that they should marry in their local church in Meryton with the minister who had baptized them, but with some of the flourishes she had originally conceived for the larger venue, only with fewer people in attendance. Mrs. Bennet thought it beneath their grooms to be found in such lowly confinement, for how would the neighbours know that her girls had married men of great distinction if they would not (at the very least) be married in a fine gothic church with a great organ and stained-glass windows?

"Such fine men of distinction marrying like a country squire..." she complained.

"No better than our father, really," Elizabeth refuted her, returning small clothes to her trunk.

"Well, your father is fine. But he is nothing to your Mr. Darcy."

"He is everything to Mr. Darcy, and Mr. Darcy has a great deal of respect for father. And he does not object to marrying in a country church. It is but you and Miss Bingley who are offended."

And thus, everything was decided and the day to leave London approached with the wedding day falling soon after their return to Meryton. On their last evening but one, Jane and Elizabeth were giggling and chatting and preparing for bed when Mrs. Bennet knocked and asked if she might speak to them both. Mrs. Bennet took the chair at the vanity, turning it towards the bed, and indicated that both girls should sit. Elizabeth could not read her face, for it was serious, but with a discomfort in the mouth and eyes, so that Elizabeth imagined that her mother might recently have sucked on a lemon, and she smiled and said, Dear mother, what terrible news do you have, and Mrs. Bennet dismissed the question with a flip of her hand, and Jane asked if her head was quite well, for you seem to have one of your headaches, and likewise received a dismissing hand wave. But nothing was immediately forthcoming. The girls, who had been bright and cheerful and animated, suddenly had to sit sedately in their shifts.

Finally, Mrs. Bennet indicated that she would speak by shaking her head and rolling her throat lightly as she exhaled noisily. "Procreation," she began. "I am here because I must talk to you about procreation."

Elizabeth pursed her lips and held them tight, dared not look at Jane, and tilted her head a little to show she was listening. Jane replied with a spontaneous and ill prepared "Oh, dear. Now?"

"My mother gave me this speech and so did her mother. It is traditional to provide this information on the eve of the wedding, but I admit to being entirely unnerved by this responsibility that I should like to relieve myself of it prematurely. It is but less than a week to your wedding and I see no reason to wait any longer finding myself encumbered by the strain of knowing I must have this conversation."

The girls nodded sagely. Expectant.

"You do understand that it is due to my terrible nerves?"

They nodded and commiserated with their mother, and granted her all rights to speak now if she must.

"And a wish to protect myself from this strain that I speak prematurely?"

Again, they nodded.

"And you will not consider this conversation in any way approbation for premature delivery of your goods to your gentlemen?"

Elizabeth had to stare at her fingers, hold her breath and count to ten to keep from laughing. Her stomach hurt and the laughter threatened to snort out her nose. She heard Jane say, Yes, Mama.

"Cleanliness is the most important thing," Mrs. Bennet stated. "You do understand which of your parts must be clean?" The chair sighed as she moved on it, shifting her body from side to side. "Also, your nails, your hair, and you may wash yourselves thoroughly before inviting your husband to your bed. It is not sufficient to cover yourselves in perfume in order to please your spouse. And of course, there is no question that when you are in your moon, you will refuse him. Please remember that formalities of behaviour are expected on all occasions but the most intimate: in your bed. You are not expected to join him in his bed. Nor are you to share intimate moments in any other room. Your room is the only place he may approach you, and you are entitled to a key to lock the door, but you are not entitled to use it except under the most dire circumstances. For instance, if you believe he is diseased." She paused. Frowned. "But I am not sure how one would ascertain whether or not one's husband has a disease. In any case, if you suspect it, or know it, please make sure that you protect yourself." She frowned again, re-orienting herself in her speech. "It is unwise to habitually sleep together as that will lead to undesirable engagements and too many pregnancies. You do understand that when one lies with one's husband one might gain children in the event? One must decide when one will be engaged and when one will not."

Mrs. Bennet was staring off at a spot beyond their heads, her eyes fixed on an imaginary audience crawling up the wall. She might wish for a fly to land and give her attention to it so as to deflect focus. "There are terrible things which can be passed from man to wife. Some will kill you." She spoke as if she had forgotten where she was in the speech. She paused, took a deep breath as if she had not breathed since entering the room. "Good. I have been as clear as possible and educated you to the best of my ability. And I would ask you to go to your husbands for the other particulars when that is appropriate. I will leave you now. Thank you for indulging me."

She stood and put a kiss on each of their foreheads. The girls did not move until their mother had completely descended the stairs and was well out of earshot. Elizabeth, imitating her mother's body posture, leaned into Jane. "There are terrible things which can be passed…"

"Some will kill you!" Jane giggled.

"Don't lose your key, Jane. Do not forget your lock!" Elizabeth chanted, all too aware that she had no such plans, that her bed would be Darcy's bed and that her lock was already tossed in the bin.

They both cried from laughing, while downstairs it is true that Mr. Bennett had to ask his wife what had gotten into the girls for they were exceptionally loud.

GOSSIP SORROWS

Miss Bingley arrived unannounced at Darcy's townhouse. It was bad form for an unmarried woman to visit an unmarried man alone, a thing she acknowledged immediately with the explanation that she wanted to give him an opportunity to hear her news secretly and in private.

"Indeed. That sounds serious. But you must sit," he motioned towards a chair. "I will send for tea and little sandwiches or such. You ladies like nibbles at this time of day, I believe."

"I am rather fatigued and a light refreshment would ease me, thank you."

"Or would you prefer a sherry to tea?"

"Yes, that would be exactly what I would like to have. I believe, with the news I bring, you might want to partake as well."

"Please, continue," he handed her the glass. She made sure to touch his hand, and to smile at him as if she were his greatest ally. He sat in the sofa opposite and crossed his legs comfortably. He had been engaged in writing a letter to his steward when he was interrupted and there was a list of instructions in his head he did not want to forget. He counted the items he must remember. Seven. Seven when he returned to his desk.

She sipped her sherry and leaned forward when she spoke her next words so that she tipped herself into him, revealing more of her bosom than he would want to inspect.

"I bring you this news for your own wellbeing."

"Then I shall thank you."

He concentrated on looking at her face.

"There are two distressing pieces of information that have been brought to my attention, both of which are – at this very moment – circulating in good society." Darcy nodded. He had done his best to avoid most good society rumours. "Well, you are aware that Miss Elizabeth leaves every morning to take a walk?" He nodded. "Jane has told me she is absent every morning and returns home quite flushed and buoyant. I believe those were her words," Caroline paused as if the matter should be clear. He smiled – yes, she would be flushed! "You smile, for you like the image of your darling fresh home from her walk. I remember you saying some such thing before. That it brightened her complexion."

"I did. I do," he answered. "My Miss Bennet has always habitually walked out, Miss Bingley. She is not content unless she has stretched her legs and freshened her senses. Those are *her* words, I believe, Miss Bingley."

"You know she and I did not get on famously from the outset. I found her simple and proud, two characteristics which do not suit one another at all. She has none of Jane's beauty, nor her sweetness. But we have reconciled since then and I have learned to see what you appreciate in her."

He wondered if she might broach the topic in the next century, but he remained polite and patient and said something bland and appropriate.

"The problem is that I will not be able to tolerate her in my company. She has a stain upon her. It is widely known that she climbs into a carriage and walks out with a gentleman." Darcy frowned. "It is true," Miss Bingley said. "It happens almost daily. I'm afraid to say, once again, that her head has been turned by my cousin. Who else?"

"Indeed. And who has been following Miss Bennet on her morning walks to establish that she is regularly boarding a carriage and to later return home... what was the word? Buoyant?"

Miss Bingley narrowed her eyes at Darcy and tossed her head to one side as if she were trying to hear something that was not in her usual frequency.

"I do not understand why you are not upset, Mr. Darcy. If you are not even married and she is already meeting with a gentleman, then surely you must rethink your intentions with her."

He spun the brandy in his glass and stared through it as if it might resolve itself into a quiet afternoon, writing his letters, anticipating his evening with his beloved Elizabeth. "Would you care to tell me how you acquired this information?"

"A reliable source, who had it from a most reliable source. Charles received it from Col. Fitzwilliam who said that your aunt said that it was well known in London society. Rumours are spreading already. Oh, please don't marry that wretched girl. She is beyond your help, Darcy. She is a foolish country girl caught in the limelight of your attention. She does not meet you as an equal."

"I do appreciate your kindness, Miss Bingley, but I am devoted to Miss Bennet. Quite completely devoted. I assure you; I will confront Miss Bennet about this situation," he paused, then decided that he might with one swift blow kill the gossip. "I will most directly assure myself that there is only one person she is meeting in a carriage."

It took Miss Bingley a few seconds to understand Darcy's meaning. She laughed, finally, uncomfortably. Darcy put his glass in the air.

"Touché." Miss Bingley replied with her own glass, but she did not smile as he did. "I suppose you do not care that your bride has acquired a reputation much like your own. That she is likely not even a virgin, Mr. Darcy?"

Although, to his knowledge, Caroline Bingley's information was correct as of yesterday, there was no reason she should know it. He had paid the cabby well for discretion.

"I see you are surprised now, Mr. Darcy. You think you know your bride but you do not. She refused to be inspected by a doctor and so it is almost certainly true. I am quite shocked that you proceed as if this has not changed everything."

He had a vague recollection of Elizabeth fleeing his aunt's interferences and was relieved that their intimacies of the previous day were not now the subject of London gossip.

"Miss Bingley, I think that if you were seized by a doctor who would inspect you, you would also refuse."

"Upon my honour… no one would think of treating me thus!"

Elizabeth stared at her face in the glass as she prepared for their last assembly before quitting London. She peered into her pupils and found, in them, a question. She is named Elizabeth Bennet, but it was not much more relevant to her essential being than a sign tied around her neck. She was daughter to such and such and sister to others, and friend to a few others, and she was engaged to Mr. This and will soon be Mrs. That, but none of these designations were what she saw in the glass. Invisible to the eye, but framed in the glass with indelible presence, were not just her parents, but their parents, and theirs, an ever-expanding proposition of people lined behind her, and she one more in the line containing a complex and profound potentiality of people coming through her in the future. Not merely her grandchildren, but theirs, as far down into the future as she could imagine into the past. A fraction of herself spilling in two directions, all real with their own particular identities, all siphoned in some mysterious way through her.

The glass was not sufficiently wide to hold all these and yet it contained them all in this one person. And the harder she looked into that glass, the more she found nothing but choice, or more precisely, a series of choices lined up along an arc of time. It was like seeing the second hand of an elegant clock, performing acts and containing them in a cabinet where their existence is fiction but not irrelevant. She lived in a stream of choices which arrived in succession and without pause. And this is what made her.

Deep within her pupils was a question posed at every second and an answer waiting. She formed herself from the answers she gave to the questions. All her ancestors, all her progeny, all her family and Darcy, they all acted on her somehow, but in the end, she must find a place in that, a place that wasn't confused, a way which provided protection and afforded her the same feeling she received when lying on the earth staring at the sky. A place in which she felt expanded and calm. She narrowed her eyes and saw nothing new in them. It was still just her. Not a virgin. But it was just still the same girl. And she smiled.

Kitty poked her head through the door and said, You had better go see Jane, and popped back out again. When she found Jane, Elizabeth had to cajole her to speak. Jane, as always, did not like to complain or speak badly of anyone.

"It is not right that I should find myself perpetually placed between you and Caroline. She goes on incessantly about how Mr. Darcy is quite mistaken in you, and then when I am with you, you at worst disparage her and at the least dismiss. She will be my sister, and she will be in my circle of daily acquaintance. She says I should not marry with you by my side, that it will corrupt my honour. What does she mean Lizzy?"

Elizabeth paled at the accusation and her temper flared a little. She did not want to answer Jane, nor say anything against Miss Bingley. Nor did she want to defend herself against such accusations. But mostly, she was horrified. It is one thing to pretend that one does not care what rumours are flying like ghosts around one's head;

it is quite another to ignore one's sister's admonitions.

"She says there is talk that you have been unfaithful to Darcy. That you enter into a liaison with another man in a carriage during your morning walks."

She considered telling Jane the truth about the rumour so that she might at least understand how it was forged, but she shrank from Jane's judgements.

"There is likewise talk that Darcy is unfaithful to me," she replied. "There is always talk, Jane. You hear it all the time. The only difference is that at home, in the village, we know who to believe. When Mrs. Gordimer sells you a loaf of bread and tells you that Mr. Littlebum's leg was chopped off, you know enough to believe that perhaps he was scratched by a rake. Here, we do not know who to believe. There, we have known them all our lives and can discriminate."

Jane responded by sobbing. "You're merely deflecting the problem, Lizzy, and it is frustrating."

"I have also heard it said that Bingley was once caught in the Thames swimming without any clothes on and that he was very drunk. I have also heard that Miss Bingley has intimate encounters with young men with barely any hair on their faces, that Lady Catherine killed her husband and that there are unicorns in Ireland. I believe none or all of it, Jane, according to who tells me the news and whether it fits with what I know. I do believe, for instance, that Bingley was caught swimming in the nude because Darcy told me and he was not only a witness but was also in the Thames."

Mrs. Bennet, drawn to excited voices like moth to the light, arrived with Kitty directly behind, smiling and shrugging as if to say, I tried to distract her.

"I will marry on another day if you prefer Jane. It was your request, in any case, that we should marry together. But I would be very upset if you do so on Miss Bingley's advisement. She has nothing positive to say about me, and never has had. She confuses sound opinion with criticism. The one requires intellect and discrimination, and the other merely a negativity which, I might add, is much simpler to devise. I too could spend my day berating everyone."

"You think so highly of yourself, Miss Lizzy, that you do not hear what your sister is telling you," Mrs. Bennet interrupted, apparently already having heard Jane's worries on an earlier occasion. "There are words flying about. Words against you. Have you not understood how they can be treacherous even when they are wrong?"

Jane nodded, drying her tears with the handkerchief that Kitty had fetched for her. "Yes, Lizzy. I do believe there is rumour that you are seeing another man behind Darcy's back and that he will break the engagement with you soon."

"That is ridiculous. Who? Will they produce this other man? I suppose they say it is Nathan." She could tell from their reaction that she was correct.

"Don't you see?" Jane pleaded. "It does not matter if he is real or not. It is only that they have created him which is enough to make a problem."

"But how does one change the rumour when one does not know who is perpetuating it. Is no one willing to step up and ask whether or not it is true?" was Elizabeth's reasoned response. "And what are we to do with Darcy's reputation, the one in which he seeks commerce with every woman? Are we to listen to every bit of information that is produced?"

"They arrive! They arrive!" Hill burst into the room, announcing Darcy and Bingley who were to escort them to the ball.

Darcy noticed that Elizabeth was unusually quiet in the carriage. Jane and Bingley, sitting opposite, were whispering and giggling as they often did. Elizabeth stared from the carriage as if the street held fascination. When he asked, she assured him that she was well enough, that she was merely tired from packing and was looking forward to being home again. "I have had enough of society, Darcy, of balls and visiting and of entertainment. Of five dresses a day, to be in morning dress, and walking dress, in gowns and street dress. To change a thousand times for each occasion. All this busyness is dizzying. I hardly know myself. Give me a simple cotton dress all day and a long walk where I shall meet not a single person but a farmer or a parson who will tip his hat and say, Morning Miss."

He kissed her forehead with a nod and held her hand. He remembered many occasions now of seeing her arrive from one of her solitary rambles, her simple cotton dress muddy, wrinkled, her bonnet upside down in her hand bearing berries, or flowers, or a stone or stick, her hair askew and her eyes shining with delight and joy. Her feet, in solid boots, wet. Even at the end of a two hour walk up and down the many fields and hills, she would be striding with long steps, agile and lithe on all terrains. He had seen her run up and down hills, step across streams with hardly a pause, refusing his hand. "When you are in Longbourn, you most often find yourself at the top of the Stemson farm, under its great hawthorn do you not?"

She laughed. "Yes, Oakham Hill, my hawthorn tree. I don't decide to go. I feel settled there, and so I often wander and it is there I seem to want to stop."

"All roads lead to Jerusalem..." he pointed out, squeezing her hand. "Pause now and think of that place. It might comfort you."

"Yes, my little tree church. My sacred apex."

Elizabeth's head was against his shoulder, but he did not feel that she was at peace. "I would wish to see you laughing again, and enjoying yourself, but if you wish to spend the evening on my arm, staying quiet, I would feel the privilege."

Elizabeth did not move, but when he looked down, he saw her eyes well with tears. He had never seen her as fragile and vulnerable, and he was overwhelmed by the tenderness he felt for her.

"We are here," Bingley announced, peering eagerly from the window. The carriage slowed and he jumped from it and lifted Jane out. Then poked his head back into the box. "We are here, Man. You are both too somber. Look lively," he ordered encouragingly.

"Aye, aye capitaine," Darcy saluted, but otherwise did not move.

"I suppose we had better get out and go be presentable," Elizabeth said, not moving, "for if we stay like this long, we will feed a rumour."

There was a little bitterness in her words that pained him. She leaned herself against him and he felt an overwhelming desire to take the solidity of his care and to pour it into her. "Ignore it, my sweet. I know it is not true. I know what Lady Catherine asked of you – the doctor – and I am so sorry for the way she has continued to interfere in our lives. I have not protected you from her."

She sobbed a little then, almost as if from relief. "Lizzy, I have been thinking of something I would like to ask of you. Perhaps it is a bad time?"

She turned and gave him a wan smile. He took it as assent.

"You have fallen into the habit of calling me Darcy, as if you were one of my male companions. And you use Fitzwilliam when you tease or scold. Have you noticed? Do you know what I was called as a child by my parents?"

She bent her face up to him slightly tossed to the side, as if letting an ear rest closer to his words, and her face relaxed, softened out of whatever preoccupation had kept it tight. Her lips likewise stretched out, opened a little, almost into a smile.

"Occasionally Georgiana calls me Will when we are alone, but mostly I am Fitz, which is reserved for her." He paused, laughing suddenly, reminded of their conversation about children's names in which he suggested Edward for the first, and she said I will not name a child who has not yet been born. Child One, in that case, he had acquiesced. Child Two. Child Three. Up until Child Fourteen, he had teased.

"My parents called me Will and I should like you also to call me Will."

She squeezed his arm but did not sit up. He stroked her hair a little, knowing that he must not mess it. "I like calling you Darcy," she answered. "I know it is what others call you, but that I have the privilege to speak to you as others do makes me feel good. Calling you Will... now that is strange, but I'll try, my dear. Perhaps," and now he could see that mischievous grin of hers as she leaned in to whisper. "Perhaps there will be occasions to cry out your name and call you to me with it."

He shook his head, smiling. "I have turned you into a vixen," he whispered back. "Where is my innocent young bride?" Her face darkened, and he knew suddenly what was bothering her. He took her in his arms and kissed her as she told him about Jane's misgivings. He held and rocked her and felt her sink into him. He handed her his hanky and she wiped her eyes and handed it back.

"I have a slight cold, if anyone should ask," she told him as he helped her down.

If either could foresee what would happen once they entered those halls, they neither of them would have attended the ball. They would have followed their inclination, hers to be quiet and his to comfort her.

CHASE AND RESCUE

The party was infectious. Elizabeth decided that the best way to face the rumours was to show herself at the height of happiness, to laugh and flirt and tease and to give strong opinions which would surprise the men and shock the women. She was in a discussion with Sir Reginald De Clare when Darcy came and stood by her side and joined in the conversation, giving information which helped prove her point. She leaned into him a little and thought she could enjoy any number of parties if he would only support her in this way. Sir Reginald eventually was called to dance, and Jane and Bingley with Miss Bingley joined them in surveying the event. Miss Bingley, attaching herself to Elizabeth, talked about the dress she had made for the wedding, pointing to colours and shapes of various other dresses so that Elizabeth might imagine it. Glad that they were engaged in suitably friendly conversation, Elizabeth listened attentively and asked appropriate questions. As Miss Bingley was describing a woman in the far corner who had a lace collar similar in style, she suddenly squealed and said, "There is someone I have not seen since I was a girl." She waved and beckoned the woman to her. "It is one of my dearest friend's sister. She married an Italian and has been away these many years."

As Miss Bingley introduced the woman to everyone in their circle, Elizabeth saw Darcy's face change. He bowed to her stiffly, and she nodded her head. Elizabeth, who was opposite Darcy, could see in his manner and face that something very remarkable had happened. He looked quite ill and, when she looked more closely, she saw that Lady Compardi had a power over him and seemed as though she had just made a purchase for which she was well pleased.

Outside, Darcy pulled his fingers through his hair and would scream at the sky if he thought it might change his life. Augusta. Here! Now! A widow. He did not know what he felt, but he remembered a promise he had made and saw how she insinuated it with every gesture and word. He knew her as well as he knew himself and was in no doubt that she had arrived on purpose without warning to present herself to him in front of Elizabeth. Although his promise was made many years ago, it was made in good faith and in all sincerity. And as much as he might regret it, might wish he could say to that young man (himself) that he was a fool to give so much to such a woman, it was long since done. The words were spoken and the promise made.

When he returned to the hall, Darcy looked for Elizabeth and found Miss Bingley.

"She is quite upset," Miss Bingley explained, "but I have no idea as to the reason. Augusta had her ear for a few minutes and then, poof, I saw Elizabeth run out."

He fled to speak to the doormen to ask them about her. Yes, they had opened the door for a lady dressed in such and such but twenty minutes ago. She had walked out the drive and out the gates without a shawl. South, one thought, she had turned left. I do remember thinking that she would be going in the wrong direction, sir, cause in a few miles there's naught but dodgy lanes and rowdy pubs. This house is protected by the park and then not far beyond it things start to turn.

As she walked, Elizabeth slowly began to feel more settled. It was as if the pace of her feet, the movement of her breathing, all contributed to giving her a sense of peace. The quiet of the evening, dusk going to dark, the men lighting the lamps along the way, the park in a bounty of low salmon sky, the streets tidy and full of pretty houses close against the roads so one might peek a little into the windows and see people there, beside a lamp, reading or talking. She heard laughter, and music and, once, people screaming. She saw children in a yard running, squealing, calling, counting. She saw a gentleman with a dog at his heels. Lovers strolling. The mere act of leaving the party gave her scope to remember all the other lives which are lived, all the other ways each one of us choose to make a world, and the pains and joys that come by accident or fate. And she, an anonymous woman strolling in a fine gown and silly shoes, was nothing in this mix.

She walked beyond the park and the fashionable houses, noticed the streets change, the houses become smaller, the industrial buildings and shops, and beyond these, narrow grimy lanes. She turned into these despite her fear, compelled by a sense that she might survive this grief if she could re-inhabit a new world, that being an entirely different person with new surroundings, family and friends, would excise Darcy from her chest.

The streets were busy and noisy. Crowded with people, vendors and pubs, people smoking, throwing dice, playing draughts and cards. Women loitering at corners, showing a little ankle to a man. Gentleman strolling, looking. Smoke coming from doorways, thick as a bad fire made with wet wood, some smelling of smouldering cook fires, others of something sweet and pungent, like a herb being burnt, which captivated her as she stood tasting it as it wafted under her nose.

"Going in?" the gentleman holding the door asked as she stood, staring in.

She had not heard of drug dens, did not know the value of opium or she might have entered at that moment to seek its escape, but she shook her head and continued down the lane. She walked decidedly on. Listened to the cacophony of street life. Smelled the dust, the grime, the body odours, all like an assault and all exciting. Except for the fact that everyone stared at her attire, which stood out as unsuitable, she was almost happy in her anonymity, as if she had broken free of something terrible by simply leaving it. From the moment Lady Compardi had told her of Darcy's promise and explained how important that he and she should be a family so that their daughter might grow in her rightful home with both her parents, Elizabeth knew that her life had changed, that there was no way she could marry Darcy under the circumstances. And the pain, the grief, the shock, were all somewhere back there, in that other life. She had left it and was never going back. She reached down and tore at her dress, but it did not give. Eventually, she found a man with a pocketknife and cut it to ankle length so that it would no longer drag behind her. She gave the excess cloth to a street woman who was delighted as it might make a wonderful, if small, shawl.

At first, Darcy was able to keep to Elizabeth's trail. A woman in a fine gown was noticed. And yet, he had met no one for some time who had seen her and he felt that the trail was cold and that he had taken a wrong turn. He wished, in that moment, he had some way of communicating with the people at the party, to determine whether she had returned, or to seek aid in finding her. He was quite upset with himself that he had not thought to take a few more minutes to at least ask Bingley to come with him. And now, also, he wished for The Dog. Despite not being a dog of impressive hunting abilities, too frightened by horses, The Dog was perfectly capable of tracking Elizabeth. Darcy, flagging down a carriage, wrote a note, handed it to the cabby and told him he'd be paid upon his successful return. After the cabby rushed off, Darcy stood on a corner feeling foolish in his formal attire. A horse, a riding crop, and a good coat was now wanted. And despite his anxiety and worry, he laughed thinking of Elizabeth's earlier statement about having to change dresses all day. The burden of privilege, his aunt was fond of saying, is that you must prove it continuously by wearing silly clothing.

The Dog arrived with a footman in the cabby and Darcy walked them back to the last place he had had positive confirmation of Elizabeth's presence, took out his handkerchief which had been bundled in a ball since Elizabeth had dried her tears, and he fed it to the dog's nose. The Dog shot down a narrow lane, one which Darcy could not imagine Elizabeth having chosen, and then further into a maze of winding paths. The smells were unbearable and the dark oppressive.

She was lost and the streets were so narrow that not a single carriage might pass. She had no money and no means to buy food from the taverns with delicious stew smells coming into the lane. She did not want to return in any case, but she was cold and hungry. She did not know what she might do. If one cannot return, but there is nothing presenting itself as a way forward, then one is stuck, and so she halted on a doorstep and sat. A man with a wide brimmed hat with a hole in it as if waiting for a feather, or some other decoration, asked if she might be aided, but his tobacco stained teeth and fingers, and the leering way he offered her a hand, convinced her not to accept. She refused him politely but firmly.

She looked about her and suddenly felt scared, as if she had climbed happily to a ledge on a cliff only to find that the way out was more difficult than she had at first thought, and neither up nor down seemed like possible routes. After some time, a woman approached, an older woman with a fine round face and friendly eyes and this woman, who had never before met her, handed her shawl over without a word, a clean smelling shawl of wool, not beautiful, but warm.

"My name is Mrs. Brown," the woman introduced herself as she sat beside Elizabeth on the stoop.

"Thank you." Elizabeth wrapped herself. "But won't you be cold?"

"When I get cold, I'll tell ye. Then we'll share."

The woman had fine strong hands, used to working. Nails cut short, fingers callused and brown. Her shoes were firm boots, the kind people wore in the fields at hay time, and her dress also was a good working skirt with pockets. She had a basket full of clothes and she explained that it was laundry she had taken in and was needing to wash that night. "I am on my way home now. My husband will be wanting somewhat to eat...He is in bed, these days, and will not get up. Not since he had an accident and canna make a living the old way. He's a man of the land, he is, and so I am also. We the two of us don't belong here, no more than you do," Mrs. Brown added.

"Well, thank you, but I must be going." Elizabeth stood. But as she handed the shawl back to Mrs. Brown, she felt dizzy and had to grab at the wall to keep from toppling. Mrs. Brown took her by the elbow and sat her down, wrapped her again in the shawl and handed her a bit of bread and cheese.

"Always carry a little nibbles wit' me." She nodded her encouragement. "Eat. 'Twill help."

Darcy was more and more astounded by the places The Dog took him. He was quite sure the hound was on a false trail despite his apparent excitement and conviction at each turn, wagging his tail, even occasionally barking. But soon The Dog was unnecessary. People had noticed Elizabeth. A woman wore a strip of Elizabeth's dress around her waist. A man pointed – she's sitting through there. Didn't want my help, he said. Then held out his hand to Darcy for change.

Darcy went left on Old Pye Street, into its smells, squalor, and festering poverty, and then into a passage the man pointed to, elegantly named George Court, but foul. Cobblestones muddled with mud supported a half dead oak at the centre of seven doorways all facing in at odd angles in various states of decay. Elizabeth had chosen the furthest to sit, a doorway wider than the others and with a small set of flagstones. She was leaning sidewise, with her back half turned to him, talking to a woman who was sitting similarly, facing

Elizabeth. They were laughing loudly. He turned to the footman and told him to go in search of a carriage. The old woman looked up.

"Do this be your man then, Lizzy?"

Elizabeth's face was sad and beautiful. Her hair disheveled and her hands perched on her knees delicately. Something passed in her face that he could not read, but he had an urge to cry. Not the weeping at sad news, but a raging howl.

"Yes, this darling worried man is he," she answered the woman without introducing them.

The Dog, who usually bound around a friend, went quietly up to Elizabeth and sat beside her, leaning into her slightly, proprietarily. Elizabeth put her arm around The Dog and leaned her head into his shoulders and Darcy was astonished at how weak she seemed.

"He do be a fine young man. Perhaps you are wrong about the situation?" the woman said as if he were not present.

"I know him well," Elizabeth replied. "His word means a great deal to him. I think the situation is intractable."

Mrs. Brown studied him as if he were someone she was inspecting for hire. She stood. "Do you deserve this one, sir?" she asked, but Elizabeth, without rising from the comfort of The Dog's affection, introduced him before he need speak. "Darcy, I quite forget myself. Mrs. Brown, this is Mr. Darcy. Mr. Darcy, this is Mrs. Brown."

As he bowed formally, he had the sudden sensation of being in a play in which some magic puppeteer was holding his strings, and he was dancing, bowing, walking, singing without any of his own agency. As if he was beside himself.

"Darcy, would you be so kind as to fetch food. Mrs. Brown gave me all she had and we are both quite hungry now."

"There is no food to fetch, except that you go into that pub nearby and eat," he said kindly. "But Lizzy, surely you do not wish that?"

"I do. I want food now."

"Then I will fetch food," he agreed, listening to himself, estranged and awed. He had never fetched food. Yet a lightness came to him, of opportunities in shadows underdeveloped, ready, waking. An engagement with possibilities. If it were not for his sorrow, he might be elated.

He went around the corner and returned with food. Stew in two bowls and spoons and two tea towels to use as napkins. He had never carried a plate in his life and as he walked across the square, he felt the pleasure in bringing them food. Mrs. Brown and Elizabeth ate on the stoop while Darcy watched. The angles of everything were wrong. The night poured into the square. The cold also. He could hear the bustle of nearby enterprises as if they were far away, through a fog. Diffused. The dead tree branch leaned in, like a hook, and the weird glow of candlelight coming through the windows sharpened angles. He did not move, just watched as if it was every day that he found himself in an alley in London talking to a Mrs. Brown.

Mrs. Brown winked at him. She winked. And she smiled, a wide loving smile. When she finished eating, she stood and gave him a big hug. She took him in her arms, all of him, and filled him with her flesh and her smell and the insistent softness of her. And she whispered in his ear, "There ain't no wrong turn, only wrong reasons for turning..." And she gave him a large wet kiss on his cheek and laughed at what she saw on his face.

"Excuse my impertinence Mr. Darcy, sir, but I think you needed that hug as much as she needed that stew. I be leaving now."

Elizabeth looked up from her bowl. "I am so tired now that I want nothing but to sleep. But please provide for Mrs. Brown. She has been such a dear."

He started to reach into his pouch, but Mrs. Brown shook her head as if it would be an insult to pay for the kindness she had bestowed, and he nodded, and thanked her.

"I've sent for a carriage, dearest, and we'll get you home."

"Darcy, I can't go home. I don't know where to go. Will you put me on a boat and send me away somewhere?"

The footman arrived saying he had a carriage no less than two minutes away, waiting on a wide street. "Come dear." Darcy reached for Elizabeth's hand and supported her as she walked leaning against him, an old lady, frail and bent and disoriented, and he worried that she would not recover from whatever it was that had sent her, haunted, into this place. "I will take you home. Tomorrow you can determine where you must go, for it will be clearer then."

"There, there, you get yerself home." Mrs. Brown took Elizabeth's other arm. "That's where you ought to be. 'Twill be alright, you'll see. If you love like that, all manner of troubles can be fixed. Me and my man, we been together forty-two years and even though we sometimes hates each other, we also go to bed ever' night content to be by each other's side. He's in a bad way now, missing his farm and the land, but we still be glad to be together. That's what you want eh? To be glad to be together ever' day."

Darcy asked Mrs. Brown if he might escort her somewhere by carriage, but she said she was but around the corner. "It was lovely to meet your Lizzy."

"And it was a pleasure meeting you," he replied, bowing his goodbye. They followed the footman to the carriage, Elizabeth stronger than he had supposed, but when he climbed into the carriage beside her, she sat sobbing. "It is terrible. They were turned out of their land. Because of the new enclosures. It has changed everything. Don't you see? You cannot do that to your people, Darcy. Promise me you won't."

It suddenly occurred to him that Elizabeth was wearing an old heavy wool shawl.

"Oh, it is Mrs. Brown's. Please, oh please, we can't take her shawl."

"Calm yourself. I'll go with it."

He stopped the carriage and ran back to the doorway where they had dined, chased into a few lanes to no avail. Mrs. Brown was gone. He asked, but no one had seen an older lady with a big laundry basket. Or more to the point, they had seen too many people who might have fit the description.

PEMBERLEY

PREPARATIONS FOR A WEDDING

Dear Reader, I know you are impatient to know how this story will end but allow me to digress for a moment to consider how best to formulate the happy-ever-after, for it is a tricky business and I would like you to know why. The standard fairy-tale romance ends in those moments at which the young girl, in peril for her life from a wicked stepmother, is kissed by the prince and recovers from her sleep, or her nightmarish cleaning duties. She finds herself betrothed to a saviour she does not know, and he to a beauty with a character that is not necessarily reflected in her features.

When the prince seeks Cinderella, the shoe size as a guide, he must stroke and smell a hundred feet and ankles in the quest. Could this be a euphemism for the many women a man must explore to be educated to the needs of a wife, and to attain the happy-ever-after which is required to our romantic ideals? Or is it the ideal of a love spawned in an evening in which the very specificity of a body part, in this case a foot, is the key to attaining the desired ending?

This story, which accompanies Darcy and Elizabeth past the moment of betrothal to their wedding night, ends successfully. We know this not merely because it is Darcy and Elizabeth, characters who have inhabited our imaginations for some years and through several mediums, but also because this is a romance which, by definition, will end happily. There are many hazards which can be put in the way of a happy ending, but not many in which the prince stays a prince and the princess a princess, in which our lovers are seen by all as admirable, and whose marriage is enviable. We wish, with this story, to maintain the fiction of the fairy story, that these two are lovers of a high order, that their love is true. The fantasy of the Cinderella ending is perpetuated in most romances by the fact that it ends, but in the backs of our minds, as we live a little longer, and by the time we are fifteen and understand the world a little better, we must be prepared to realize that the ideal is only sometimes true.

Our princess is now on Jane's bed watching Kitty arrange Jane's hair, playing with different styles for the wedding. Elizabeth is determined not to marry the man of her dreams because she understands him all too well. She understands that his honour and pride will not allow him to revoke a promise without dire consequences of loss of face and sense of honour. That she knows him so well is the reason he is her true love and that this prevents her from marrying him has a special irony that is all too clear.

"I hate to see you so sad, Lizzy," Jane sympathized, looking at her sister through the glass. "I cannot think that I will be married soon and that you will not be by my side. I will delay the wedding. I will. I cannot be happy when your grief is so heavy on my heart."

"Don't do that Jane!" Kitty scolded.

"No: you shall get married," Elizabeth answered. "For me. I can't pretend to be happy, but I am happy for you, Jane. I'm happy that you are with a lovely man who you adore. And I'll do my best to lift my spirits. I will. Say nothing else about it. Can you imagine how my pain would increase if I thought I was the cause for your not marrying?"

Meanwhile, Darcy was stunned. Shocked.

"Mr. Darcy! I did not expect you. Were you not intended for Netherfield and your wedding?" his housekeeper and once governess, Mrs. Reynolds, asked as he arrived at Pemberley.

"I had no time for a note." He stormed past her, striding through the main hall. "Where is Sherwood?"

Mrs. Reynolds trotted after him. "He is, I believe, downstairs polishing silver with Mr. Holmes."

"Lord, will he not give that up? Tell him to come. Please."

He strode into his study. Elizabeth's letter to him burned in his chest pocket. He sat to write two letters. His face was caked in the dust of travel and his horse was exhausted from too much riding. His boots were dripping mud. His hair fell into his eyes. His hand trembled as he picked up the pen. The paper shifted beneath his tired eyes, fell in and out of focus, shimmering because of both his exhaustion and emotion.

Fitzwilliam Darcy to Miss Elizabeth Bennet, Longbourn, April 1813
Lizzy,

Sherwood arrived before he could pen any more words.

"I am slow."

"And greetings to ye, too."

"Go back to your polishing."

He did not look up to see Sherwood wince.

"Are we a little grumpy?" Sherwood mumbled as he turned to leave noisily. Darcy had for several days of hard riding failed to compose any words in reply to Elizabeth's letter. Only one refrain had repeated itself and it was the one he put to paper.

I do not accept your breaking of our engagement. I will marry you.

D.

He picked it up and stared at it. He thought he should add more words, little bits of love or explanation or arguments to convince them both that his first sentence was true. But he did not since all were empty promises, placating excuses and to her point, that he was promised elsewhere, insufficient to repeal the facts. He folded the letter and sealed it into an envelope, then dipped the pen again in ink with a fresh sheet before him. This letter would be easier.

Fitzwilliam Darcy to Mr. Charles Bingley, Netherfield Hall, April 1813

Dear Bingley,
Charles. I wish I could avoid the circumstances in which I find myself unable to be at your, at our, wedding. I will not here explain anything since Jane, through Elizabeth, will have provided amply. Please accept my deepest regrets and my most sincere wishes for your happiness.
D.

Re-reading this letter, he had the same urge to add more words. A good friend should have some words of encouragement. "Well done chap" sort of words. Best man words. Pat on the shoulder, "you'll do fine on the first night" sort of words. And perhaps even, "don't worry about me, old chap, I'll be fine", sort of words. But these, too, did not come. He called for Sherwood, yelling loudly without moving.

Sherwood, rather quietly, said "Yes sir. I am here." Darcy looked through the big doorway to see Sherwood seated in a large wingback in the entrance hall reading one of the rags which seemed to thrive on obituaries. Sherwood dropped the paper and looked squarely at Darcy who could see that the man would not budge. He got up from his desk. He looked down on his dear uncle and noticed suddenly how small the man seemed to have become. He hadn't noticed it, but suddenly Sherwood seemed old and frail. He wondered when that had happened, when the vulnerability of age had begun to enter his uncle's bearing.

"Please deliver this letter for me. Would you run it down to the village. It will not wait for tomorrow's delivery, and I trust no one to take it but you."

Sherwood stood and bowed with mock servitude. "As you wish. But please note, *sir*," he said facetiously, "I'll protect ye from havin' to interact with anyone but meself only if ye agree to go rest. I've seen corpses look more alive than ye."

"Please leave me," Darcy asked quietly. "And thank you."

Back at his desk, he put the letter destined for Elizabeth in his vest pocket beside the one he had received from her a few days earlier, the one in which she broke their engagement. Mrs. Reynolds entered with a maid who carried a jug of warm water and a washing bowl. He waved it away, but Mrs. Reynolds ignored him. "I am sorry for your sorrows. But remember to take pains for the little things, for even when something terrible arises and disturbs one's peace, those little things are fodder for our lives, the way we keep going. The care we give ourselves by taking nourishment and washing our hands is the care that is the bottom of it all."

When she left, he cupped the water and put his face into it and focused on the water on his skin, the way – despite his terrible agitation and pain - his skin enjoyed the water's gentle caress. He focused on that one feeling, letting it sooth. And then, when he brought the towel up to dry hands and face, found that the truth of his future life, the unhappiness that crouched before him like a beast in a jungle, would not be relieved with a bowl of water or soup, mead, or a thick slice of bread. Although his room was as comfortable as ever, he did not sleep. He feared that he would never sleep again. On the morrow, he would wake and for the rest of his life he would bury himself in Pemberley and live alone. He would make a life dependent on no one. And he would force himself to be content.

Elizabeth cried a great deal. She went for walks, forced herself to eat, slept fitfully, listened absently while Mary read to her, and whether or not there were tears to show for it, she ached all the time.

Three days since his arrival at Pemberley and not a word from Lizzy, though he did not expect one. Instead, one from Augusta. Later that evening, while using billiards as a kind of distracting salve, Darcy handed Augusta's letter to Sherwood.

Lady Augusta Compardi to Fitzwilliam Darcy, Pemberley, April 1813

My dearest Will,
I am yours still. You know that I have always been yours.
I am sorry I did not write. I wanted to see you, to tell you myself that I am free, that my life, fortunes, duties are all discharged and that I care not at all now whether or not you have aristocratic title. I have done my family duty. I have been married at the age of twenty to an aged man who treated me fairly. But you and I were children in love. We have been betrothed since then. We are adults now and can make our own lives.
I have seen our daughter. Yes, she resembles your mother a great deal. I told her that I was her mama. I told her that she is a great lady and that she stands to inherit a good living. She will come live with me when I have found a place to settle.
I had only just arrived in London when we met, you and I, and it had not occurred to me that your life had moved on. I believed your promise to wait. I believed you would be happy to see me. I believed that you, as did I, pined for what we should have been to each other all this time.
I understand and forgive you. That you despaired that we should ever be reunited and that you might propose to another woman. I do believe that it was fate interfering before you married, fate that prevented us from being separated again. You know how that would have broken my heart, again and again.
Dearest: we are free. It is not too late. And you may comfort yourself, for she will find a suitable man easily, especially since you have given her your blessing, and introduced her to fine people and finer ways of living.
Oh, dearest Will! Can we not speak of these things together? You have

disappeared from London so suddenly that I must put all these words to paper. I know this must be terrible for you, to feel how you must hurt her at the cusp of your wedding.

Please, do not stay long from London. We must talk about our future, about our daughter's future.

> *I know that you are a man of your word,*
> *Yours with love,*
> *Augusta*

Sherwood sat and read the letter while Darcy chased a few more balls around the table, sinking none.

"You lived through that terrible period of my life, and you remember how angry my family was when they learned of Augusta and my tryst. How despondent I was that Augusta was taken away. You know how much I wanted to do the right thing and marry her. You are the only person who gave me sage advice. But tell me? Do you believe what she says in this letter? My first instinct is that she planned an ambush."

"Hmm. And ye believe yerself bound to marry her? On account of that promise…? And what of your Elizabeth? Do ye not 'ave a duty to 'er which is more legitimate?"

"Miss Bennet has relieved me of that duty. She believes that I am required to honour my daughter by marrying Augusta and she has broken our engagement." Darcy slammed the cue ball into the pink, and it bounded off the band and caught a corner pocket. "I will not marry. I will marry no one. You and I will live here together and play backgammon."

"Aye. T'is one solution. But 'am afeared that ye'll outlive me by a number o' years - and then who shall you kiss?"

Darcy smiled and leaned over to give Sherwood a dry peck on the cheek.

"My esteem of Miss Bennet grows," Sherwood added. "She is a remarkable woman."

"Do you think Miss Bennet hates me because I was betrothed?"

"You've been betrothed to a married woman, Darcy. T'is not a betrothal! I care not a whit about a promise made when ye were but a lad. Pah! This is foolishness."

"But I gave my word, and I broke my word. Elizabeth is so disappointed in me that she now refuses me."

"T'were those her words, exact? I t'ink she knows ye better than you know yerself. And she has good courage and integrity, she does."

"Damn her integrity."

But Sherwood's words woke him in the middle of the night. He imagined marrying Elizabeth, a beautiful church wedding, with Elizabeth's beaming face and Augusta scowling, glaring while he spoke the words "I do" to both. And he thought about his daughter who he might protect if he did indeed join Augusta.

Mr. Bennet asked Elizabeth into his library and told her that Mrs. Bennet had charged him with going to Pemberley and to make Darcy come back to Longbourn so they might talk. She knew what it cost her father to propose such an outrageous act, for he disliked confrontations as much as he disliked travel. She shook her head and told him he didn't understand. He asked her to explain it and Elizabeth did her best to describe the situation.

"And what of it?" he replied. "You knew that he has a daughter. That there should be a mother did not occur to you?"

"Well, I did, yes. Of course. But he told me explicitly that she was married and in Italy. That she was married. You see. It is not so."

"Not so?"

"Her husband is dead, father, and she is now available. He must marry her now. And care for his daughter properly. It is the right thing to do, don't you see? And he still loves her. It is obvious to me."

"And did he agree that he must marry her."

"I believe he did. I believe he agrees with me."

"He said as much."

"Well, father, it has been a week and not a word from him. Is that not sufficient confirmation?"

"There is a wedding in a few days and you will not be marrying?"

"I don't think so, father. I ended the engagement."

Mrs. Charlotte Collins to Miss Elizabeth Bennet, Longbourn, April 1813

Dearest Eliza,

I am sorry to write to you at such a terrible time, Lizzy, when you must be pre-occupied with your own sadness. It is about a matter that very nearly does not relate to you in any way, but I am beside myself as to what can be done!

Yes, I am fine, so it is not about me nor Mr. Collins. No, it is about Miss Anne who is lately returned from London. A doctor, who currently lives at Rosings and fills our heads with such nonsense about female diseases (the way he speaks, we are all diseased in every one of our female body parts)... He confines Miss de Bourgh in a room and she is almost always in paroxysms of despair. I believe she is tied, for I have inquired at the back door where the servants come and go and asked directly of them, for there were terrible rumours and I felt I must learn something of the truth to dispel them and I find that the truth is worse than the rumours. (It sounds quite risqué, does it not, me six months with child, an espionage?) I have a little of your gumption after all. They tell me — oh it is too terrible — that the doctor's cure for Miss Anne is to abuse her every day three times daily. It is true: he relieves himself on her as treatment! Who has heard of such a thing!!!! And does Lady Catherine know?! Please, tell Mr. Darcy. I could not write him myself in case he was also involved in this nastiness — you will know. Oh please, something must be done!

I do hope that you are slowly recovering from the pain as regards your difficult relations with Mr. Darcy. As I have said in previous letters, I would come to see you, to walk and keep you preoccupied if I could, I would, so believe me to be there with you, Lizzy, with this letter and these words of care.

Yours with love,
Charlotte

"You must send it on to Darcy, Elizabeth," Mr. Bennet told her after reading the letter. "There is no reason Charlotte should have sent this to you. What can you do?"

Tired and wanting only his bed, his mornings in the breakfast room, the familiarity of Pemberley and the comfort of his home, Darcy rushed back to Kent to save Anne from his Aunt Catherine's misguided attempts to make her a different person.

"I'll come with ye."

"It is unnecessary Sherwood."

"But I will come."

Before Darcy left, he sent a letter to Augusta arranging a meeting in London as he passed through. He did not arrange a meeting with Elizabeth and would not send his measly letter, yet he still had no words to add.

Nathan returned to Netherfield to be best man at Jane and Bingley's wedding. He sent Elizabeth a short note of commiseration about her own thwarted plans and asked if he might walk with her. One morning, before the dew had completely dried from the short grass, they climbed the hill to her favourite tree, and all about them the light glistened, and their footsteps made dark pathways where they lifted the wet with their boots, like forming trails in sand or snow. The sky was hazy and lifting slowly and the morning was full of birdsong and the unmistakable calls of males making promises to attract a mate.

As they climbed, Nathan was strangely silent. When they reached the hawthorn tree and stood looking out across the valley, past the little farms to the pretty river which wound its way between round hills and the open rough patches of pasture, he announced in a strangely formal voice that he had something serious to ask her, and when she turned to look at him, he dropped to his knee and proposed marriage.

THE PRINCES

Darcy was back in London in a foul mood waiting for Augusta. She had let a suite at the newly opened Mivart's Hotel. Hotels were a new concept he was sure would fail for he could not understand why anyone with money would choose to deprive themselves of their own servants to eat with a group of strangers and share public lobbies. To not find oneself at home. Although, he had to admit the lobby was tastefully decorated and designed with many coves of sofas and chairs from which little islands of furnishings provided independent if not intimate space. Of Augusta's suite, he knew nothing, but he was convinced she would use the hotel's novelty as a conversation starter. Yes, it is the latest thing, she would say. It just opened, and there are boys who carry things as a footman would, and other amenities without the responsibility of hiring anyone. I may not find a house at all! Who needs servants when one has a hotel suite?

He smiled. All the tones of her voice were firmly established in his mind. He watched her arrive, the poise and grace of her walk as she crossed the room, ignoring the men as they stared, her smile only for him. She walked into his arms and kissed his neck.

"Sit, please. I am so sorry about your father. I just heard. Miss Bingley has not kept me as well informed as I had hoped. She tells me who is in Bath for the season, or who has fired their housekeeper, but does not tell me when an important member of society dies."

"It has been a few years now, but I miss him still. Thank you."

She sat in a large divan, and he took a chair opposite her.

"When I saw you the other night, I thought how unchanged you are. Since you were sixteen! A few pounds heavier, but that same proud bearing and straight figure. Your hair thins not at all. And your face keeps that stiff ostentation which I always admired. You should have been born to higher people, Will, for you have a way about you that reminds one of a king."

"And you also are more queenly than ever. I once loved that you called me Prince, but we have both of us lived many years since then. As you say in your letter, we were children."

"Ah yes, all the years. But we remain the same essentially, don't we? There is only so much change that is possible. A piece of stone can become a work of art, but it will not become animate despite having fingers or toes and every vein reproduced."

"The analogy misses the mark."

"No, it hits so close that you refuse it. You cannot possibly think that marrying a young girl, daughter of a country squire with no property and no education should be a wise choice for you. I know you; she would soon run out of things to inspire your mind, her lack of taste and breeding would reveal itself with time, her prettiness would fade. She is, I must admit, a handsome girl. Lively in a fresh way. But she is no beauty, Darcy. Not a woman other men will admire. You want, on your arm, a woman who makes men think, immediately: there is a man to respect. His wife is impressive, and so too must he be."

"It is true that Miss Bennet would not give me that kind of stature when we walk into a great hall. In fact, you are correct in thinking that there are those in society who would ask why a man of my distinction should want to be attached to such a woman. Once, long ago, however, I remember you saying to your parents most vehemently that you did not care that I was not a viscount, that your love was sufficient."

"Touché, but I can't imagine you believe the two situations compare."

"Of course they compare. They compare exactly."

"Oh, then you suppose yourself to be in love." Her voice was surprised, but when she continued to speak, it was modulated. "You do! Of course you do, for otherwise you would not marry such a girl when so many are at your doorstep."

"You use that word as if I might be inspecting a mare for purchase. Is that what you have become, Augusta? Do you believe now that we are all of us just pawns to be bought and sold on a marriage market to keep the ranks strong and the blood pure?"

"No, of course not." She scowled a little at him. "This is not how I imagined our reunion. I am hurt, Fitzwilliam. Thoughts about you kept me alive these years. That is the truth. I lived to see you again, otherwise, without it, I should not have survived."

He sat in front of her, finally, and took both her hands. "I am truly glad that you are well. And that you are home and ready to make a life for yourself. But I cannot marry you. I do not love you."

"Because you marry that child. She knows nothing about how people like us live. And you will hate her within a year."

"No, I will not marry her. She has broken the engagement."

"She has broken with you? Oh, that is rich. A poor little country girl, and she has the gall to break her engagement with you. Well, that is obvious then. You are free. Why will you not make me happy? Why will you not welcome me and our daughter – our daughter, Fitzwilliam, who we made with love? It is unacceptable."

He found no words to refute her. His care for Lettice Rose and his promise to her mother both occupied him. It seemed only right that he should mend that mistake. But he could not will himself to say yes.

"Oh, your heart would mend. You would remember who we are Will, how we loved."

Hearing her use "Will" was painful. He wanted to hear it from Elizabeth, to hear her whispering it in his ear, tenderly, her lips tucking into his earlobes gently. In Augusta's mouth, it sounded blemished, even cursed. The tenderness grated against him. She handed him a well aged note, bent into itself on several creases revealing only a date and a "Dear", the rest of its contents still hidden in its folds. He did not open it but laid it to rest on the table at his side.

He was silent. He remembered vividly how much he had loved this woman. He would have become a pauper for her, to fly in the face of both sets of parents and elope to Scotland. To give up his inheritance and to work for a living. He had yelled at his father, I am capable of working. His father had replied caustically, You are sixteen. You know nothing of labour. You know nothing of life. Darcy was furious. To what do you object? She is of superior wealth and birth, and excellent in all ways that you would want. Why disinherit me? I have no objection to her, Will, but her father is my dearest friend and I owe him my life. He asked, and I agreed, to make it difficult for you to elope. So, you see: it is no use. I agreed to make it hard for you. Traitor, Darcy had yelled. You betray your only son to appease a "friend" who uses you to do his bidding and returns nothing in its stead. But in time he had understood. In time, he had accepted his father's decision with an unspoken reconciliation in which both men ignored the past.

"Read it," Augusta commanded.

"I do remember how I loved you," he replied not looking at the note. "I remember it all. But I have not come to discuss our wedding plans. I would like to speak with you about our daughter."

"They are one and the same issue. It is time we take care of her. Have you seen her?"

He nodded. "Occasionally during the past year. Before that, I did not know where she was."

"She is beautiful. She stands out among that brood, and she will not last long in that little village, hidden away, a princess among common folk. She is thirteen now and is sprouting. It is time she learns to sit, to walk, to stand like a lady. To hold herself and to speak properly. A few more years will be too late."

"I do not think she should be taken from there. It is her home. She is happy there."

"How can she be happy? They do not even have a water closet in that cottage. I will never forgive my parents for putting her in a situation so below her class. Abominable."

"He seems a good man. It is a happy family. Did you see how they are with one another, how they play, how the parents love all their children equally, how they take care to spend time and to be with them? Have you watched it?"

"You have become sentimental. What does it matter that they love their children equally? What did you know of your parents growing up? Nothing."

"I beg you to leave her there. That is why I have come. To ask that of you."

She refused, as he expected her to. He stood and handed her back the letter.

"It seems unfair of you to hold me to this childhood tryst. Many years ago, you also made a promise to me, which you also broke. You came north with me and disappeared the moment I revealed that I would be disinherited if we married." Augusta paled. Her mouth tightened and her eyes narrowed. "I have no wish to play a game in which we blame one another, Augusta. It is long over and you made your choice…"

"I was removed from you against my will…"

Darcy shrugged. He knew from his father that this was not entirely true. He let her words sit in the air, suspended between them and losing power in the silence. He smiled and shook his head sadly, a gesture not intended to mock entirely, but to indicate his refusal to bite, to play the game, to fight. She began speaking again, reiterating and pleading, arguing her point for several more minutes and he listened. He gave her all his attention. When she leaned forward into him saying, "You must see!" with an insistence that there was but one point of view, he smiled tenderly. He could see very well now. She had no hold over him and he wondered how he could have been led so easily by her in the past. There was no appeal in marrying her except the one of helping Lettice Rose and keeping his promise.

"I find it hard to believe you would want to be with a man who is no longer in love with you. You have lived that once already. Do you really want to do it again?"

The truth of his sentiments caught her unawares, but she recovered quickly. "I will wait, because I do love you, Will. I love you terribly. If you remember, we made that pledge again and again since we were children."

He nodded. She stood and put her hand against his cheek, tenderly. She looked directly into his eyes. "It is true. Every minute I spent with him was a minute I longed for you. Why do you not return these affections? How can you have forgotten?"

He took her hand and held it away from his face. "I have changed. I don't think I want the same things as I did even six months ago. I recently carried plates through the street, like a servant, and bowed low to a Mrs. Brown, a washer woman." He looked up to her. "I don't know who I am. And I don't think I want to be that person you love. Within a year, you would resent me. I will marry you if you insist. I will. But not soon and not until you understand that if you do insist, I will want to live my entire life at Pemberley with no other society. I will sell the house in London. I will refuse visits. The only people I would welcome would be family and Bingley. If you will marry me under those conditions, then I will honour my promise."

"You can't be serious."

"You're right. I do love you, dearly. You know me better than anyone, or rather, you know the person I was until a year ago. Perhaps the one you know is underneath it all and I'm still the same prince as I ever was. The only thing that may have changed is that I don't want it. Simple. I just don't want to be the prince anymore."

As there were often tears at a wedding, Elizabeth hoped that hers would not be out of place. She cried because it was a beautiful wedding, elegant yet simple and Jane was full of loveliness and poise and Bingley shone with delight. Elizabeth cried at times because the beauty was not hers to have, and she could not help but feel sorry for herself. And at times she cried because the wedding moved her. But whether for one or the other reason, her eyes were not dry.

While the vows were being spoken, she imagined that Darcy would come riding in on his grey, arrest the proceedings by smashing the church doors open. The Dog would run ahead of his master, wagging and elated, and Darcy would arrive with a great deal more dignity than The Dog and say, I will marry you. But of course, no such thing happened, and glad she was that Jane's wedding was not disrupted with such nonsense. She smiled through tears and gave hugs and found Mary's elbow as often as Nathan's and her father's, for they all three supported her gently. And then Jane rode away to her bridal tour to visit family who had not attended the ceremony and then to Europe wherever war had not ravaged the art. And it was over, except for her mother's nattering about how disappointed she was in a daughter who could not keep a good man.

Nathan agreed to wait for Elizabeth's answer. She kept his proposal entirely to herself. He stood by her side, whispered funny things in her ear, entertained her, and provided tidy handkerchiefs from multiple pockets. With a smile and a flourish, he would draw another and brandish it with a bow so that as she cried, she also smiled, or laughed. Despite his unexpected proposal, things were not awkward between them. The fact that she had not answered him did not seem to bother him. "I am leaving for India in five weeks. If you are coming, then that is the deadline."

He told her that some months earlier (when the family was away in London) he had proposed to Mary, for he had fallen deeply in love with her. Her mind, her wisdom, he said wistfully. Her refusal had given him deep sorrow, but she had been very forthright in explaining herself. That she would never marry.

"I thought I might distract myself elsewhere," he explained to Elizabeth. "But being a pretty boy to a sad mistress has no charm. We *are* friends, Elizabeth. We could be good mates to one another.

We would have a good life, I believe. Perhaps respect and fun are more important than passion, which is all about heartbreak anyway." His proposal was full of such words. Words which come from decency and care and thoughtfulness, but also carried resignation and resolution. "I have missed you these months. But not the way I should, I know. Not the way I have missed your sister. But come with me. To hell with love. I love you. You know I do. And you love me. Many marriages are built on much less. And maybe a night or two will cure some of that," he laughed that deep roaring laugh which she found so infectious.

She blushed and laughed and pushed him away from her. "You are so rude..."

"I'm just being honest, Liz. You know we could have fun. I'm not half bad looking, at least..."

"You're positively Grecian. Blue eyes, blond hair. Chiseled muscular gorgeousness."

"Well, that may be so, but I think I am too pretty. Too many women think I am easy because I smile at them. You are the only woman (except for Mary, of course) who didn't see me as a pretty boy, and didn't flirt, and didn't blush and didn't get stupid around me because my good looks intimidate them. So, dearest, lovely, smart, wicked Lizzy? Are you going to come with me?"

"It is tempting," she answered.

"Yes. That is startlingly romantic."

"It makes sense to me now. I can't stay here, and to run away with you would be such fun. Does it make sense to *think* ourselves into a marriage?"

"Better than to be assigned one!"

She laughed again. "Oh, how can I be serious? You haven't a serious thought in your head, ever."

"I do, I do. I asked you to marry me very seriously. You know I did. I'll do it again, if that will help."

He dropped to a knee again, but when she did not stop laughing, he dropped to both knees and crawled along after her as she backed away, laughing.

"Stop my princess," he called to her with mock drama. "I am trying to propose to you! Stop! Lady: my knees will be green if you refuse me thus!"

Elizabeth was laughing so hard that she charged into the woods to relieve herself.

Darcy left Augusta and continued immediately to Rosings Park to solve the second of his two great problems. When he arrived, he took the stairs by twos and rushed past the nurse who was like a sentry at Anne's door. He found her room empty of everything but a bed to which Anne's wrists were bound. She was practically unconscious and, after sniffing at the glass beside her, he determined that she was opiated, probably with laudanum. He unbound her wrists, wrapped her in her bed clothes and carried her out. Sherwood, who had insisted on joining him, went up to ask a maid to pack Anne's bag. Lady Catherine, alerted to the disturbance, hobbled out of the throne room and yelled down to him "If you take her like that, Fitzwilliam, then you must marry her, for she is not good for anything else." He did not look up. His rage was so out of control that he was afraid what he might do. Sherwood climbed into the carriage to deliver news that Anne spends all her time in wanting to end her life.

Once on their way from Rosings Park, perhaps for the last time, Sherwood said, "I might 'ave done summat a little inappropriate. I went into your chambers to look for those cufflinks ye lost. Thought I might as well, and 'ere they be." Sherwood shrugged, producing them. "Collins and another man was in t' library. They… well… they got righteous about us taking Anne. I got my fists hot, a little, on t' doctor's face ... I thought ye might want to know."

"How old are you, Sherwood?"

"Must be seventy-three by now."

"Going on seven?"

"Saved ye from 'aving to do the dirty deed."

"I suppose I should thank you then."

"So? You'll be marrying Miss Anne after all?"

Darcy laughed. And then he laughed more. And his laughing seemed infectious. But it was the raw laughter of a bitter man.

He did not leave Anne's side for two weeks. He trusted almost no one else. In that time, he thought a great deal. He thought about how he had changed in the past two years, how much he had learned about how he wanted to live his life, and more importantly, about how he did not want to live his life. He was glad that he had not married young before he had learned what wealth had hidden from him and what his priorities must be. He was grateful for the opportunity to choose wisely. And as he sat with Anne, as he talked with her, and reassured her, and comforted her, and listened to her, and felt fear for her, with his family around them, with Pemberley and his land and all that he loved surrounding him, he knew that he had spoken the truth to Augusta. That he could eventually be happy to live a simple life at Pemberley, just as he had described to her.

ELIZABETH AGREES TO BE MARRIED

It is possible to recover from loss and grief. Initially, when we are shocked by a tragedy, a calamity of great proportion, or even the apparently minor death of one's horse, the pain is overwhelming, and its weight convinces us that we may never rise out of its excruciating darkness. Our intellect will tell us, along with people who wish us well and seek to alleviate the sorrow, that it will pass, that time heals. Mary, who was overly fond of such aphorisms said it quite too often. At least, Lizzy, she said, you found love. Knew what it is to be loved, and to love in return. There is a great deal of solace in this, is there not? But Elizabeth knew that there was no denying the fact that she had met the person with whom she wanted to spend her life and that there was no interchanging that person with another. She might live another kind of life, might even be happy with Nathan, for she could not imagine that it would be terrible with him; but the person who would be her one person, the person who somehow completed her, made her feel that she was more herself in his company than she was on her own, that person was gone, and the life she would have lived with him would not happen.

The wind shifted overnight and a slightly colder air ventured in. Rain coming, Mr. Bennet remarked at breakfast. The farmers will be disappointed, he mumbled through blood sausage.

Rain meant the stacks would get wet and delay the gathering of hay. But no rain interfered with the farmers' harvest and only a few darkish clouds swept down the valley. The sun came and went as large clouds flew by and the wind was instead a blessing, drying the hay faster than mere sun would have.

"You should have married Mr. Collins. Then you, like Charlotte, would soon be bearing a child."

"It would be me *instead* of Charlotte, Mama."

"What is that?"

"Well, had I married Mr. Collins, Charlotte would not have a child."

"Oh, well of course Lizzy. I am not a fool."

"But you said *like* Charlotte. It would not be *like* Charlotte. It would be *instead* of Charlotte."

"Oh, you Elizabeth Bennet. I hope you find a man soon for your attention to details and sudden need to correct is quite driving me mad. I cannot say a word to you that you do not find in it something to mince."

Elizabeth begged to be excused.

"But you have not finished your breakfast."

"I have eaten sufficiently, Mama, of everything."

It was a little dig that her mother did not notice. All the better for that, she decided as she stood in the hall searching the hooks for her bonnet. Her father came up behind her as she bent to her laces. He had received news from Mr. Collins that they were celebrating Mr. Darcy's engagement at Rosings Park. He paused a little and she stood to look at him quizzically. His face was not celebratory, but reticent, as one bearing shocking news. Her stomach contracted as it armed itself. She had been harbouring hopes that her beloved Darcy would be hers, and she dreaded words that would, might, come one day to announce his betrothal to another.

"Married. Mr. Darcy married?" Mrs. Bennet shouted. "He is contracted to our Lizzy except that she could not keep him."

"Mrs. Bennet that is quite unfair."

"Well, that is it then," her mother pouted.

"I am glad for him," Elizabeth said bravely. "He should be married. It is what I want for him."

"But it is not to whom you are thinking."

"Who is it then that he marries?" Mrs. Bennet arrived in the hall. "I knew it. He had too much of a reputation to stick with any one girl and he goes off like this with any girl who will give herself to him. A floosy here and a floosy there. He will offer to marry anyone and then leave them when he has had his way, is it not so?"

"Mrs. Bennet, please quit for a minute. I would like to talk to Lizzy."

"Then why are you in the hallway where I might listen."

"That, Mrs. Bennet, is a very good question. But it is done now, so please mind Lizzy. I have news for her. Lizzy, he does not marry Lady Compardi."

"Why should he not marry the mother of his daughter, and marry someone else? Oh, that is too terrible father..."

"He is marrying his cousin, Miss de Bourgh."

"Anne?" She stopped tying her bonnet and sat on the little bench at the door. "Anne?" she repeated not understanding, not believing. "Impossible. No, very possible. It is his fate, after all, to marry the woman his mother had intended for him."

"I know you held hope that he would return and that you would still be married. I know Lizzy, for you cannot keep these things from me. I am very sorry for this news for I must admit that I had also hoped that he would return and ask you again."

"It is too much to expect a man like Mr. Darcy to ask Lizzy three times to be married," Mrs. Bennet said. "And if Elizabeth Bennet thinks that she will sustain his interest through all this fussing, she thinks more highly of herself than she should. You were too good for Mr. Collins, is it Lizzy? But it is too much for you to think that you are too good for Mr. Darcy."

"I will live with Jane at Netherfield and I will be very content."

"If your father dies, we should all go to Netherfield," her mother replied.

"No Lizzy," her father said, laying a hand on her shoulder and making her look at him directly, "you would not be content to live at Netherfield as Jane's spinster sister. It would not suit you at all, and more to the point, you know it. It is not necessary to feel such resignation when you are still young. You will see. Young people recover from heartbreak. You must allow yourself to forget Mr. Darcy. No doubt there is another good young man who will see, as did Mr. Darcy, that you are a fine girl. That you are my best girl," and his smile, his tenderness, caused tears to well in her eyes.

"Nathan will marry her," Kitty speculated, yelling from the drawing room and then appeared in the doorframe. "They are good together, do you not think? They have such fun. Why should they not marry?"

"Oh, that is well. It is good of you Kitty to leave him for your sister," Mrs. Bennet agreed, jumping quickly on this idea that had not yet occurred to her. "Elizabeth, see if Mr. Nathan will marry you. Such a sweet man and you would be twice related to Jane!"

"I won't marry him..."

"Well of course not, you must first acquire a proposal," her mother said. Elizabeth bid them adieu.

Hay season was in full swing, and the fields were covered with lines of villagers cutting, stacking, and hauling bushels. Although they wore old colourless clothing, their movement in the fields was bright and cheerful. The flat plane of green field was alive with lines of scythes swinging and children running behind, sometimes playing, sometimes working. Women in handkerchiefs bent into bundles and older ones arrived with baskets, calling their families and friends to the shade to eat.

Elizabeth sat on the low hills looking down at them wishing she could join. Not just wanting the hard labour to alleviate her mind, but to feel a part of that community, their teamwork a force of invisible threads to hold her. She rose from her spot on the hill and wandered to the edge of a field where a woman was setting out a picnic blanket. She looked up at Elizabeth, said morning miss, and Elizabeth nodded good morning, but didn't know what to do. She watched the younger women at their bundles, saw their strong hands moving quickly as they tied the shafts and poised the haystacks like little chimneys everywhere. She admired their strong forearms, ribbed with muscles and the tough chapped brownness of their skin. The woman stopped preparing her picnic and Elizabeth gave her a forced smile. "Just go on," the woman said. "They'll show ye how. Ask for Beatrice."

Elizabeth stepped forward into the group and asked for Beatrice, and Beatrice showed almost no surprise at receiving the request. She demonstrated how easy it was to make good haystacks and set her to work with the children who teased her in a friendly way for her ignorance, but then showed her tricks to getting it right. They were soon a jolly bunch laughing and playing and teasing one another.

Darcy re-read Augusta's letter. *Gawd, Darcy, who are you? How did you become so boring? The girl is with me. She will thank me some day.* He crumpled it, took out a match, and burned it. The flames slowly spread and the paper turned to ashy dust. He lay back against the tree and looked up through the branches, the myriad of leaves feathering the sky. The horse wandered nearby listening as he prepared a speech.

In his imagination, he would arrive at teatime with the entire family sitting in the garden, under the cottonwood, and he would propose to Elizabeth in front of them all. "You were correct in thinking that I felt some responsibility towards Rose and Augusta and to the pledge I had made her," he would announce, "but I am relieved of those obligations and I am glad of it. And now I am free to be your husband, if you would be so kind as to accept me..."

That was pathetic. What had he said to her last autumn? When he realized that she had feelings for him, not of outrage but of care. He had blurted something without thinking. I love you Elizabeth Bennet, I will have you to hold...

He should not prepare. He should blurt. He should beg her forgiveness. He should swallow all pride and tell her that she was always meant to be his. He should...

His mind stopped as he saw a hawk circle above the field workers in the valley below. He watched it rise on a thermal. He felt a sudden calm and thought, there, nothing else matters but this great vision, from those sky heights. And he lay against the tree and watched the clouds pass, waiting for teatime.

When Elizabeth finished helping with the hay gatherers, she walked up Oakham Hill towards her favourite hawthorn, to sit and meditate and mend, but before long she heard horses trotting in the lane and Nathan rode towards her, breaking away from his party who passed them by with whistles and calls. Nathan bounded from his horse and gave her a big hug. "Well met, my dear. We have got a stag!"

She looked at him, his boyish generosity and his great lovely joy and she knew that he would drive her mad. He picked up her hands and spun her around.

"I have terrible news, Liz. I've been lying awake all night thinking about my proposal. I will marry you if you want, but I want us to be friends. I want to be your brother. I want you to come to India. And I want to love you the way I do now. I am sure we can't do all that if we marry, do you see? It seemed a good idea, did it not? You know I was trying to help you. I thought I could ease your sadness. But it will not do any good? You're not upset, are you?"

He blurted all this without pause, not waiting for her reactions, but when he took her hands, she smiled and assured him that she was not upset, that in fact he was the best brother and friend a person could have. He kissed her on the cheek, bounded to his horse, and cantered off, leaving her feeling unexpectedly bereft.

Elizabeth continued her walk, thinking of Darcy's marital plans. She was proud of him. She admired that he would care for Anne even though it would give him little satisfaction. And she, Elizabeth, could certainly more easily produce another husband. She was feeling rather altruistic. Darcy was a good man. He was a good man, and she was proud of him. And maybe, once they were both married, they might see one another. Surely, then it would be possible for them to be friends. Or she might write to tell him of her children, and how it is with her, how she is happy in the cottage, or the manse, or the farmhouse, or even Netherfield, for surely if she lives at Netherfield, she will see Darcy. And when she visits Charlotte, she will see Darcy. She will see him everywhere in her future.

As she climbed the hill, she understood that she must never see him again. She must go away to some missionary, must go to India as Nathan's sister, as she has heard other women do when they are stuck in a scrape and cannot do anything else but convert the wicked from heathenism. Bitter choice: to see Darcy everywhere or to leave for India.

She almost turned around before arriving at the hawthorn tree. But a shadow in the tree moved a little and she decided she would meet whoever it was in the world who sat beneath her beloved tree. She climbed, the deep grasses muffling her footfall. The tree, whose girth was thick as a door, hid all but the man's riding boots of fine leather.

"Hello, sir," she called out. "Do you love this tree as do I?" The light blazed on her as she stood below it, not wanting to approach and startle the man.

"I believe I do." He stood, and she raised her hand against the light which came through him, the tree, its branches, all highlighted by the rays coming from behind them. She had dreamed to hear that voice again, but that he should be here, under her tree, was unexpected despite all the many times she imagined his arrival. He had caught her by surprise.

"It is you." Her voice felt like it was blowing through a reed, trembling on fragment of grass.

The tidy garden scene at tea, the joy in her face at his arrival, the pretty proposal he would miraculously devise, were all now lost. She was dishevelled. Her hair was strewn everywhere and bound with strands of hay. Her smock was dirty and had at least one handprint on it. Her boots were dusty and she was not glowing in a radiance of delight but frowning up at him with a puzzling consternation.

"If you have come for congratulations, then I beg you turn and leave for I can be happy for you, but I cannot bear to be with you."

"Lizzy, for what could I possibly seek congratulations?"

"For your matrimonial intentions of course, Mr. Darcy."

"I see." He did not see, but he waited.

"I believe you have made a wise choice."

"You do." He came forward out from under the tree and moved slightly so the sun was not in her eyes.

"Yes. I do," she spoke stoically. "I believe the woman you have chosen to marry deserves you, for she needs you desperately."

"Does she?"

"She does."

"That is good. I am glad you approve. It means a great deal to me that I have your approval."

He took her hands and she looked confused.

"Then I have your blessing to choose the woman I am to marry?" he asked her. "To shelter her with my care, to be my best companion and dearest friend? To love and to hold and to be held, and to be understood as this man, not this man who is Pemberley's master, nor this man who is Rose's father, nor even this man who will be a husband, or a father, or anything, but this person, here before you full of all that you know so well?"

"Please, do not torture me so. You know you must do whatever you need to, Will."

Every time he realized his love for this woman, he disbelieved that it could ever be stronger; yet over the past several months, he marvelled how that feeling returned, each time a surprise, each time like a new awakening. It had started with a girl flitting about a room, with a smile, a fine set of eyes, a quick sparking wit that was turned against him. His love didn't increase with each realization, was not greater in size nor impermeability, nor did he idealize her and ignore her imperfections; but whenever he felt a great care and admiration for her, it was added to all the previous occasions, solidifying as they added one to the other.

"Here, in my pocket. I have been carrying it these weeks. I didn't send it, but it's my answer to your last letter. It has always been my answer."

It was worn and bent. It had coffee stains. And it had been once crumpled. It was dated over a month previously and it told Elizabeth that he would marry her. He handed it to her, but before she had time to read it, he bent on his knee for the third time. "Miss Elizabeth Bennet, would you do me the honour of being my wife. I'll not ask again, and I will not accept no as an answer."

"But I thought..."

She did not finish her sentence. He picked her up and kissed her. "It's too late for thinking. I do not want you to think Lizzy. I want you to say yes."

"Then I shan't go to India to be a missionary."

He laughed "Why in heaven's name for?"

"To seek new friends where I should not find you."

"In that case, your old friends will suit. You haven't said yes."

"Well, let me think about it..." she smiled.

"Say yes, you brutish thing, you terrible tease."

"Oh, fine then, if you insist."

She jumped into his arms, hung around his neck and they kissed. There was no crack of lightning, no storm, no fire, no change to the weather at all, though the sun came out from behind a cloud and then disappeared again as they kissed, for they kissed longer than what is commonly described in many tales, they kissed longer than is interesting except for the participants in the kiss. Finally, they stopped kissing and, holding one another, they walked hand in hand down the hill, Darcy's horse following beside like a large hound on a leash.

"What took you so long?" she asked finally. He heard the cheek in her voice, the not so subtle reprimand full of love and fun.

"Well, I had to be refused by two other women," he laughed. "One had no interest in me, so you were lucky in that."

"Anne."

He nodded.

"Mr. Collins wrote to us," she told him. "We received the news just this morning that you were marrying her. It seemed unbelievable to me at first, but then I was proud of you." She paused a minute. "I still think we should be caring for her."

He nodded. "It is why I have been away. She is recovering at Pemberley as we speak." He stopped walking. "Forgive me, dearest.

I could not send you a letter. I wanted to be here when you said yes."

"I almost married Nathan."

"You didn't!"

"He proposed. Out of kindness."

"That was big of him." Darcy thought how he could have done the same, taken Anne as his wife, to keep her safe, except for the fact that it had never occurred to him to do such a thing.

"He's a better man than you," Elizabeth teased.

"He is. But I must object a little to that comparison, for marriage to you and marriage to Anne aren't quite the same sacrifice."

"I don't know. Anne is rather sweet and docile. And the other woman?" she prompted.

"The other, well, she took a little convincing. I told her I wanted to sell the London house to be a country squire and raise lovely children and a few dogs."

"I see. And she thought that was a terrible life?"

"She thought I had become a boring old fool."

"Ah, and so you are. *My* boring old fool." Elizabeth laughed and hugged him. They talked for some time, she telling stories about Jane's wedding, he of his discoveries about Anne, but as they crested a hill, she broke away from him and ran down the hill as if gravity would catch her. He watched her old boots popping in and out of her simple cotton dress, the way the shape of her formed as the dress gathered here and there around her as she ran, her arms out slightly like wings to balance her as she easily took the steep hill, the rocks and the grass mounds. "You will swallow the mountains around Pemberley," he whispered. "And you will be my boring old matron, Mistress of Pemberley."

But she seemed to hear and stopped.

"But we won't sell the house in London, will we?" she called up to him.

"Not if you don't want to. But I thought you hated London?"

"Well, I do, but it's good to see a few plays and art and to visit some people who have interesting things to talk about, not the weather, and we can't become entirely boring old fools, for then we would be quite sick of ourselves and hate that we were quite so boring."

He started laughing loudly, stopped walking he was so overcome by it.

"But Darcy, surely it wasn't that funny?"

To which he laughed harder. It wasn't funny at all, he thought to himself. Not at all. Yet laughing made him laugh more, and then Elizabeth could not help it, for she began laughing and he laughed at her laughing even though there was nothing particularly funny.

He took her firmly by the hand and led her along the lane. And if you were a stranger or a friend, walking opposite them on that late afternoon, you would have seen two people walking quickly side by side with purpose, almost entirely in silence, their faces two bright wide open smiling grins as if they had just seen a miracle.

GREAT CHANGES

For the next several generations, great changes came to the world. In but a few years, the steam engine train cut through the English countryside and created the possibility for casual weekend visiting. Time to travel from France to England, or the New World, decreased by degrees until it was possible to travel from London to anywhere in the world in less time than it took Elizabeth and Darcy to travel by carriage to London. Although for Darcy and Elizabeth, there were three posts a day in England moving notes and letters with reasonable alacrity, and soon the telegraph could deliver urgent missives within a half a day, it is now true that the death of a celebrity is well known around the world to billions of people in less time than it would take Elizabeth and Darcy to walk from one room of their home to another. Now, the speed and scope of communication makes it almost impossible *not* to be in communication.

All these developments, however, did nothing to change the basic landscape of human intimacy. No technological train has been developed to increase the proficiency and mastery of deep communication, to avoid the pitfalls of misunderstandings, to avoid the damage of unrequited love, or to guarantee great sex. Nothing has moderated the necessity of opening one's heart and bravely saying "I want to spend my life with you," exposing one to the fear of rejection and the elation of acceptance. And there are no tools to eradicate the potential for further complications, trials, and misunderstandings despite sincere words of devotion.

Romantic tales may have done us all a disservice in suggesting the opposite. They have lied to us. Our romantic ideals lull us into a false belief that Sleeping Beauty, once awakened, will live forever in the bliss of love and that Cinderella, once the prince has obtained the precise measurement of her shoe size, will be endlessly content. I am sorry that I must say this, to sound bitter, but the pursuit of idealistic endings bars us from seeing the reality in the dangerous present. It bars us from confronting the work that must be done. The work is not a magical cure, or perfect shoe size, or a technology that will fling us into the past to remake a happy ending. It is to produce daily, no, momentarily, the constructive care for each other. To love each other well, with grace and tolerance despite all the many ways we can accidentally cause grief. The greatest test is to be decent even when there is hatred, to be careful with one's enemy, not out of fear, but in the deepest and most precious attention for one's own inner peace and sense of integrity.

I know this sounds obvious and incredibly simplistic. I do. But I am mystified by the incredible developments in technology mirrored by a lack of progress in the art of decency and care. And with the technology, the power to cause greater damage and disregard is increased. But I digress, and I sound like my great, great, great Aunty Kitty.

Years after Darcy's third and last marriage proposal to Elizabeth, they were comfortably lounging in bed. The curtains were open to a summer morning sun, low slung and buttery. The windows were wide open to chattering birds. A pigeon on an eave nearby was regaling his mate with a high whistling sound. Darcy had a coffee by his side, and she a tea. His paper was on his knees, unopened. Their children had already bounced on the bed and visited and had all left again, except for the baby who was sleeping between them. In this momentary quiet, Darcy described his dream, and although he could remember little of the dream itself, he had woken with memories of Lady Catherine filling his attention.

"Well, no wonder," Elizabeth interrupted, "given the nature of the letter we received last night. Will you go tell Anne, or do you want me to?" she asked.

"No. I'll ride over later."

"Sorry, I interrupted."

"You're good at it," he said kissing her cheek.

"The children train me! You were dreaming...?" she prompted.

"No: I was remembering. After mother fell ill, and I went to stay for many months at Rosings, Auntie Cate tried very hard to be kind. I know," he responded to her smirk, "that sounds like an oxymoron, but she tried. She brought me into her presence and gave me things, such as books and opportunities to talk, and she told me stories of my mother, stories from her childhood.

"Anne was very sick most of that time (almost a year) and I was required to read to her for an hour a day. Anne once said to me 'Please Fitzwilliam, if something happens to me, please take care of my mother.' Aunt Cate was devoted to her husband, but he was not particularly kind and they lived somewhat separate lives in the two wings of the house. In her appeal, Anne was telling me something I didn't understand at the time but was suddenly clear to me this morning."

Elizabeth sat up and turned around so that she was looking at Darcy. He continued. "I just understood that Anne's confinement and her incredibly submissive acceptance of Lady Catherine's will throughout her life was a way of protecting her mother."

"Darcy! That is so interesting. But is it true?"

He shrugged his shoulders. "I never believed that she was sick. When I went to read with her, and the nurse left us alone, we laughed and played cards and she didn't seem all that sick."

"Oh, that is tragic."

He put his hand on the baby. He felt its round belly in his palm and closed his eyes. His life was a mystery. He woke at times with the knowledge of his children sleeping nearby, their tidy little fingers curved, and their lips perched open, and the weight and glory of it was more than he could bear.

"How do you think she will respond to this news?" Elizabeth asked, putting her hand on his.

"I'm not sure. It's so hard to tell with Anne."

He kissed her and rose to dress. "I'll be back to dine with you. I'll see to some things in the village while I'm out."

She nodded and lay back on her pillow.

Later that day, Darcy rode out to the cottage where Anne was living. When she first arrived at Pemberley, she would not venture beyond the gallery or patio, and then, on Elizabeth's advice, Anne had gone travelling. Kitty had accompanied her and they had returned seven months later with a groom for Kitty and a brightened complexion and several new and wonderful hats for Anne.

She had said, at that point, that she would be happier living in a home which was not so busy with people, for despite their attempts to keep out their friends, there was a constant stream of visitors at Pemberley. Darcy had immediately made the folly available to her. It was at the heart of a mature forest near a lake at the east corner of their property, connected to the main house by a lane which followed a creek, the same creek which fed the small lake nearby. Along the way were the groundskeeper's cottage, stables, gardens, forests and a large greenhouse wherein was a small indoor pond which contained seven large carp who roamed all day in their small quarters, and which Anne loved to watch in the winter months. They called this folly the Hunting Cottage, for it was built to function as such, despite the fact that his father, Mr. Darcy, had not been particularly fond of hunting. Mrs. Darcy had asked that his hunting friends, with their loud brash calling and shouting to one another, reside away from the manor house when they visited, and so he had taken the opportunity to build a folly which reminded him of his youthful days in India.

It was a fine little house, with many rooms, several turrets, a round staircase, and oddly shaped windows as it was hardly square anywhere. The light fell into it so that there was at least one room with wonderful light, and it had been richly furnished with elaborately inlayed furniture from the east. Anne was delighted with it and lived there with the understanding that Darcy and Elizabeth might occasionally spend time together there alone, for they loved the house quite as much as she.

Anne was quite isolated there, which she had wished for, with a handful of servants, most of whom lived in nearby cottages, and she had developed the habit of rescuing small animals and nursing them to health as well as pursuing her old love of writing wild stories about fantastical creatures which she would read to the children to great acclaim.

With the letter in his breast pocket, Darcy found Anne wrapped in a large quilt, sitting on a big chair overlooking the lake. The water seems to absorb my thoughts, she had once explained. And in her dreamy way, continued, As if it is a sponge and I can lose myself into the water every day, lose myself in that way which relieves me of all pain. He had replied, laughing, It is a miracle that you get up from the chair at all, if that is the case. Indeed, she had agreed. It is with a force of intention that is all. An intention to act, every minute. To live. Her seriousness and sincerity had been palpable, but she had smiled and touched his arm, and said, And it is a glorious one.

As he walked up to her, he regretted that he must disturb her serenity as she read the letter he had brought.

"It has taken me years to grant myself the right to believe that I am worthy to be human. That I am not a corrupted, evil disease. Fitzwilliam: you know how hard it has been, how my correspondence with Mary has helped. But now, now with this news, I feel a weight lift. The person who I love the most and hate the most can no longer tell me who I am."

Then she wept quietly, tears streaming down her face that was sober and relaxed despite the tears. He waited patiently by her side until she spoke again.

"I suppose we should go to Rosings and make arrangements." She started crying again. "Oh dear," she apologized. "I'm so sorry. It's just that I actually don't know if I can go back there. Not even for a funeral." He wondered for a moment if she would not say more about the memories of living at Rosings Park. "I will not live at Rosings again, you know. I'll leave it to your Bruce."

"He'll be happy to have it when he can understand what it means. For now, his mother's milk is quite enough to make all his joy."

She laughed. "I am so happy here. Are you sure I might stay even though I now have a house of my own?" And he assured her that of course she might. In fact, he could not imagine Pemberley without her. They sat some time thinking their own thoughts and he too felt the great effects of the lake, its stillness on a fine day, the sounds of life in the noises of bugs and birds.

"I'm so glad I have spent some time with Mama, that we reconciled as much as possible."

"I was just thinking the same." He reached across and took her hand. "That she goes in peace. That's all we ever wish, isn't it?"

As for the other people of this story, and their happy endings, I will say a few brief things. Jane and Bingley eventually moved into the Lake district, not far from Pemberley, and the two households developed a great traffic of children back and forth between them, full of noisy activity, pony rides, fishing trips, and picnics. The girls of this tribe were permitted activities which Darcy, initially, found difficult to accept, for even though he allowed that Elizabeth was an active person, he thought that it was her particular quirk. But she soon persuaded him that it was a blemish in social fashion to confine girls and that putting them in a paddock limited their natural development, and so they were taught to throw a ball, fly a kite, and toss a fishing line off the side of a boat alongside their male cousins and brothers, as well as to read and study. And they all grew to be variously productive and happy members of their society with obvious and natural rough patches along the way.

Charlotte's child was born, and when Mr. Collins arrived at the bedside to see, for the first time, his son cradled in Charlotte's arms, he wept openly. He doted on the child - their only one – in the most wonderful way, for the boy thrived in these attentions until he was a young man and had to naturally break away from the values and ideas brokered by his father to adopt his mother's quiet wisdom. Charlotte spent many years loving Mr. Collins for the simple reason that he adored their son.

Nathan, who went to India almost immediately after Elizabeth was married, returned some years later with a wife, three children and a governess, Prisha. She was the daughter of a wealthy Indian merchant who refused an arranged marriage and joined Nathan's family to avoid the retributions. She did not return with the Bingleys but stayed as Anne's housekeeper and married the very handsome groundskeeper. Anne remained a true spinster and never loved again.

Darcy's daughter was abruptly taken from her childhood home to bathe in the activities of high London aristocrats. Since we know so little about her, except that she was happy, we can only assume that this was both pleasant and shocking. Her birth mother doted on the girl until the novelty wore off and Lettice Rose proved to be a human with failings and Augusta handed her to an auntie for safe keeping. Let us assume that Lettice Rose was happy there and did eventually find herself with a life she might call her own. Reading Fanny Burney several times, she would have seen how the good Evelina and Cecilia managed their trials and won out in the end without compromising their good names.

It is quite certain that she did not return to the blacksmith for Darcy and Elizabeth went in search of Lettice Rose and when Augusta refused to disclose her whereabouts, they sought the blacksmith's help. It was not until a much later date and another story of long complicated trials and betrayals, that Lettice Rose finally learned who was her father and where he resided.

Mary lived a long time in the Bennet house, caring for her aging parents until her mother died suddenly of a stroke and Mr. Bennet moved to Pemberley where everyone seemed to be having such fun. Mary refused to stay alone at Longbourn and moved to live with a widow she had known for some time. Mary was beloved in the community for her good works with the poor and she played organ in the church until arthritis confined her fingers to mere chords. There never were any rumours about the nature of her living arrangements with Sharon Carr, the widow, as there was no reason for anyone to suspect that they were providing anything but comfort to one another, where Mary required lodging and the widow a helpmate. But it will be admitted here that they were very much in love. And although they sometimes sat in their kitchen discussing their sadness at not being able to express that love in a public way, they enjoyed very happy familial ties. With great sex.

And we must not forget the brave and loyal Sherwood who had already lived a long life and died peacefully in his rooms at Pemberley, but not before he had a chance to greet and grumble about all four of Darcy and Elizabeth's children.

But I have managed to push into the future quite too far, into new generations and large global changes, without really telling the most important story, the one of Darcy and Elizabeth leading a grey horse down the hill into Meryton after he had proposed marriage to her for the third time in a little over a year. As it was dinner time, they ate quickly at a little inn after having popped by the church to speak to the vicar. It was almost dark when they arrived at Longbourn and Mrs. Bennet opened the door to them exclaiming, "Oh Lizzy, I have been most worried for your safety!" And she hugged her daughter and was sobbing with the relief.

"Oh, I had quite forgotten that I should send a note. I am so sorry to have distressed you."

"And here you are with Mr. Darcy. Oh, that is a surprise. We were not expecting you."

"I too did not send a note." Darcy smiled and bowed and was amused by Elizabeth's mother's quick emotions which ceased as quickly as they appeared.

"Are you well?" she asked, picking up the required formalities after she had dropped them.

"I am well," he answered. "And you are quite well, Mrs. Bennet?"

"I am. I am quite well. I am quite well now that Lizzy is safe returned to us. She must not be wandering in the dark as you must know, Mr. Darcy, and it is cold." But of course it was neither dark nor cold, since the sun did not set until quite late and the summer heat remained quite late into the night.

"Then let us in the house, Mama, and we will explain all."

"Explain. Explain. What is there to explain?"

"Why we are late in our coming here."

Elizabeth would say no more but waited until everyone had gathered in the drawing room to hear that she would be married the next day. "But the banns, the banns must be heard!" Mrs. Bennet exclaimed, but Mr. Bennet reminded her that, as they were to be married so recently, there was no need to repeat the banns. They agreed that Jane, who had already sailed to the continent, would be upset to miss Elizabeth's wedding, and it was sad not to have Georgiana and Sherwood attend. But Darcy proposed a gathering of the clan at a later date to celebrate the families. And so, on the morrow, Elizabeth and Darcy were married in the little church in Meryton. There were rumours that she was with child and that they had had to rush into a wedding for that reason, but two years went by before any progeny were born to them, so the rumours proved to be unfounded. The wedding was too short for Mrs. Bennet's taste, and too ill attended, and not very grand, for none of the neighbours were invited to witness the ostentatious marriage of her daughter to a man of distinction with ten thousand a year, imagine, and Mr. Bennet reminded Mrs. Bennet that she had had that privilege when Jane was married and that she must not be overly greedy with her ostentation.

Some days later, after travelling quite steadily, Darcy and Elizabeth pulled up to a beautiful little cottage in a large wood.

"A folly," she exclaimed.

"My father's hunting cottage" he told her.

The folly was set on a rise above a small lake surrounded by a mature forest of beech and elm. The trees were massive, with girths wider than a stable door and one could walk anywhere beneath them for they were clean and sparse at their roots. The house was decorated everywhere with gardens, lavender and foxglove and lilies in bloom, and oxeye daisies dotting the edges between yard and forest. The door and ornate shutters were yellow, which struck Elizabeth as delightfully whimsical and with closer inspection, were carved with creatures, peacock and elephant, large fish and strange lion beasts. It was not a square building, and although not immense, it had turrets and round curves and looked in some places as if rooms had been piled unevenly to form the structure.

"This is my surprise?" Jane had gone to the continent.

"We can travel any time. I have waited too long to be with you and I don't want our intimacies to be on the road in inns and such."

"And this is my surprise bridal tour?" she repeated.

"You don't understand Lizzy. We are here alone."

The driver emerged and said their luggage was upstairs and everything was in order. "The maids has come and lit the fires to take the damp and 'tis cozy and inviting in there, sir." His voice winked, if such a thing were possible.

"Thank you, Brown."

Elizabeth did not immediately notice the import of this name, although she would eventually meet her Mrs. Brown who was hired to help with the Pemberley gardens and to later buy her a beautiful shawl which might keep her warm on cooler evenings.

"Most entirely grateful to be of service, Mr. Darcy sir. Me and my wife is both of us very glad." And he bowed to them both and drove away down the lane and left the recently married pair in total silence. Elizabeth tossed her head as she did when she was thinking and said "Brown?" Darcy smiled but remained silent, for he could see that Elizabeth understood. "You are a good man, Mr. Fitzwilliam Darcy, and I am proud to be by your side. But this is my bridal tour?" she asked for the third time. "You mean there is no one here, not even a servant?" She was beginning to form a picture. "I will clean and sew and make you food, Mr. Darcy? Oh, you show such incredible consideration, so that I will feel welcome, yes? And not so estranged from my former life?"

"I will help" he laughed, and she pushed him for he knew nothing of boiling water. "They will come with food and to clean. We are not entirely abandoned as there is a stable and the gamekeeper's lodge not far away. He is a very handsome single man, so I hope we don't meet him for he has a reputation with the women."

"I will be sure to look for him, Will. I'm still disappointed we are not going to the continent. Or Bath. Or Wales even. Wales is supposed to be beautiful. And what are we to do?"

He smiled again and picked her up so that she was cradled in his arms with her face on his neck, the warmth of her breathing in his shirt down through him. He smiled inwardly. His whole body smiled.

Her momentary disappointment was about to end. "I'm sorry you're disappointed. We can leave in a day if you want...But I'm quite sure we will organize ourselves here admirably."

"I see. And how would you like to organize us Mr. Darcy?"

"If we were travelling, we would be doing the same thing we will do here. Bless the sofa, the chairs, the dining room table... yes, the table!... Travelling would be wasted on us for we would see nothing of any of it but the inside of lodgings."

"Oh, that's what you think, is it?" she teased, pulling at a vest button.

"Ah, I see you are now understanding the point," he answered, pulling her hand from his buttons. "Not so quickly. We have nothing but time." He carried her over the threshold and stood with her in his arms. "What room would you like to bless first?"

"Right here is a good start," she smiled.

"The front entrance?"

"Is a good start."

He put her down, and somewhat elated, picked her up and spun her joyously. She ran from him, kicking up her long dress. She fled so slowly that he caught her and held her. She squirmed, and struggled, and laughed and bit him gently on his ear as he bent to undo each one of the buttons along her back.

"One," he counted, and kissed her. "Two," he counted and kissed her until, when the dress was a puddle of beads and lace at her ankles, his face having shifted from tender, to joy, to care, to desire, he stood back and his mouth and eyes narrowed, and a fierceness she recognized as desire, and restlessness and power, came into his entire countenance, and he grinned a mischievous crooked smile and took both sides of her undergarment in his strong hands and tore at it until she was naked.

Standing before him, he still fully clothed, made her feel vulnerable to him in the most delicious way. She stood coquettishly, with her hand on his chest as he pushed into her, refusing him softly, achingly, with her mouth wide, part with joy and part seduction. She was quite enjoying herself and the freedom she felt to be charming for her husband (her husband! the word was like a blessing, a salve, a promise of beautiful trust and care for the rest of her life with this man).

"My, my Mrs. Darcy." He pinched gently at her nipple. "Aren't we going to have fun."

Darcy woke curled around Elizabeth. The light was bright. Morning had arrived some time ago. They had made love, talked, made love, slept, talked and made love all night and he could not imagine what time in the day it might be.

He stretched and thought about his morning coffee. There was a flaw in his plan to be here alone with his dearest, and the flaw was rather late in making itself known to him. "Lizzy dear...are you awake?" She grumbled, stretched, looked at him, and said, "Oh, you're still here?" Poked him, then announced that she didn't think she could do much more of *that* for a few more hours anyway. And he laughed and suggested they might swim and go for a walk up the mountain nearby.

"Tomorrow the mountain."

"Quite right. Today we might just sleep beside the lake and drift in a rowboat. But Lizzy dearest, I must go to Pemberley first. Unless of course you know how to make coffee."

ACKNOWLEDGEMENT

This project's completion is thanks to many people, but there is a single person who stands out among them. It is a person who is beloved by many and gracious in all her dealings with us, and she has worked tirelessly to produce the final product of this novel since I presented her with the first draft. Her name is Kay Flanagan.

Putting a final manuscript into print involves many skills and experience which I did not have, and I am grateful to a number of people who shared their experiences of publishing, editing, web site design and graphics. Among these are Isabelle, Dahna, Sam, Elaine, Marlene, Lise and Keira. There have been many enthusiastic cheerleaders, but I am especially indebted to Rick who has given not only advice and support, but also helped create the most important requirement: time to work. I thank his generosity for the opportunity to devote myself to my lifelong passion.

This is aJbishop's first published novel. She is a lifelong writer of fiction and poetry and is a lover of all things literary. She wrote the first draft of this novel after a year of burying herself in the syntaxes and attitudes of Regency and Victorian England, by way of Austen, Eliot, the Brontës, Fanny Burney and more. She hopes to publish three other completed novels, all different one from the other. All seek to uncover deeper mysteries of human consciousness of mind, body, soul connections. She has occasionally earned lunch money from her published poems. For more, please go to www.ajbishop.com.

Printed in Great Britain
by Amazon

81429200R00150